BELOW ZERO

AN INGRID SKYBERG THRILLER

EVA HUDSON

VENATRIX

First published 2016.
This version published by Venatrix 2020.

978-1-9160195-5-3

For Angela Dees

BELOW ZERO

1

Special Agent Ingrid Skyberg pulled her scarf up over her chin. Not only did it help to hide her face from any surveillance cameras, but it insulated her from the icy wind scraping over the water. She had waited in her cabin until the rumble of footsteps and trundle of cases had peaked, timing her exit to disembark with the greatest number of passengers.

She had spent the overnight crossing from Riga alone in her cabin. She could have saved money by sleeping in a recliner in the lounge, but she needed to minimize the chance of being spotted, or being engaged in conversation, or getting hit on by a truck driver who thought a woman traveling alone must be up for it. The instructions she'd been given could not have been clearer: no one was to ever know she had been in Stockholm. No ID, no credit cards, no trace. If something went wrong, if her body was found floating in the docks of Djurgården, or she was arrested and imprisoned, there could be no way of identifying her. There was no backup, no FBI, no Fortnum Security, no Phone-a-Friend. Out of an abundance of caution, she had wiped over the vanity unit in the restroom and the handle of her cabin door before tucking her short blonde hair inside her hat and joining the crowd in the corridor.

Ingrid was relieved to see she was dressed like almost

everyone else on the ferry: gray beanie, black padded jacket, black jeans and sneakers. She knew she should have worn boots, but she had packed in a hurry. At four in the afternoon she had been approached at Nick Angelis' wedding by a man who introduced himself as 'James', and by five past four she was in no doubt that her debt to Fortnum Security was being called in. Before midnight she had touched down in St Petersburg.

That had been two days ago. She'd then left her US passport and cell phone in a locker at Pulkovo airport and traveled on her Russian papers to Latvia by train. She left her Russian ID—issued by the FBI for her undercover work in London—and her credit cards in another locker at Central Station in Riga before buying a ticket, in cash, for the ferry to Stockholm.

Shuffling like penguins off the ramp and onto the dock, Ingrid was careful not to make eye contact with the other passengers or draw attention to herself. Just another traveler, no one special. There were no passport controls between Latvia and Sweden—hence her choice of route—but a random customs inspection was still a possibility. All she had with her was a change of underwear, a toothbrush and slightly less than $5,000 in cash in three different currencies: she really didn't want to explain the contents of her backpack to the authorities.

The last time she had arrived at the docks at Frihamnen, Ingrid had been met by her cousin Anna. Born only weeks but an ocean apart, they had first met aged four at a family reunion in Minnesota. Aunts and uncles had said that the two little blonde girls who played so nicely together could have been twins. But by the time Ingrid was studying in St Petersburg and spending regular weekends in Stockholm, they couldn't have looked more different. Ingrid had stepped off the ferry aged twenty-two to be met by a punk with piercings and green hair. Anna had officially become a rebel and Ingrid had never felt so square. Now it was Ingrid who was the outsider, the renegade, on a mission so secret and so dangerous that she was a liability to both the FBI and her government. She knew how the State Department graded their priorities: while her mission had level five importance, she was deemed expendable. 'Below zero' was how Nick Angelis had put it. Given the temperature of the Stockholm air, that seemed fitting.

Ingrid walked behind two young Latvian men, carrying canvas holdalls and wearing work boots. In London, in recent years, she'd overheard increasing numbers of conversations about the 'bloody Poles' or the 'scheming Bulgarians' bleeding the state dry. In Sweden, she noted, the immigrants were also commuters: arriving on a Monday morning to do five days' hard labor then returning to their families for the weekend.

The constant flow of arrivals meant the double doors to the terminal building were perpetually kept open, and the air inside was barely warmer than the external temperature. The passengers followed markings on the ground that showed the way to customs and the exit. A cordon of officials monitored their slow progress, examining them from beneath the peaks of their black caps, scanning faces, assessing the threat. Ingrid kept her eyes down and her gait casual, though her heart was hammering inside her chest. A dog handler and an excited spaniel patrolled as they all shuffled forward. A family—exhausted, ragged—who spoke in Arabic were ushered to one side. Refugees from Syria, most likely, and a reminder of how important her mission was. If she could stop one more family having to cross Europe in search of a new life, if she could contribute to ending the war in Syria sooner, then the risks she was taking would be worth it. She stared at the family as they started a conversation with a border guard, a conversation they must have rehearsed a thousand times, a conversation that would likely last for hours, if not days.

"Ursäkta!"

Ingrid carried on walking, keen to escape the port as quickly as possible, and felt the money pouch strapped to her ankle rub against her pants leg.

"Ursäkta mig! Miss!" A small part of her brain thought the guard was trying to attract her attention; the rest of her brain feared that was the case. "Miss! Stop!" he said in Swedish.

She could pretend she didn't understand the language. She

could act dumb. She exhaled deeply, blowing into her scarf. She could feel her pulse in her neck.

A hand tapped her shoulder.

She swallowed hard and turned. The woman behind her said something so quickly Ingrid couldn't understand her. Sensing Ingrid's incomprehension, she repeated herself in English. "I think he wants to speak to you."

A security official was jogging toward her. She felt her cheeks flush but told herself it was OK. She'd worked out a cover story. *You can't blow it this soon.*

"Miss," he said again, a little out of breath. His brilliant blue eyes were imploring her to stop. His expression looked desperate as he approached. Ingrid gritted her teeth, readying herself for the inquisition.

He raised his right hand, and Ingrid saw the red leather glove dangling from his grasp.

Relief surged through her, forcing sweat through her pores under her hat. She couldn't remember the Swedish for glove, but beamed at him and held up her hands to show him the lost item didn't belong to her.

"*Tack*," he said. Thank you. Of all the words Ingrid wanted to import into English from Swedish, '*tack*' was her favorite. It reminded her of her grandmother. Whenever Ingrid helped her clear the table, or brought her a morning coffee, she would always say, "*Tack*", despite the fact she had been born in the US. *Tack*, along with blonde hair and blue eyes, was part of Ingrid's Swedish inheritance.

She smiled at him and quickly turned away, keen to be unmemorable and eager to escape the terminal.

Safely through customs and back out in the brittle Stockholm air, Ingrid decided not to take the bus to the city center. It was just another opportunity for someone to remember her. Instead, she set off on foot and within a couple of hundred yards was marching through Gärdet, a light dusting of snow beneath her feet.

It was a little before ten thirty in the morning. If all went according to plan, she would return to Riga on the same ferry she had come in on when it departed at five thirty. She shoved her hands deep into her pockets: it was going to be the longest seven hours of her life.

2

Ingrid tried to calculate the odds, as she walked quickly west through a light flurry of snow, of bumping into Anna. She knew her cousin was in town as it had only been a couple of days since she'd liked a photo of hers on Facebook. It had been a shot of her cousin—the piercings and mohawk long since replaced by expensive clothes and a sophisticated elfin crop—and her husband Björn in front of their Christmas tree while their toddler screamed his head off, raging against the indignity of posing for the camera.

It was just about the only contact they had these days, tiny electronic reminders of each other's existence, although it hadn't been so long since Ingrid had read about Anna in the *Guardian*, causing her to splutter her coffee. A bill Anna had introduced in the Riksdag had been approved and her cousin had been photographed shaking the hand of the British Prime Minister. Of course Ingrid was thrilled for Anna, but her cousin's success only gave her mother more ammunition to berate her for her own lack of career progression. "Look at Anna," her mother would say, her accent as heavy as the day she defected in 1976. "See what people achieve when they work hard." Sometimes, Ingrid was amazed that the inheritance from the Russian side of her family tree had never forced her into therapy.

At ten thirty in the morning, Anna Skyberg would most likely be in her office. Maybe she was in the parliament building, righting wrongs at that very moment. And if she was between meetings, the Minister for Climate and the Environment would be in a chauffeur-driven car, nose buried in briefing papers or on the phone to her nanny. Ingrid reasoned that even if they happened to be in the same grid reference at the same time, the only person in Stockholm who knew who she really was would be too busy to recognize her. After twelve years, it was possible Anna could look straight at Ingrid and not even see her. She was a ghost. She didn't need to worry.

Ingrid looked down at her feet: ghosts didn't leave footprints in the snow.

She carried on searching for the kind of store that was on every street corner in London, but although she stopped at each intersection to check the retail outlets, she couldn't see what she was looking for. The center of Stockholm was just too damn classy. *Where's a bit of urban decay when you need it?* At this rate, she'd have to walk all the way to Central Station.

She finally found what she was looking for and ducked inside, instantly grateful for the fan heater that rumbled on the worn linoleum floor. The store owner was wearing a woolen coat over his salwar kameez. He was on the phone, talking in tones that indicated he was arguing with his wife. Ingrid was fine to wait. She had rehearsed what she needed to say countless times, but it had been so long since she had spoken Swedish that she was worried she wouldn't be able to make herself understood. In a city where residents slip into English as easily as changing gears in a car, it would be hard to resist the convenience of speaking in her mother tongue. But that was one of Nick's rules. At no point was she to speak English. No one could be left with a memory of a blonde woman, five ten, one hundred and thirty pounds, speaking in an American accent. If her schoolgirl Swedish failed her, she was allowed to try her Russian or her Italian, languages in which Ingrid was fluent. *Capisce,* Nick had said. She understood perfectly.

The man ended his conversation, slammed his phone down on the glass countertop and looked at Ingrid with the same contempt he had shown his caller. Ingrid guessed he was Pakistani, possibly Afghan.

"*Ja?*"

"*Hej. Jag behöver en mobiltelefon?*"

"What kind?" he asked in Swedish. Thankfully, it was a question she had rehearsed an answer to.

"An old one. Just calls and texts."

"No iPhone? I have iPhone."

"No, something basic. Something cheap."

He couldn't hide the disappointment from his face as he bent beneath the counter. While he was on his knees, Ingrid took a look around. The store sold the kind of merchandise found in street markets the world over. Replica watches, personal fans, pocket warmers and air fresheners to hang from your rearview mirror.

The man placed a Tupperware container on the counter and pulled out an old Nokia handset, a Samsung flip phone and several grime-covered chargers and leads.

"They work?" Ingrid asked.

"*Ja*. Of course."

"How much?"

He shrugged. They were virtually worthless and they both knew it. "One thousand kronor."

"For both?"

He nodded.

"I'll give you five hundred. With the chargers."

He looked at her, considering if he could be bothered to haggle. Ingrid took his hesitation as capitulation and reached into her pocket for her wallet. Before she opened it she remembered that it only contained dollars. She shoved it back in her pocket then searched inside her backpack for the envelope her Swedish currency was in. She placed a five hundred kronor note in front of him and pushed another one into her jeans pocket.

"OK?"

"You want SIM card?"

She shook her head.

"They need SIM card."

"That's OK. I don't need a SIM."

He looked puzzled.

"They are for a play. The theater." She didn't know the Swedish word for 'prop'. It was possible he didn't either.

"Ah."

He took the money and she threw the phones in her backpack. "*Tack*," she said and smiled as she walked back out into the cold. She pulled off her beanie and turned it inside out so its bright orange lining was on the outside. It had taken longer than she'd hoped to buy the phones and she didn't have time to waste finding the SIM cards she had been instructed to get from a separate retailer. She knew there would be one in Hötorget station, but she also knew that entering the public transport system massively increased her chances of being caught on CCTV. She hoped a distinctive hat would confuse anyone who might be tailing her, or anyone who wanted to recreate her movements in the event of her... her what? Her failure? Her disappearance? Death?

She bought two pre-paid SIM cards in the station, and stocked up on painkillers and a packet of Libresse sanitary napkins after feeling the first twinges of period cramps. When she returned to street level, she quickly found a branch of Wayne's Coffee and chose a seat next to an electricity outlet. She set down her Americano and pulled the Samsung flip phone out of her backpack, realizing too late that she had already taken her gloves off. She examined it closely: it was absolutely covered in dirt. She reasoned there would be so much DNA on it, some of which—given how she'd acquired it—would almost certainly match at least one record already on the Stockholm police database, that it would be a challenge to get her profile from it. And given that it would soon be at the bottom of the harbor, she hoped removing her gloves wasn't the first in a long line of mistakes.

Transcript from Riksdag Comittee Hearing 23

December 14 2015

BILUNGS: For the record, please state your full name and rank.
HOLM: Detective Sergeant Sami Holm with the Stockholm City Police Department.
BILUNGS: And what was your primary role in the events of December last year?
HOLM: I was the officer who responded to the one-one-two calls from the Republik café. The calls claiming the minister had been taken at gunpoint.
BILUNGS: Claiming?
HOLM: Well, we now know that wasn't true.
BILUNGS: We do indeed. I presume you have been briefed on the purpose of these hearings?
HOLM: Yes.
BILUNGS: You understand that we are not here to apportion blame. This is about discovering the true facts of the events of December 15th and 16th last year. Nothing you say here will have any bearing on your future career prospects and no one will be subject to sanction on the basis of anything they reveal to this committee.
HOLM: I do. But I didn't do anything wrong.
BILUNGS: Then you should have no problem speaking freely. If you could start by telling us what you remember of the morning of Monday December 15th.
HOLM: Where do you want me to start? Breakfast?
BILUNGS: The beginning of your shift will suffice.
HOLM: [Refers to notes] I was late. The road closures had already started—
BILUNGS: The road closures around the National Museum?
HOLM: Yes. So obviously I stopped to see if I could help. I spoke to an officer [refers to notes], Constable Eklund, who told me it was precautionary. A bomb threat had been called in.

BILUNGS: And after that, you went to the station house?
HOLM: Yes. It was not an emergency. There had not been an explosion. Not yet. There were no injuries. The situation was under control, so I went to work as normal, arriving for my shift at eleven fifteen.
BILUNGS: This was one of the most serious security situations in our nation's history and you simply carried on to work. You walked away?
HOLM: I followed protocol. I didn't have my radio with me, it was at the station—as it should be, I should add. I had cases to work. I had a suspect who'd been taken into custody overnight. All we knew at this point was that someone had made a bomb threat. It's not uncommon. I was not being neglectful.
BILUNGS: You are not being accused of such behavior. And this committee has already heard from your colleague, [refers to notes] Sergeant Engström, that hoaxes of a similar nature had been made in the months leading up to December 15th. What happened when you got to the station house?
HOLM: [Takes sip of water] Well, obviously, because of the incident at the National Museum, most of the uniformed officers were out. I remember the phones were all ringing. On almost every desk, all the time. I guess people had heard the news and they were all calling their friend the cop to get the inside story, you know. And of course no one was there to answer them. Lots of ringing. Endless ringing.
BILUNGS: So.
HOLM: I grabbed the case files for the suspect in custody, reviewed the arrest report and made the arrangements for him to be interviewed. Making sure his lawyer was present, that sort of thing.
BILUNGS: And, just to be clear, does this have any bearing on the events that happened that day?
HOLM: No, but you asked me to tell you about my morning. I am telling you.
BILUNGS: Perhaps if you could speed things up a little bit, Sergeant Holm.

HOLM: I guess it was around twelve forty-five when a call was patched through to me from the dispatch office. They had received several calls claiming that Anna Skyberg had been kidnapped. At gunpoint.

3

Ingrid punched out one of the SIM cards from its plastic casing and inserted it into the phone. She replaced the battery, attached the charger, plugged it in and prayed. The phone immediately vibrated. Then a blue light behind the keys flickered and finally the screen brightened. She relaxed a little, sat back in her seat and took a sip of her coffee. She had forgotten that there is no such thing as a bad cup of coffee in Sweden—even in a chain like Wayne's—and smiled. If only she was back in the land of her ancestors for a different purpose.

The Samsung trilled with the sound of a new message from the provider, presumably welcoming her to the network and advising her of the call tariffs. That meant it was working. She took a deep breath, then pushed up the sleeve of her jacket to reveal the phone number she had written on her arm.

She had rewritten it three times since Nick's wedding on Saturday, each time on a different part of her body. With each transfer from limb to belly and from belly to limb, she had checked and triple checked that she had written it down correctly. But now that Ingrid had to use it, she feared she might have made a transcription error.

She inputted the number and started to write the text message, just as she had been instructed.

I am waiting for you.

That was it. Just that. She dropped the phone back on the table and took another sip of coffee. Then another. She kept looking at the Samsung as if the power of her stare would be enough to make it ding with the sound of a reply.

By the time she had finished her Americano, there was still no text. Had she used the wrong number? She checked the scrawl on her forearm against the single number in the phone's memory. They matched, so she licked a paper napkin and scrubbed the ink from her skin. All she could do now was wait. She ordered another coffee and her first Swedish *bulle* in over a decade. It was sticky and sweet and just what her exhausted body needed. She had always thought that Sweden's greatest gift to the world hadn't been ABBA, but the tradition of *fika*: strong coffee and sweet cakes, ideally twice a day.

She reflexively checked the phone. The display flashed 00:00. Ingrid had left her watch in London and there wasn't a clock on the wall, but she guessed it was now eleven fifteen or eleven thirty. Which meant it was ten thirty in London where she was about to miss a meeting with an art collector who was interested in acquiring a Kandinsky. For the past several months, Ingrid had been working undercover for the FBI as an art broker, matching ultra-rich Russians in London with twentieth-century masterworks. Her brief was to gather intelligence on the Russian oligarchs in Britain and to piece together where they kept their money and how they moved it around. After spending most of her career in child protection, it was work Ingrid enjoyed.

Her undercover role meant she was less tied to her desk in the criminal division at the US embassy in London. She was now often absent from the office for days at a time and she hadn't needed to call in sick, or arrange a vacation day, before she'd boarded the flight to St Petersburg. For a day, no one would miss her.

Ingrid took a sip of coffee. She didn't want to think how long she could actually disappear for before anyone would notice. With no family in London and the kind of friends she tended to see spontaneously rather than casually, not to mention the sort of neighbors who avoided eye contact in the elevator, the only person who would think to report Ingrid missing was her assistant Jennifer. But right now, Jennifer was on vacation, visiting her folks in California.

"Damn you," Ingrid said softly under her breath as the realization dawned. "You goddamned bastard."

Nick Angelis knew that Jennifer was away. Nick had worked it all out, and as she licked the sugar off her fingers Ingrid had to accept she'd been played. She should have been suspicious the moment she'd received the last-minute invitation to Nick's wedding, given their status as acquaintances-with-benefits. At first, she had assumed Nick simply wanted to make it clear that their arrangement had come to an end, or maybe he had wanted to prove to as many people as possible that an inveterate lothario was truly capable of settling down, or at least saying 'I do'. On Saturday afternoon, Ingrid had considered whether perhaps the wedding was a way of telling half the women crammed into the pews of the St Andrew's Greek Orthodox church that they simply weren't good enough. It was only when the laconic James —silver-haired, bespectacled, Savile Row suit, and with a handshake that could split bedrock—had handed her a glass of champagne at the reception and said, "Do the words 'Arding Manor' mean anything to you?" that she realized her invitation had been a straightforward business transaction.

Ingrid shuddered. Was it the cold air that burst into the coffee shop every time the door was opened, or was it recalling what had happened at Arding Manor? It had been the biggest screw-up of her career, and Fortnum's—one of the world's elite private security companies—had, quite literally, disposed of the bodies. She had always known that one day her debt would be called in, and here she was, waiting in a coffee shop in Stockholm for a phone to ring.

Nick's parting comment to her before he'd taken his bride—twenty-six years old, a doctor with MSF, as beautiful as she was intelligent, and who would have no reason to marry so young to a man with a past as checkered as Nick's—on honeymoon to Venezuela was that Fortnum's would never ask her to do something she was not capable of executing perfectly. While the remains of her coffee grew colder, it dawned on Ingrid that the real reason she had been selected for this mission wasn't that she spoke Russian, or could pass for Swedish, or even that she was available—it was because it was so risky Fortnum's could not allocate one of its own. Nick must have calculated that she was expendable, that if anything went wrong no one would notice Ingrid's disappearance until Fortnum's had been able to cover their tracks. A small dagger of resentment thrust its way up from her waistband and under her ribs. They might not be sleeping with each other anymore, but Nick Angelis had found another way to screw her.

Ingrid couldn't stay in Wayne's any longer. The girl serving at the counter had smiled at her too many times and there was a risk she'd be able to identify Ingrid, to confirm to investigators that, yes, she had indeed been there and that all she had done was quietly drink coffee and stare at a phone that looked like a prop from a ten-year-old movie. She pulled the beanie over her blonde hair, bent down to unplug the phone and grabbed the Samsung from the table. The moment she dropped it into her bag, a muted trill announced the arrival of a message. She scooped it out, figured out the unlocking sequence, then read the message:

Grand Hotel. Spa. Midday.

She flipped the phone shut, suddenly feeling like Fox Mulder or some other vintage TV cop from a time when flip phones had felt like the future. The spa? It was obvious now she thought about it. What better way to make sure she was unarmed than to force her to be naked.

She picked up the napkin and wiped the rim and handle of her coffee cup, then checked herself: she was taking things too far. The cup would be washed before the lunchtime rush, long before any forensics specialist might come searching for evidence. Ingrid took the battery out of the phone and removed the SIM, which she wrapped in the napkin and dumped in the trash can.

Back on the street, Ingrid hailed a cab, but before she climbed in she knelt down and carefully placed the Samsung's battery under the car's rear tire.

"*Nationalmuseum, tack,*" she said. The National Museum was just a block from the Grand Hotel but it disguised her true destination.

The driver pulled out into the traffic and Ingrid heard something crunch beneath the wheels. Ten minutes later, after waiting for the cab to disappear around a corner, she crossed the street and threw the Samsung into the harbor and watched it sink beneath the frigid water. Then she turned back, looked up at the Grand Hotel and took the deepest breath of her life.

4

Ingrid took the towel from the receptionist and followed her directions to the changing rooms. Still, at the age of thirty-three, nothing could make her feel like an awkward teen as reliably as a changing room. Lurking somewhere inside Ingrid's five-ten, size-four frame was the second fattest kid in the class. The same old feelings of revulsion tightened the muscles beneath her tongue as she pushed open the locker-room door.

One of the things Ingrid had come to appreciate after two years of living in London was British prudery. It was rare that a store or a fitness club had communal changing rooms, but this was Sweden, the country where entire villages took a sauna together. Just as she had done as a teenager, Ingrid moved to a far corner, hoping to be invisible.

There were two other women in the changing room, both older. Ingrid had no idea who she was meeting and it was possible her contact was the overweight woman with sagging, rippling flesh who was struggling to keep her towel tucked under her armpits. The woman was red-faced, her wet hair flattened against her thick, wobbling neck. Ingrid tried to make eye contact without appearing to stare, but the woman was more embarrassed than Ingrid and did not look up.

The other woman—wiry, gray ponytail, black Lycra gym gear—seemed a more likely contact, but her smile was an awkward expression of locker-room solidarity rather than one of greeting. Ingrid slipped off her sneakers. A burning memory of Middleton Junior High flashed into her brain. Her and Megan, the fat girls, holding up towels for each other so that the other kids wouldn't point. It didn't stop them. Two little piggies. Ingrid blanched.

Fuck them.

She stripped quickly, defiantly, even waiting until she had folded her clothes before grabbing the towel and securing it over her breasts. She had worked hard—in the gym, pounding sidewalks, rock climbing—for her physique and a tiny bit of her wished the girls from the catty clique at school could see her now. Although, no doubt, they'd still point and laugh at the bruises Ingrid was collecting below the knee. She couldn't tell which ones came from whacking her shins on the foot pegs of her beloved Triumph Thunderbird, and those she'd acquired in parkour training. She'd like to see one of those cheerleaders attempt a twenty-foot leap from a high-rise parking lot onto the story below.

Ingrid picked up her neat pile of clothes, carefully hiding her runner's ankle pouch containing around two thousand euros between her tee and her jeans, and walked over to the bank of lockers. She felt two sets of eyes boring into her. She turned to face the women, who both had open mouths. The gray-haired woman blinked and turned away. The obese woman bowed her head. They weren't looking at her bruises: they had seen her scar. A dark, pinched purple welt under her right shoulder blade that was so obviously a bullet entry wound that no one ever had to ask how she got it, only when. Ingrid's teenage awkwardness, her yearning to be invisible, was instantly reignited.

She slammed the locker door hard and turned the key before pinning it to her towel. There was a pyramid of rolled towels by the door. She grabbed one, flung it over her right shoulder and strode out into the spa.

The place was beautiful, with muted lighting, soft classical music and a series of columns that hinted the spa may have been based on an original Roman design. There were, unusually for a spa, several people in the pool, three naked men, one naked woman and another woman in a black swimming costume. Ingrid was willing to bet the woman in the swimming costume would be British. She found a wooden lounger facing the deep end of the pool and sat down. Presumably, whoever she was meeting would approach her?

She carefully checked the entrances and exits, an occupational necessity. She could see three doors: one to the locker rooms, another to the treatment area and a third marked 'Staff Only'. She watched one of the women climb the steps out of the pool and grab a towel, and wondered if she was the person she was meant to be meeting. Nick and the mysterious James had only given her need-to-know information, and that definitely hadn't included a description of her contact. What the two men had impressed upon her, however, was the strategic importance of her impromptu city break in the Venice of the North.

"Do you know about the Vienna negotiations?" James had asked. They then ushered Ingrid out of the room where the wedding reception was taking place and led her down the corridor into the Reform Club's library. They spoke quietly but firmly so that she would understand and no one else would hear, despite the fact that they had the room to themselves. Ingrid realized now that their isolation would have been arranged in advance.

"The Iranian thing?" she had said. Never had the attempt to find a settlement to nuclear proliferation sounded so casual.

Nick had nodded. He had run his hand through his hair, and she remembered thinking the new gold band on his finger looked preposterous. Nick Angelis had committed himself to one woman. Until death did they part. "Right now there is a side negotiation happening."

Ingrid put her champagne flute on a bookshelf. The dark wood was worn, polished, ancient. "Should I know about it?"

The two men looked at each other.

"It's probably a very good sign that you do not," James said. He was well-spoken, and Ingrid thought that, unlike Nick, his crisp upper-class consonants were the result of breeding and education, not affectation. "While various foreign ministers were in the same room, a few decisions were taken about Syria."

"There is a plan emerging," Nick said. He had loosened his tie and unbuttoned his collar. Ingrid remembered hating that she had noticed. "There is an opportunity to apply some pressure, but—"

"But," James interrupted him, "no one, no nation, can be seen to be applying that pressure."

"And it is in these sorts of situations that organizations like ours are asked to do what governments cannot be seen to be doing."

"Or ever be known to have done."

Ingrid had wished her glass wasn't empty. "And what has this got to do with me?"

James turned to Nick. "Don't you have a bride to attend to?"

He nodded. "I certainly do. I will leave you in my colleague's estimable hands." He gave Ingrid a tiny wink and retreated back out into the hallway.

"Shall we?" James said, an arm extended toward a table and two chairs near a leadlight window overlooking Pall Mall.

Nervously, Ingrid followed him and he pulled back a chair for her.

"Relax, Ingrid. Nick has assessed that you are more than capable of carrying out this task. And when it is done," James sat down, brushing invisible specks from his pressed black trousers as he did so, "you will never hear the words 'Arding Manor' again."

Ingrid bit the inside of her lip and fought the instinct to stare at her lap: she was damn well going to look him in the eye if he was going to send her into the lion's den. "I don't know very much about Syria. There is probably someone better placed than me for whatever it is you need."

"Nick assures me you are perfect for this." He reached inside his tuxedo jacket and pulled out a white envelope which he slid across the table. "That is five thousand dollars in cash, a mix of US, euros and kronor."

"Kronor?" Ingrid stretched out a hand and quickly shoved

the envelope into her clutch. A small but significant act of compliance.

"Don't look so worried," James said, his jet-black eyebrows inclining toward the middle of his forehead. Did he dye them, she wondered? "Your task is straightforward. We only require you to collect something, and then deliver it."

Ingrid's lips were dry. She wanted a drink. "What has this got to do with Vienna? With Syria?"

James spread his fingers and pressed them into the table. His cuffs were starched, his cufflinks gold. His watch, just visible, was a Breitling. "Your government," he began. "Your State Department, to be precise, is attempting to build a coalition within Syria. I presume you know the basics?"

"I think it best if nothing is presumed."

"Very sensible." He cleared his throat. "After the Arab Spring, the country fell into civil war. This much you know?"

"Yes."

"President Assad refused to step down, and the rebels, notably the Free Syrian Army, could only provide robust opposition for a limited period of time. They simply didn't have the supply chains, the command structures to hold out against a trained and funded military."

Now Ingrid wished she hadn't had a drink at all. She needed her brain to kick up a gear, but she was having trouble working out how the hell this could possibly involve her. Didn't they need special ops? Delta Force? She was a fed. A glorified cop. What did she know about the military and civil wars? She didn't even speak Arabic. She was convinced they had chosen the wrong person.

"As a consequence, to oversimplify things, the opposition crumbled and Daesh moved in."

"Islamic State?"

"Or, if you're toeing the line, I believe we are supposed to refer to them as the 'so-called Islamic State'. Or maybe that's just on the BBC." He looked at his watch. "So, now we have a situation where we—or rather you, this is coming from Washington—wish to oust both Assad and Daesh and the only way we can do that is by supporting and consolidating the moderate opposition forces on the ground."

Ingrid was gripping the clutch bag in her lap so tightly her fingers were starting to hurt. She didn't want to interrupt James, or whatever his real name was, she just wanted him to tell her why she had really been invited to Nick's wedding.

"And this, my dear, is where you come in."

5

The spa of the Grand Hotel was a classic piece of restrained Scandinavian design. The Swedes, as a rule, were too pragmatic for luxury. Wool over cashmere, ceramic over porcelain, steel over chrome: understated, utilitarian and just how Ingrid liked things. She didn't do bling. Her earrings were simple silver hoops, and even they sometimes felt like overkill. She couldn't accessorize. Hated drawing attention to herself. Whether or not that had something to do with her Swedish ancestry she had no idea. She lay back on the lounger and scanned every person who entered the pool area, anticipating that one of them would approach and ask her about the food in Bolivia or the weather in Jakarta. Or was that just what happened in spy movies?

Ingrid stretched out on the lounger, trying to affect a pose of relaxation. A couple in their forties appeared from the archway that led to the treatment rooms and Ingrid scrutinized them as they headed for the locker-room exit. They only had eyes for each other: they were not who she was meeting.

It seemed impossible that her visiting a luxury spa in Stockholm could have anything to do with the war in Syria, but if the Fortnum plan was implemented effectively and on schedule, she was assured her actions would enable the State Department to pave the way for a new coalition in Damascus.

"I believe," James had said to her as she looked out the window at an ambulance forging a path through the traffic on Pall Mall, "it is important that you understand what is at stake, agent."

Ingrid turned to him. "For me, or for the State Department?"

"For the people of Syria."

There was no reply to that.

James continued: "Right now there are several factions fighting each other, presumably because they know they cannot defeat Assad or Daesh. To be blunt, we simply need them to stop."

Was this how the British behaved in diplomatic negotiations? Talking to warring factions like a headmaster at an ivy-clad prep school? Ingrid was starting to feel cold. In the other room, slung over the back of her chair, was a shawl that she wanted for her shoulders. But whether sitting next to a drafty Georgian window in a thin silk dress in the middle of December was the cause of her shivering she couldn't be sure: she had never been sent to a war zone before.

"What is it you need me to do?" she asked, her throat tightening as she spoke.

James pursed his lips and narrowed his eyes. Ingrid had done several training sessions on reading facial expressions: she understood that he wanted to reveal as little as possible. "Let's say there are two factions. We'll call them Faction A and Faction B, and let's also say that we—the West—is backing the A team. Your job is to help persuade Faction B to capitulate. By Thursday."

Was he serious? "How? And why Thursday?"

"There is another meeting in Vienna. By the end of that meeting, A and B must be in agreement if we stand any bloody chance of making a difference in Syria."

"I don't see what I can do."

"You only need to do what you are told. And to follow your instructions with absolute precision and discretion. Nothing else." He looked down at his hands and Ingrid followed his gaze.

The immaculate silver hair and tailored tux were in contrast to his rugged fingers. They looked like they belonged to a gardener or a sailor: weathered, lined, callused. Ex-military for sure. Probably SAS. Hands that could kill. Hands that had killed. Without the need for a weapon.

"And how on earth am I supposed to get Faction B to play ball?"

"Fear not, Agent Skyberg. You won't be doing it single-handedly. You will be part of a team, and—" he interrupted himself. "Do you watch sports?"

"Yes."

"Then you'll know the teams that win matches are the ones where the individual players stay in position, follow their manager's instructions and don't need to look behind them before they throw the ball because they trust their teammates will be there." He paused, weighing up if he needed to say more. "It is also important that, as a manager, you choose the right players for the opposition. If you're a flyweight, you're not going to do well against one of the Klitschko brothers, are you?"

One of the swimmers in the pool climbed out. With no magazine to read, it was hard not to watch him, a choice she regretted when he caught her staring at his penis. The man—thirties, southern European, judging by his olive skin and dark hair—was muscular with a tattoo on his upper left arm. Some sort of insignia. A regiment perhaps. She smiled at him, hoping he would recognize it as a greeting rather than a compliment. He tied a towel around his waist and walked off toward the sauna and steam room, leaving foot-shaped puddles in his wake. He didn't look back.

Not him.

Ingrid had been waiting on the lounger for fifteen minutes, making it well after midday. She wasn't sure what else she could do apart from make herself both visible and approachable. She had no idea if the person she was conducting the transaction with had her description or not. Perhaps she didn't fit their idea of an arms dealer.

James had explained to Ingrid that her role was to acquire a component from one organization and deliver it to another. 'A simple courier job' was how he'd put it.

"What kind of component?" she had asked, fearing the answer.

James nodded. "It is better that you understand. There is an argument for saying you should know nothing, that you should not open the package, but I like my players to know the role they are performing. It generally leads to better outcomes." He sniffed in sharply through his nose. "You will be aware, of course, that there are restrictions on the weapons we can supply to the combatants on the ground. Officially."

"And unofficially?"

He leaned forward. "Have you heard of the Haze missile?"

She shook her head.

"Ballistic. Laser guided. Damned effective. Can practically turn on a sixpence at 400 miles per hour. SAMs are useless against it."

"And you want me to, what? Go to an arms fair and buy one?"

"No, my dear, that would never be allowed. How best can I explain this? Faction A, as I shall continue to call them, already have a supply. Via the Israelis, oddly enough. But they are all useless. They were supplied without... how can I describe it to you? You don't know about ballistic weapons, do you?"

"No."

He nodded. "Nick tells me you ride a bike?"

"A Triumph Thunderbird."

"Ah, a beauty."

"Thank you."

"Now, tell me, what would be an excellent way of preventing a thief from using it?"

Ingrid gave it some thought. "Disconnect the battery? Remove it? Or the spark plugs?"

"Bingo. These missiles are missing their spark plugs. Your job is to obtain these components—discreetly, without incident—and deliver them. You won't know who you are meeting. You will not be able to join the dots. But if you play your part, by Wednesday morning Faction A will have released the first Haze attack. And by Wednesday evening, Faction B will be in the mood to negotiate and the talks in Vienna will achieve the aims of the US government."

"And if they're not?"

"What a good question, my dear." He took a sip of his Scotch. "That is why you will be collecting three of these spark plugs. It is entirely possible that the first Haze attack will be assumed to be a one-off. Faction B will likely take stock. Launching a second Haze missile should convince them Faction A have a good supply… that's generally when we get people willing to negotiate. Same thing happened in the Iran-Iraq war."

"It did?"

"Yah. You remember Oliver North and all that, don't you?"

Ingrid had barely been born at the time of the Iran-Contra scandal. "Of course."

"It was the second missile that got Saddam to the table."

Ingrid wondered what kind of missile he was talking about. Chemical? Worse? "So why the need for a third…" Ingrid searched for the right words. "The third spark plug?"

"Insurance. Just in case one of them is defective. And besides, we have been offered three of them. By Thursday, the Vienna negotiations will be on the cusp of a breakthrough and no nation, not yours, not ours, will have breached the arms control agreements to which we are signatories." He looked at her closely, making sure that she understood. "Needless to say that —if those aims bring about the intended result—many, many lives will be saved. You will have done a good day's work, agent."

"I have a question."

"Go ahead."

"You want me to collect these 'spark plugs' from Peter and deliver them to Paul?"

"Correct."

She took a breath. "Why doesn't Peter just take them to Paul?"

"Ah. Yes. Obvious question." James rattled the ice cubes round his tumbler.

"Well?"

He pressed his lips together, then spoke carefully. "It is important that the receiver has no way of identifying the supplier. For obvious reasons."

She supposed it made sense. "And I can buy these 'spark plugs' for five thousand dollars?"

He bit the inside of his lip, pulling the skin tighter over his chin. "No, I imagine they cost a great deal more than that. The money is for you."

"I am being paid?" She knew she sounded indignant.

"To cover your travel expenses."

He laid out the plan to her: get to Stockholm by midday on Monday without any means of identification and without being followed; buy two burner phones and two SIM cards from separate retailers; send a message to the number he wrote on the palm of her hand; wait for instructions; follow whatever instructions she received.

So far, Ingrid had obeyed James's instructions to the letter. But the longer she was made to wait at the poolside, the less sure she was she hadn't forgotten something. Or made a mistake. Was there another Grand Hotel she didn't know about? Had she been followed? Compromised? She was breathing deeply, her chest rising rapidly beneath the cotton towel.

She had to try something else because waiting wasn't working. She got up and walked back toward the locker room. From her vantage point on the lounger, she hadn't been able to see either the fat woman or the woman in Lycra leave, but she reasoned that enough time had passed for either of them to have placed the spark plugs in her locker. If someone had the contacts to deal in ballistic missiles, was it really so ridiculous that they'd be able to get a duplicate key to a changing-room locker? Ingrid marched up to the locker room and pushed the door open with such force that it slammed into a bench. Five shocked faces turned toward her.

"I'm sorry," she said. In English. Dammit. She clenched her jaw in annoyance. "*Jag år ledsen.*"

The women—none of whom Ingrid had seen before—returned to their excited conversations about massages and pedicures. Ingrid reached down and unpinned her key. Then she took a step toward her locker, tensed every muscle in her body, and inserted the key.

Transcript from Riksdag Committee Hearing 23

December 14 2015

BILUNGS: If we could continue, Inspector. When did the Stockholm City Police first learn that the suspect had been at the Grand Hotel?
LUNDBERG: I wasn't aware of it until the Wednesday, so the 17th. It's possible some of my other colleagues had heard something sooner.
BILUNGS: And you spoke to staff at the hotel?
LUNDBERG: Yes, but not until the following day.
BILUNGS: It was not a priority?
LUNDBERG: You have to remember, on Tuesday 16th I was out at Västerås, where the cell phone had been traced to. That had been my part of the investigation. It wasn't until the hotel got in touch, after our appeal for help, that we knew she had been in the spa.
BILUNGS: Understood. So please tell us what you found out from the hotel.
LUNDBERG: Sure. Of course. Well, there had been some thefts. A few guests reported belongings had been stolen from their rooms, and another—possibly two, actually—guests had complained of things going missing from the changing rooms in the spa. Ilse Fredriksson, the duty manager, had reported it to the police. On the Monday. Though, obviously, given what was happening next door at the museum guests were issued with crime numbers, so they could claim on their insurance policies, but it was not followed up until the Wednesday, by which time the hotel had carried out its own investigation. [Pause. BILUNGS motions for her to continue] Miss Fredriksson had already matched the spa guests against the main hotel guest list and had eliminated everyone who was staying at the hotel. She told me she was satisfied none of the hotel guests were responsible, so that left the day visitors.

BILUNGS: And the suspect was one of these day visitors?
LUNDBERG: Yes, there is no CCTV footage from the spa, but we believe the suspect is the woman you can see in Exhibit 38, the screenshot from the security camera in the hotel's main lobby.
BILUNGS: [Holding A4 photo] Is this the photograph you mean?
LUNDBERG: Yes. It's not a great image, but when we showed that photo to the patrons at Republik, several of them said they believed it was the same woman. Anyway, as I was saying, the hotel started to do its own research into the day visitors, most of whom we were able to trace through credit card usage, but the receptionist remembered this woman who had paid in cash. When uniformed officers followed up the theft reports on the Wednesday, and they saw this woman in the photograph, they immediately called my team. By this stage, there wasn't a single cop in Sweden who wasn't looking for her.

6

Ingrid checked the pockets of her jacket and her jeans. She checked inside her sneakers. She opened the runners' armband she had strapped to her calf.

"Have you lost something?" one of the women asked.

"I'm sorry." Though she understood her perfectly, Ingrid replied in English. "I do not speak Swedish," she said in what she hoped was an authentic Russian accent.

The woman, probably part of a bachelorette party, repeated herself in English.

"No, thank you. Nothing is lost."

It occurred to Ingrid that she had no idea how big the components she was collecting were. Would they fit in a pocket? Would they even fit inside her backpack? Ever since James had called them spark plugs, she had been envisioning exactly that, but she had no idea if she'd need a suitcase to transport them or if they'd fit in her pockets. She peered inside the oak locker: even if they were the size of a stamp they weren't there.

She put her clothes back in then went over to the mirror and made a show of fixing her hair while examining the five women as they undressed. Never had five women needed a spa day less: they were all manicured and waxed, without a dimple of cellulite between them. What happened to the universal law that in every group of five women there always had to be an ugly one? Or had that law not been in force since the dawn of the Spice Age?

She decided she should go for a swim. Not only would it deal with her 'hat hair' situation, but she had been instructed not to draw attention to herself and it had to look odd that she had paid for the spa's sumptuous facilities and wasn't using them. A little exercise might also soothe the menstrual cramps that were beginning to tighten around her abdomen. Then she remembered that she didn't have a swimming costume.

To hell with it. She was part Swedish, wasn't she? She was in the shape of her life. And maybe, just maybe, she was being watched and someone would only approach her after she had demonstrated, categorically, that she was unarmed.

Ingrid left the hens to their chatter and didn't miss a beat between dropping her towels on the first lounger she came to and diving in. Within a few strokes, the water didn't seem so cold, and by the end of the first length she wondered why people didn't swim in the nude more often until a guy switched to her side of the pool so he could swim in her wake. Then she remembered exactly why: because most men are creeps. He was too slow to get close enough for an eyeful, but when she reached the end, she climbed out, as modestly as she could, and wrapped herself in one of her towels.

She ran the other towel over her short hair and looked again at the people using the spa. It had to be twelve thirty by now. Surely one of them was looking for her?

"Hi."

Ingrid turned. The man was in his twenties, wearing a tracksuit. Her heart released an explosion inside her chest. "Hi."

"You have booked a massage?" he asked.

"No, no I have not." Her Russian accent was holding steady.

"You are not Mariam?"

Ingrid's teeth started to chatter as the water on her skin evaporated. Had James forgotten to give her the script? Was there a code she was supposed to give him?

"No. I am not."

"Ah!" He spotted someone over her shoulder. "I think that is my client."

He was just a masseur, not a black market dealer of military hardware. There were goose bumps all over Ingrid's skin and her teeth were graduating from a chatter to a shudder. She covered her scar with the towel she had been drying her hair with and walked toward a door that she presumed led to the sauna and steam rooms. It was the best way she could think of to warm up.

There are certain things that some nations do better than others. No one, in Ingrid's estimation, could barbecue meat quite as well as an American, not even an Australian. No nation has better cheese than France. New Zealand makes the finest Sauvignon Blanc. And no one does a sauna like the Swedes. The moment she pushed open the door it was apparent why the rest of the spa was so empty: everyone was having an earnest conversation about whether or not the Vasa Museum was worth a visit.

"*Hej*," one of the women said to Ingrid as she stepped inside.

"*Hej*," she said back and took a seat on the lower bench. A man sitting on the tier above her shuffled across to make space for her. She listened as they spoke, as ever, in English, about how much time the Australian tourists in the sauna would need to allow to see everything at the museum. Ingrid smiled: if the hotel's guests had been Brits and Yanks, the towels would be up to their armpits and the conversation would range between non-existent and stilted.

There were eight people in the sauna, including her. Swedish tourists, mostly, in the city to do some Christmas shopping, the Australian couple and a striking woman from Germany with long black hair, shaved eyebrows, piercings and tattoos. Ingrid wondered if she was making a Lisbeth Salander pilgrimage. She made eye contact and the German stared back. Something about the way she stared at Ingrid told her she had either found her contact, or the German woman was a little lacking in social etiquette.

The German woman gave her a wink.

Or, as the Brits would say, she had pulled. She couldn't risk being remembered, so she got to her feet. "*Förlåt,*" she apologized. It was bad form to open the sauna door so frequently.

A little further down the tiled corridor was the entrance to the steam room. She looked behind her to see if anyone had followed her, then pulled open the door and went in.

The sharp menthol vapors pricked the sensitive skin beneath her nostrils as the door closed behind her. The steam was so dense it took a few moments to see that she was not alone. A pair of feet was visible on the dark granite floor. She could just make out that they belonged to a pair of hairy legs. Too hairy to be a woman. Above the noise of the steam generator she could hear the short, labored breaths of a fat man.

She sat down. This was it. Her skin tightened, her whole body stiffened and the muscles in her throat tensed painfully. She placed her hands on the stone bench either side of her and straightened her arms, almost as if she was bracing herself. Exactly as if she was bracing herself.

Someone tapped on the door. A short, firm knock. Whoever it was did not enter.

The tightness in Ingrid's throat spread upwards, creating pain in her ears. She was experiencing all the symptoms of a cold in very rapid succession. Her skin constricted like she was under pressure, a free diver exploring deep inside a dark crevice, holding her breath.

"You may need an extra towel," the man said. Eastern European accent, possibly Hungarian or Czech. He made a slurping noise as his corpulent flesh peeled off the tiled bench. "There is one for you here."

He padded over to the door and pushed it open. She could see as he walked out that he was Caucasian, balding and had a particularly hairy back. He did not look back.

When the glass door closed behind him, Ingrid took a deep breath and instantly spluttered as the hot air rushed against the back of her throat. She gulped hard, trying to suppress the urge to cough. She swallowed again, and held a hand to her sternum, forcing the irritation to stay where it was.

When she had recovered, Ingrid stood up slowly and crossed

over to where the fat man had been sitting. She bent down so she could see the stone surface of the bench through the steam and her hand stretched out in search of the towel. Her feet slipped a little on the wet floor and she fell against the bench, breaking her fall with her extended arm.

Ingrid could feel her pulse in her ears as she touched a folded towel. She patted it. There was definitely something inside it. She lifted a corner of the towel.

"Don't do that."

Ingrid gasped. Someone else was in there.

7

The steam swirled and Ingrid caught a glimpse of a woman, sitting like Buddha, observing her.

"You wait," she said. "Five minutes. Then you can leave." An Australian accent.

"OK," Ingrid said, her voice unusually tentative.

"Don't speak."

Ingrid peered through the steam, trying to make out who she was. She desperately wanted a sip of water for her scratchy throat. There had been a fountain in the corridor outside, but she swallowed, trying to lubricate her itch with saliva.

"And don't look at me." The woman was sitting next to the steam outlet where visibility was at its worst.

Ingrid turned to face forward and shuffled backwards so her spine was touching the stone wall of the steam chamber and lifted her feet off the ground. She tucked them under her knees and sat cross-legged. Her right hand stayed firmly planted on the folded towel.

"Don't touch it, you understand?"

How was it that the woman could see Ingrid more clearly than she could see her? Ingrid had been in enough negotiations to know complete capitulation was foolish. The opposing party needed to respect you, to value you.

"I am checking that everything is in order." Ingrid spoke slowly and deliberately.

"I told you not to speak."

"So you did." That was it. She had done enough to make the woman see she wasn't some dumb mule to be pushed around. Ingrid defied the instructions and kept her hand on the towel, her palm pressed against the hard shapes within its folds. Ingrid exhaled deeply, creating eddies in the steam. The woman did not stir, did not make a sound. Whichever organization she worked for, she had no doubt been hired for her ability to be invisible on stake-outs, to observe without being seen. Special obs, Ingrid joked to herself.

No one entered the steam room. Someone had to be acting as a security guard, guiding unsuspecting tourists back to the pool area. Ingrid wiped the moisture—was it water or sweat?—out of her eyes and noticed how smooth her skin felt. How ironic that while she was doing the government's dirty work, her pores were getting cleansed. She used her towel to dab the drips falling between her breasts and saw that a vein in her chest was pulsing fast. She was so hot she thought she might faint.

The two women sat in silence for several minutes and Ingrid tuned in to the sound of the steam generator, finding its rhythmic whirr oddly comforting. Her thoughts drifted to her old apartment in DC, where her bedroom window had been above the extractor fans of the store below, and how she had loved those hot sticky nights with the window open, the gentle burr guiding her toward sleep.

"The person you're looking for," the woman said, "is Magnus Jonsson. You hear that? Magnus Jonsson."

So now she was allowed to speak. "Yes."

"Repeat it back to me."

Ingrid swallowed, trying to lubricate her dry throat. "Magnus Jonsson."

"Good."

The woman got to her feet in one swift, sharp movement. Ingrid instinctively leaned forward, pressing down with her hands, ready to lever herself up.

"I told you not to move."

"You also told me not to speak."

The woman reached down and grabbed Ingrid's wrist.

"What the—" Ingrid tried to stand up, but her feet slipped beneath her. She twisted a shoulder into the woman's torso, hoping to barge her to the ground, but the Australian had both hands firmly around Ingrid's left wrist. There was a clunking noise, the sound of something snapping shut. The woman let go but Ingrid could still feel her grasp. She raised her hand to her face and saw she was now wearing a thick plastic bracelet. "You're tracking me?"

The woman stayed standing.

"It's a little insurance policy."

The vein in Ingrid's chest pulsed harder. She grabbed the bracelet with her right hand and tried to push it over her fist. Even with the steam and the sweat, there was no way it would slide off. It was black, about an inch wide and tight. Furious, she slammed her wrist against the wall but the only damage she did was to herself.

"You want it off, you make the drop."

Ingrid was indignant. "Why wouldn't I make the drop?"

"We just need to be sure." The woman's ankles were visible beneath the steam. Her skin was light brown and she had a faded tattoo of a Chinese pictogram on her ankle. The ink was at least twenty years old: the woman was older than she sounded.

Ingrid's breathing was deep and painful as the hot steam reached the bottom of her lungs. "So who takes this off?"

The woman stood perfectly still and her body above the knee remained wreathed in steam. "When we receive confirmation we can unlock it remotely."

"And if you don't receive confirmation?"

The woman sighed heavily. "Then we come and find you." The menace in her voice was steel-coated. She took a step toward the glass door. "You need to stay in here for another minute before you can leave." She pulled the door open and Ingrid watched as she stepped out into the corridor where she was briefly visible. Petite, slim, short jet-black hair with a towel around her neck and nowhere else.

The door clunked shut and Ingrid fell against the hot stone wall. She wanted to scream. She wanted to punch something. Was this standard practice? Was this how black operations really worked? All need-to-know and obscured in steam? She had questions she wanted to ask, answers she needed to get. Who the hell was Magnus Jonsson?

Her jaw tightened and her insides churned like wet washing in a drum. Out of nowhere she remembered she hadn't booked her bike into the garage. A flash of the case files on her desk popped into her head. It was as if her brain could not process what was happening and wanted to go to somewhere safer, somewhere familiar and mundane.

Had it been a minute?

Ingrid stood up, planted her feet hip-width apart, straightened her back and focused her eyes on the end of her nose. She had to get a grip. She breathed in slowly, then out. In, then out. Expanding her chest, and letting it constrict again. Ujjayi breath. When she felt calm enough, she carefully picked up the folded towel, tucked it close against her side with her elbow and walked over to the glass door. She reached for the handle and stepped out into the empty corridor.

8

There was no sign of the Australian woman in the locker room, so Ingrid dressed, dried her hair and made good use of the lotions and potions the hotel provided. When she was ready to leave, she looked at the folded towel lying on the wooden slatted bench next to her tattered Russell Athletic backpack. She scanned the room: three women. She tried to guess what their reactions would be if she simply lifted the towel, complete with contents, into her bag. It was too risky. Even if there was only a one per cent chance that someone would call her a thief, it would be followed by a one hundred per cent chance that someone would check her bag. She was going to have to leave the towel.

She angled herself so that her body shielded the towel from the line of sight of two of the women. A third would be able to see what she was doing in the mirror. That was fine. It wasn't as if the women would recognize what she was handling. Unless, of course, they too were connected to the operatives she had encountered in the steam room. Ingrid checked her paranoia, and reminded herself of all the witness interviews she had carried out where members of the public had seen nothing and heard less, despite being yards away from a crime in progress. *People don't care. People don't notice.*

Gingerly, she unfolded the towel. Lying between the middle

layers were three cylindrical objects, like clear cigar cases or Perspex test tubes. Each one was six inches long and a little over an inch in diameter.

She stared down at them. She wasn't sure what she had been expecting. Maybe something with a hazard warning and safety seals, but inside the cases were what looked like computer circuit boards. Long thin circuit boards. She unballed her spare pair of socks and slid the tubes inside them, hoping an extra couple of layers of protection would prevent damage, then quickly placed them inside her backpack. She pulled on her jacket, which briefly snagged on the tagging bracelet, and left the locker room without making eye contact with the other women. Instead of leaving by the lobby, Ingrid navigated to the rear of the hotel and left by a side door, pulling on her hat as the freezing air hit her pampered skin.

She headed toward Norrmalm, the commercial center of the city, and kept an eye out for a branch of Wayne's or some other anonymous place where she could plug in the Nokia and send a message. Having been so hot inside the steam room, Stockholm felt five degrees cooler than it had an hour before. Ingrid buried her chin in her scarf and picked up speed.

It took a couple of blocks for her to notice that there wasn't any traffic on the streets. Her head had been so full of circuit boards and evading CCTV that she hadn't even tuned in to the constant police sirens. Up ahead she could see uniformed officers taping off the street. The last thing she needed was to get caught up in whatever was going on, so she turned back toward the harbor, breaking into a trot to escape.

By the time she had reached the water's edge she could hear the rotors of a helicopter getting closer and crowds of people, tourists mostly, were being ushered along the waterfront away from the National Museum. Some looked confused, others fearful.

"What's happening?" Ingrid asked a couple of women as they hurried past. "What's going on?"

They spoke so quickly Ingrid couldn't work out exactly what they had said but she was absolutely sure they had used the word 'bomb'. Really? In Stockholm? She was about to dismiss what they'd told her, but then she remembered something Anna had put on Facebook, something that hadn't made the international press: a man had tried to blow himself up on one of the city's main shopping streets. His bomb hadn't detonated, but if it had, hundreds could have been killed.

Ingrid hadn't heard an explosion. Even inside the steam room she would have felt something, surely? Despite the fear on everyone's faces, she decided the road closures were just a precaution. Some tourist at the museum would have left their lunch box unattended.

She carried on walking. It didn't matter what was happening down by the museum, so long as she didn't get caught up in it. Not only did she have a ferry to catch in a little over four hours' time, but she didn't want the contents of her backpack to be examined by anyone manning a cordon. She pressed westwards, away from the museum, as more and more police vehicles arrived with their sirens blaring.

When she reached Strömbron bridge she made the decision to head south and take lunch on the island of Gamla Stan. The old town. Away from the roadblocks and the uniformed officers. Anna had posted something about a café somewhere nearby. Ingrid conjured up a photo of a perfectly poached egg sitting on top of an English muffin, garnished with pickles and rösti. It was just what she needed.

Crossing the bridge gave Ingrid a good view of the city and its shorelines of solid merchant buildings fringed with chains of moored boats. It had to be one of the most romantic capital cities in the world. A cluster of islands linked by a matrix of bridges and walkways. She remembered how green it was in summer, how she'd swum in the harbor, diving off wooden jetties and drinking beers with Anna and her friends. It was no less beautiful in winter: the gray light and dusting of snow made the place monochrome and cinematic. She glanced across at the Riksdag, the parliament building, and gave Anna a little wave.

Although Ingrid hadn't been to Stockholm for over a decade it hadn't really changed, and she quickly navigated her way onto

Gamla Stan's waterfront. She couldn't recall the name of the café Anna had posted about, but she remembered it was by the docks and its name was vaguely political. Possibly even Soviet. Republik. That was it.

The noise of the sirens was amplified by the water. Ingrid looked across the canal at the National Museum. There was no smoke, no gaping hole. *They are probably just using it for practice, making sure their terrorism protocols are fit for purpose.* It would be over soon. The ferries would run just fine. She'd get out of Stockholm, no problem.

Ingrid found Republik on the ground floor of an old merchant building that would have been the headquarters of a shipping company in the days when Sweden had an empire. She walked up to the door and pushed it open. It was only when she was inside that she realized she had made a terrible mistake. This was Anna's favorite café. This was a dumb idea. Of all the places where she might conceivably bump into the only person in Stockholm who could recognize her, this was it.

The door slammed shut behind her.

9

There was a line of people ordering take-out and several more seated at tables. Ingrid kept the scarf over her face as she scanned the place, making absolutely sure that her cousin, or third cousin, or second cousin several times removed—they had never worked it out precisely—wasn't there.

The café was long and narrow. The style was industrial with subway tiles and exposed pipework. A marble counter laden with pastries ran down one side of the main room with several tables beneath the windows opposite.

"*Hej.*" The girl behind the counter smiled broadly at her.

"*Hej.*" Ingrid ordered the poached egg and English muffin with an Americano.

"*Vill du senap?*"

Ingrid's brain scavenged her memory to recall that '*senap*' was Swedish for mustard. "No, thank you," she said in Swedish.

"You sure?"

Ingrid nodded.

"OK." The girl seemed surprised. "Take a seat."

The place wasn't full, so Ingrid took one of the tables rather than a seat at the counter. At the table behind her, four co-workers were switching off their laptops and exchanging good-byes. In front of her, two women who had to be mother and daughter were enduring a silent lunch with one another. It reminded her of lunches with her own mother, half of which were exercises in contained fury, while the other half were showdowns worthy of a daytime soap opera.

Ingrid opened her backpack and felt around for the Nokia and its charger. Her fingers brushed up against the components wrapped inside her socks, then the charging cable that was sticky with age, and finally pulled out the phone. It reminded her of the new Walkie-Talkie building in London. A hideous piece of architecture that had apparently been modeled on the ugly lump of plastic in her hand.

She inserted the cable into the port and ducked beneath the table in search of an electrical outlet. There wasn't one. She looked behind her at the group of co-workers who were packing up their laptops. She would switch tables when they left.

The counter girl brought over Ingrid's Americano. "There you go."

"Can I please get a glass of water?"

The girl looked at Ingrid with such puzzlement that Ingrid assumed she had completely mangled the language, but the girl pointed to a cabinet near the door that was groaning with cutlery trays, the napkin dispenser and a jug of cold water wearing a glittering cloak of condensation.

Ingrid smiled at her: "*Tack.*"

The backpack was on one of the chairs: even though the counter with the jug of water was no more than fifteen feet away, she was reluctant to leave her bag unattended. Not because anyone would steal it—there was no way they'd be able to escape Republik without Ingrid tackling them onto the hard stone floor—it was in case the people at the table behind nudged it when they got up to leave. She had no idea how fragile the circuit boards were.

They're weapons components, aren't they? They're probably tested to withstand Mach 2.

Nevertheless, she carefully put the bag on the floor and got herself a glass of water while the co-workers at the next table packed their briefcases and left. Ingrid placed her glass on their table, moved her coffee, grabbed the backpack and sat down on the cushioned window seat. Ingrid removed the Nokia's battery, inserted the second SIM and plugged the phone into the outlet beneath the table.

Nothing happened. It didn't bleep. Or flash. Or buzz. Nothing.

She glugged several mouthfuls of water but her throat still felt dry. She checked the cable was inserted properly. It was. Ingrid looked around the room. Perhaps she could use someone else's phone? Put the new SIM into their handset? No, that wouldn't work. She needed to receive a message too.

She gulped down more of the water.

She was going to have to steal someone's phone. There wasn't time for anything else. She looked around the café, clocking the phones on tables and poking out of back pockets.

Ingrid shook her head, took a centering breath and bent under the table to push on the plug. It gave a little and above her head she heard a tiny electronic ping.

"Duh!" She hit her head on the table in her haste to check the phone. A tiny amber light flickered. She squeezed out a vortex of air through pursed lips.

A cook in a white apron appeared from the kitchen and brought over Ingrid's lunch.

"*Tack.*" It looked just as good as the photo on Anna's Facebook timeline.

Despite the beckoning aroma of melted butter, she put her lunch to one side and grabbed the phone. It had a signal. She picked up her gloves and turned them inside out, exposing the care labels where she had written down the number she needed to dial. She keyed it in then typed out the message just as instructed, getting frustrated by the lack of predictive texting.

Are you here yet?

There was no way of knowing if the message had sent properly. No reassuring 'delivered' icon. No comforting bleep. So she picked up the cutlery and tucked into her lunch. Egg and pickles. It shouldn't work but it did.

Ingrid wiped her mouth with a napkin and smelt traces of chlorine on her hand. Somehow, with the police activity and the need to send the second message, she had managed not to think about what had happened in the spa. In particular, what had happened in the steam room. She felt the bracelet dig into her wrist as she cut up her food and recalled the threatening tone the Australian woman had deployed. *Then we come and find you.* Ingrid shivered: she would make the drop.

She had no idea who the Hungarian man and the Australian woman were. If she was right about their nationalities, it was extremely unlikely they worked for the same government. Most likely another private agency like Fortnum's, probably delivering the component on behalf of… she didn't have a clue. The Saudis? A former Soviet state? It was possible they worked for different organizations. It was all so far removed from her day-to-day life that she could almost understand why she had been chosen: even under torture she wouldn't be able to reveal anything because she simply didn't know anything.

She glanced at the phone. The tiny amber charging light pulsed slowly but there was no sign of a message. *Come on!*

She took a sip of coffee—another fine Swedish blend—and started to slowly shake her head. Ever since she had called Nick Angelis and asked for his help to clean up the mess she had created at Arding Manor, she had known there would be a quid pro quo. Payback. And for fourteen months she had wanted to be free of the debt and to have that obligation removed. She had never properly thought about what form that payment would take, but had assumed it would be something like accessing an FBI database, or maybe placing a bug in a meeting room at the embassy. She never expected anything like this. Ingrid closed her eyes and exhaled slowly. She had needed Fortnum's then, and now they needed her. An eye for an eye, a crime for a crime. She could hear her mother, in her undiluted Russian accent: "Never a borrower or a lender be, Ingrid. Don't never owe nobody nothing." Svetlana Skyberg wasn't right about much, but Ingrid never wanted to owe anyone anything ever again.

She opened her eyes as a shaft of steely air blasted in, followed by a man in a woolen coat. He smiled at her, and she smiled back. Athletic, evidently employed judging by his smartly tailored clothes, slim and with no visible deformities: why didn't she meet men like that at home? She watched him as he chatted to the girl behind the counter, who was clearly flirting with him.

The phone bleeped.

Ingrid swallowed hard and swiped it from the table. The display told her there was a message, but the Nokia wasn't a touch screen. She scrutinized its faded buttons for an envelope symbol and punched it. She read the message and gasped.

Stortorget Christmas market. 9am tomorrow.

Tomorrow? She didn't have until tomorrow.

10

Ingrid's head slumped into her hands. Really? Tomorrow? In Stockholm? She had always assumed she'd be delivering the components somewhere else. She felt her cheeks redden at the realization she'd been naive to assume she'd be returning to Riga on the ferry she'd come in on.

She looked down at her brunch and couldn't imagine taking another mouthful. She did the math: if she wasn't leaving for Riga until Tuesday evening, the earliest flight she could get back to London from St Petersburg would be on Thursday night. She had meetings. She had a goddam job. She couldn't just not turn up at work until Friday. She worked for the FBI not some voluntary organization that was grateful if she showed her face. There would be a disciplinary hearing. Reassignment was a possibility. Something hard and heavy sank from her sternum to her stomach: she could lose her job.

Ingrid's gaze settled on the middle distance, her eyes seeing almost nothing as her brain flicked through a sequence of worst-case scenarios. She bit the inside of her cheek, trying to determine how long it would take before she would be missed, assessing when someone at the embassy or the Bureau would start looking for her. The last thing that she—or Nick, or Fortnum's or even the warring factions in Syria—needed was to have the FBI track her down and blow her cover. Tracking people down was one of the things the Bureau was really good at.

Her stare returned to the old Nokia lying uselessly on the marble tabletop. What if their text was a mistake? Surely they meant nine in the evening? The market would be busy then. She pictured a postcard scene of Stortorget strung up with Christmas lights, and snow-dusted tourists buying mittens and reindeer skins. Isn't that how illicit deals take place: in plain sight, with hundreds of witnesses who can never recall a thing? So much less suspicious than meeting in the early morning when their liaison would stand out against a tide of commuters and bleary-eyed stallholders.

A single typo—the difference between a.m. and p.m.—could ruin the entire plan. Then there was the issue of where she could stay for the night without needing a passport or a credit card. Nor had the message said who she was meeting. Was it the mysterious Magnus Jonsson? Had he been given a description of her? She needed more information.

"Is this seat taken?"

Ingrid wrenched her stare from the phone and felt her features soften when she realized the voice belonged to the good-looking man, who was removing his scarf, the cute smile still on his lips. Involuntarily, she smiled back. There were plenty of empty seats elsewhere in the café.

"I'm sorry," she said. "But I am waiting for someone."

He looked disappointed. And disbelieving.

Ingrid conjured up a slightly wicked thought: if she stayed with him for the night she wouldn't appear on any hotel register.

"My boyfriend."

He knew she was lying, but gave her another smile before taking his coffee into the room in the back. Another day, she wanted to tell him, and she would have gladly shared her table.

Staying with Anna and her husband Björn would be another way of keeping off the accommodation radar screens, but Ingrid didn't have Anna's number. Finding a computer and logging into Facebook while she was in Stockholm was absolutely out of the question. She'd have to come up with another solution.

Ingrid ran her fingers through her hair, in an attempt to redress the damage done by her beanie and possibly to rub some sense into her skull. She picked up the Nokia: she had to make sure they hadn't made a mistake.

Are you sure? 9 am for the Christmas market not 9 pm? Please confirm.

She reread the message several times. Typing with one finger without predictive text was too damn frustrating to finesse it any further. She probably couldn't make it any clearer anyway; she just had to decide if sending it was the right thing to do.

Ingrid felt the blast before she heard it, her head instinctively turning toward the door that rattled with the force. A fraction of a second later, everyone else in Republik fell silent, and then in unison they all faced the direction of the explosion. The girl behind the counter was the first to reach the door, peering across the harbor toward the National Museum.

"Was that a bomb?" someone asked as they ran toward the glass door.

Ingrid had heard enough explosions in her career to know that's exactly what it was. A small one. Maybe just a couple of hundred pounds. Possibly a controlled explosion. A group of people crowded round the door. The kitchen staff crammed behind the counter, staring out of the only window to have a direct view of the harbor.

The mother and daughter practically screamed at the throng around the door, demanding information.

"*Herregud,*" Ingrid heard one of the cooks say. Dear God. "There's smoke coming from the National Museum."

Outside, drifting over the water, came a surge of sirens. Ingrid braced herself, expecting a second blast. Her body was stiff, her muscles taut, her breath still, her eyes fixed on the plume she could see above the heads of the people in front of the door. But there was no second explosion, and her body softened slightly with the knowledge it was unlikely anyone would have been killed because the area had been evacuated.

People reached into their pockets for their phones. Some filmed the smoke through the window, most sent messages or updated social media, and the café was filled with a tuneless chorus of dings and bleeps. Ingrid looked down at the Nokia and wondered again if she should send the message.

A young woman ran through from the back of the café, shouting over her shoulder at someone and then insisting she be let through to leave. The small crowd parted and she pushed the door open, sucking in cold air from the harbor. The door then stayed open as three men pushed their way in. The patrons by the door regarded them with disdain, presumably for letting the place get cold.

They were carrying several bags each and they seemed awkward and clumsy. They were African. Somali, Ingrid reckoned, judging by their high foreheads and narrow features. Two in their twenties, one closer to forty. Ingrid looked at the older man again as he reached inside his canvas duffel bag. He wasn't Somali. A case report would describe him as 'of Mid-Eastern appearance'. North African maybe.

Instinctively, Ingrid knew what he was about to pull out of the bag. Her reflexes hit the send button on the Nokia and she leaned on the table, pushing herself to standing as he shook the duffel bag to the floor, unsleeving an automatic rifle. Some variation of a Kalashnikov. One of the younger men rammed a plank of wood under the door handle, wedging it shut, then pulled a pistol from his belt.

11

The small crowd near the door backed away with their hands up. The mother and daughter started screaming and the muted sounds from the back of the café faded into silence. The man with the Kalashnikov stared at Ingrid as he shouldered his weapon. It was chipped and dented, like something scavenged from a battlefield. Ingrid sat back down, her sneaker instinctively pushing against her backpack, making sure it was still there, protecting it. The girl behind the counter dropped a coffee cup and it shattered into pieces that scattered across the floor. Ingrid swallowed hard.

"Give us your money. Give us your cell phones. Give us your watches. Your jewelry." The man's voice was quavering but he smiled as he spoke: the classic, dangerous, mix of fear and adrenaline. "Now!"

One of the Somali men approached the first table and stood over the mother and daughter, waving a Glock 19 in their faces. The women opened their handbags and offered up their purses, which were thrown into a small, tattered holdall.

Maybe, Ingrid thought, the hold-up was just a way of confusing the cops, to throw them off the scent. She kept one eye on the older gunman as he rushed past her, still shouldering the Kalashnikov, into the room at the back. Now she was confused: hadn't they come for the components? Weren't they there for her?

Surely they must have followed her from the hotel? Or intercepted the texts? Why wasn't he thrusting the muzzle in her face and demanding she hand them over?

A flurry of electronic dings meant several people in the café had just sent a text. It didn't matter if they had contacted the police or a loved one: either way it wouldn't be long before the cops arrived. The Somali man continued to collect wallets, watches and phones from the other customers. He checked wrists, hands and necks, pulling off necklaces and demanding rings.

Ingrid knew she could not let him take the Nokia. She needed a reply to her message. Using her elbow, she surreptitiously pushed it onto the cushions on the window seat then bent underneath the table. Her heartbeat ricocheted inside her chest as she reached up, grabbed the phone and shoved it under a cushion. She could see the skinny Somali's legs—filthy sneakers, stained jeans—walk toward her. She grabbed her backpack and felt inside for the tubes: she damn well wasn't going to hand over weapons components to armed thugs. Not without a fight. She slid one of them up inside her sleeve, held in place by an elasticated cuff. She could see the feet of the skinny boy collecting the valuables step toward her. She slid a second tube up into the other sleeve, above the bracelet, just as he slammed his fist onto the tabletop above her head.

"Wallet."

Ingrid reappeared from beneath the table, holding the open Russell Athletic backpack.

"I look for it." Her Swedish was faltering. She couldn't parse tenses. She couldn't think of any words beyond the basic. Quickly, she rummaged around inside the bag and felt for her wallet. She fished it out, dropped the backpack back down onto the seat and handed the wallet to the man. He looked at it suspiciously and indicated she should throw it into his battered North Face holdall, utterly unaware it contained over a thousand US dollars.

"Phone."

There was an argument escalating in the room at the back.

Someone was obviously refusing to hand over their valuables. Shouts of 'please' and 'do as he says' were going unheeded.

"No phone," she managed.

"Phone." His eyes were wide. She could see the pulse in his carotid artery thumping hard and fast.

"No phone," she repeated.

"Then iPad."

"I no have one."

His expression was one of incomprehension. He dropped the holdall onto the table and grabbed her bag off the chair. He unzipped it further and looked for a phone. Ingrid tried not to think about his fingers touching her underwear, or her toothbrush. Somehow, even at that moment, that was what her brain latched onto, not the fact that he was about to find one of the circuit boards.

And if he found one of them, presumably he'd want the other two? Sweat prickled between her shoulder blades.

His left arm pushed and tugged inside her bag, searching frantically for something, while his right hand gripped the carry handle of her backpack and the Glock 19. Ingrid knew she could kick it out of his hand while he was searching. It would be easy. But with the other Somali at the door holding a Beretta firmly in both hands, it wasn't worth the risk: there'd be a bullet in the back of her head before she'd picked up the Glock.

The man holding her bag looked up at her, confusion condensing his features into the center of his face. "Phone," he repeated.

"I no have." It was the best sentence construction she could manage.

He dropped her bag onto the table, pushed the zipper apart and laid the Glock down on the marble. Ingrid's right hand began to twitch in the certain knowledge that she could pick it up and take him out. If it was the only gun in the place, that was exactly what she would do, but she wasn't about to start a firefight and put so many lives at risk.

Her attention was drawn away from the Glock as he removed his hands from inside her bag. She could barely look, but told herself that the third component was a backup. If she could still deliver the other two, the peace negotiations in Vienna could be concluded as planned.

She gasped: he was holding the envelope stuffed full of kronor. Over a thousand dollars' worth.

Take it, she said to herself. Take it.

He opened the envelope and inspected the contents, then raised his eyes and looked her in the eye. He smiled and maintained eye contact as he dropped the envelope into his holdall. Then he picked up the Glock and pointed it straight at her. "Pockets."

Ingrid couldn't work out why he hadn't grabbed the Perspex tube.

"Pockets," he repeated. "Give me your phone."

Ingrid stood up and pulled the gloves out of her jacket pockets and dropped them on the table.

"No phone," she said again.

He shoved his left hand through the zipped openings of her pockets and felt for a phone. When he realized she wasn't lying, he raised the Glock up toward her face and made a clicking noise with his mouth.

Asshole.

She exhaled as he moved on to the next table, quickly swiping her bag and checking the circuit board was still inside. In case it got damaged, she tore a hole in the packet of Libresse and stuffed the Perspex tube inside. The shouting from the room at the back got louder. Ingrid hoped the older guy wouldn't be stupid enough to fire a round. He had to know the people in the café weren't worth a murder rap. Everyone except her, that was.

The gunman at the door kept looking over his shoulder, out onto the sidewalk and across the harbor to the plume of smoke. He would be the one to call time when it was over, to tell them when the getaway car was outside. A little chubby, he was sweating heavily and sporting the kind of facial fuzz only found on teenage boys. He was never going to be able to grow a jihadi beard.

It was while she was staring at him, and listening to the

screaming mother and the arguing voices from the room behind her, that Ingrid noted that the three of them weren't wearing masks. And it was at that moment that she understood just how bad things were going to get. The bomb wasn't a coincidence. This was all part of a coordinated attack. The gunmen intended to become martyrs. Probably ISIS.

"No!"

Ingrid turned her head quickly. A man, thirties, balding, a little out of shape, was refusing to hand over his valuables.

"Give it to me."

"No."

The older gunman was jabbing the muzzle of the rifle into the man's paunch.

"Put it in the bag."

"No."

He flipped his weapon and jammed the butt of the rifle up hard into the man's jaw, snapping his head backward. He fell hard against the edge of the marble table and slumped onto the floor.

Ingrid ran over. She could help. She could administer first aid. But as she approached the unconscious man, the gunman rammed the rifle butt into her chest, winding her and knocking her from her feet. She fell to the floor, her head cracking as she landed heavily on the cold stone slabs.

12

"Get up!"

Ingrid couldn't quite move. She tried to shift an arm, but it was as if she didn't know how. How long had she been out for?

"Get. Up. Now."

She tried again. Her limbs were so heavy. Her head felt stuck to the stone floor. She closed her eyes, willed her arms to work and rolled over onto her front. She felt the tubes inside her sleeves move with her. Then she pushed herself up onto all fours—tabletop pose—and was grateful for the elasticated cuffs. She tried to arch her back, her head dropping forward as she did so. Cat pose. Her spine from her bra strap to her skull was sore.

"Now!" the man shouted.

She looked up at his red face. He took one hand off the rifle and wiped his palm on his trouser leg. Dirty, faded denim. Not been washed in weeks. But his palms were sweating. That meant he was nervous. Good.

"Up. Get up."

"I am trying."

He bent down, grabbed her collar and hauled her to her feet. "Move!" He shoved her toward the Somali gunman on the door, making her step over the injured man on the floor who was prone and bleeding from his temple.

"Where are they?" the older man said, agitated.

The Somali looked over his shoulder at the road outside and shrugged. "Don't know."

It took Ingrid a beat to realize they were talking to each other in English.

"They should be here." The older guy, Moroccan, maybe Algerian, was jittery. "Hold her."

The Somali man—tall, muscular, trembling—grabbed Ingrid, put one arm around her shoulders and held the Beretta to her head. She now had her back to the door and could see that everyone else in the café had been made to sit on the floor, their hands on their heads, everyone apart from the mother and daughter. Frailty and obesity had apparently offered them an exemption. It reminded her of something she'd seen in the ferry departure lounge in Riga: the TV news had been showing images of a siege in a café in Sydney. Her blood ran cold: maybe this wasn't a hold-up, maybe they were being held hostage.

The man grabbing her kept twisting around to look out the glass door. Was he looking for their ride out of there or watching for cops? Ingrid didn't know who she wanted to arrive first. Her instincts and her training meant she wanted the gunmen to be arrested, but when she thought about being asked her name, or having to provide ID, she hoped their getaway car arrived first.

The Somali tightened his grip: why wasn't she being made to sit on the floor with the others? She immediately understood: she was a bargaining chip. They were going to take her with them out to their vehicle. Insurance. A human shield to make the cops think twice before firing a shot. She tried to swallow, but her throat was too sore.

The Skinny Boy appeared from the back room of the café.

"You got them all?" the Moroccan asked.

"Yeah." His bag was alive with cell phone ringtones. "Where's the car?"

The Moroccan shrugged. "Coming." He didn't sound convincing.

Ingrid stared at the man who had hit his head, motionless on the floor, blood still seeping from his temple. She couldn't tell from twenty feet away if he was breathing, but it didn't look like it. Now she really hoped the getaway car got there before the cops did: the worst thing you can have in a hostage situation is a dead body. They tend to breed.

The cell phones continued to ring, the bank of refrigerators hummed and the rumble of the ovens drifted in from the kitchen. Outside, the trundle of traffic merged with the wind and the distant sirens, but inside no one said anything. A tableau of compliance and fear. Ingrid's gaze shifted to the cushioned window seat where she had hidden the Nokia. What if it rang now? The skin on her scalp tightened. Then something else caught her eye: her backpack, the orange packet of Libresse visible through the open zipper.

The roar of a diesel engine vibrated through the door, sending shivers up her spine.

"It's them," Skinny Boy said.

"Let's go."

The Moroccan yanked the door open and the man holding Ingrid pressed the muzzle of the Beretta into her temple. "You come with us."

"I..." Her throat was so tight it was hard to speak.

He pulled her to one side, almost making her stumble.

"I... My bag," she said in English. She couldn't leave one of the circuit boards for crime scene investigators to find. "I have my period." His grip loosened. "I need sanitary napkins." The gunmen looked at each other. Ingrid had heard of abductees escape by quoting the Bible or claiming they were diseased, but never because they were menstruating. Sensing her moment, Ingrid tried to pull away but the Somali tightened his grip around her waist.

"Get it," the Moroccan said to Skinny Boy.

"What?" Ingrid didn't understand. She watched in confusion as Skinny Boy swiped up her Russell Athletic backpack from the table, zipped it up and darted through the open door, shoving his Glock into his waistband as he did so. The thrum of the engine pulsated outside.

The Somali shoved her toward the Moroccan, who held her

even more tightly. "You will walk out this door. You will get in that car. If you do not, these people will die. Understand?"

Ingrid tried to pull away from him but he raised his left hand: he was still holding the Kalashnikov.

She nodded.

He pushed her out through the doorway and down the steps to the sidewalk. A black Subaru SUV was in front of her, its rear door open. Her backpack was already on the back seat. Ingrid glanced left and right. No cops. Where the hell were they? She looked back over her shoulder at the Moroccan. He stood in the doorway, training the rifle on her torso. Skinny Boy stood on the sidewalk. He lifted his jacket to reveal his Glock.

Why weren't they getting in the car? Why weren't they making their getaway? It made no sense.

"Get in," the Moroccan said.

The only risk Ingrid could take was that the guns weren't loaded. She could run. If she could reach the side street there was no way Skinny Boy would catch her. Even if the guns were loaded, they might miss. They probably would. But then there was the bag on the back seat. The component.

The frigid air encapsulated her. She stood stock still. Run or comply? Run or comply?

They had already let one man die and done nothing to save him. There were twenty or so people in the café who would go home tonight if she just got in the car.

She looked into the open door. Black tinted windows. Black leather upholstery. Glistening with melting snowflakes. She didn't want to do it, but she had to. She had no choice.

She walked toward it and climbed in. A man—white, twenties, unshaven—was sitting on the back seat. He was holding a Beretta M9.

"Close the door."

Ingrid pulled it shut, and the driver put the car into gear. The wheels spun as a hood was pulled over her head.

"Lie down."

13

When Ingrid was fourteen, she had been walking home from a carnival with her best friend Megan. It was late. Nearly ten. They should have been home hours before, but there had been teddy bears to win and cotton candy to eat. Ingrid hated cotton candy now.

They had taken a short cut, past the softball diamond, beyond the boating lake toward a path through the trees. Even now, Ingrid could plot out every step in her mind. She relived each step most weeks, if not most days.

They were still in earshot of the organ from the carousel and the cheers from the pirate ship ride when the man jumped out into the path in front of them.

"Hey girls," he said. "Want to have a little fun?"

Ingrid had only looked at him for a second before she'd dropped her cotton candy, turned and run. Megan followed. She'd heard her footsteps. They'd called out to each other. Encouraged each other to run faster. But they were slow. They were overweight. The biggest girls in their class by twenty or thirty pounds. They couldn't run far, or fast, and Megan was heavier, slower.

In the intervening years, Ingrid began to wonder what percentage of her memories from that night were true, and which parts were just wishing. Maybe some details never happened but were implanted by the unskilled questioning of Deputy Morris. Inventions that became memories, memories that became facts.

What Ingrid never admitted to anyone was that she can't actually remember looking back. In her head she can see the path, and she can picture Megan's reddened face, but she cannot be sure it happened. It was possible Megan never even ran. Maybe she had been too scared. Maybe she simply knew she wouldn't get very far. Whatever actually happened in those hideous seconds, wherever the truth lay between hopes and nightmares, for nearly twenty years Ingrid had been tortured by the thought she could have done more to save her friend.

Megan's disappearance changed Ingrid. That night she lost her innocence, her accomplice, and her belief that somehow things would be all right. But she also found something too: purpose. She started dieting and exercising so that by graduation she was one of the slimmest girls in senior year. And those inept, brutish questions of Deputy Morris made her want to become an investigator herself. She never wanted another kid to be interrogated in the way she had been, but mostly she never wanted another child to suffer the way Megan had.

By the time she turned fifteen, Ingrid Skyberg had already worked out her career path to the FBI's Violent Crimes Against Children unit. She studied languages at college—adding fluency in Italian and French to her semi-native Russian—then joined the Jackson County Sheriff's Department the same month Deputy Morris retired.

Ingrid served the obligatory two years before applying to Quantico, during which time she reinvestigated every line of inquiry into Megan's disappearance. She re-examined all the evidence, liaised with law enforcement across the country about other abductions near traveling carnivals in the mid-nineties, but by the time she was accepted into the Bureau, she had never found a single trace of Megan.

Ingrid never gave up hope. Elizabeth Smart, Jaycee Lee Dugard, Natascha Kampusch, Michelle Knight. Every time a story about an abductee being found after years in cellars and attics hit the headlines, Ingrid went back over the original investigation notes, desperate to find something she had previously overlooked. She never stopped hoping that she would be the agent to knock down the door, to finally save her friend, to make amends.

Although she was never offered the chance to take the FBI's hostage negotiation training, Megan's disappearance meant it was a subject Ingrid knew plenty about. She'd read the Bureau's manual, made a point of playing softball with the lead negotiator when she'd worked in the Cleveland field office, and read extensively about how some hostage situations are resolved without the loss of life, and why so many end in a bloodbath. Right now, this was knowledge Ingrid almost wished she didn't have as she inhaled the scent of the polished leather upholstery.

There was no point in trying to work out where they were taking her. She didn't know Stockholm well enough to follow every turn. But there was a lot of traffic noise, a lot of gear changing; she was sure they weren't leaving the city. Her knees were in the footwell, her head resting on the back seat with the constant pressure of the Beretta against her collar bone. The man on the back seat did not speak again for several miles.

For some reason, she remembered her meeting in London. Caviar at Berlinsky's to talk about the Kandinsky. She pictured Ekaterina Volitova, wife of the owner of a Kazakh mining company, leaving endless messages, tapping the screen of her gold-plated iPhone with her pink talons, enraged that her art consultant had not turned up for their meeting. No one stood up the Volitovas. Somewhere out there, Ingrid thought, is my life, my career. Somehow she was going to have to find a way back to it.

The heating system in the car did not extend to the footwell, and Ingrid's legs were getting cold. Goose bumps were forming and she started to shiver.

Below zero.

Would Nick Angelis really betray her? She didn't think so, but as the SUV surged and swerved through the Stockholm streets, Ingrid couldn't be sure. She pictured him, leaning against the bookshelves of the library in the Reform Club, his bow tie loose around his opened collar, a tumbler of Scotch in one hand. He would pretty much do anything if it could be filed under national security. Nick Angelis, patriot and traitor.

You bastard.

Forget him. Forget the past, she told herself, focus on now. Concentrate on the present. *What do you know? What can you learn?*

She thought about the men who had taken her. The gunmen in the café were Somali and North African. Almost certainly Muslim. Possibly connected to Islamic State, Al-Shabaab or some affiliate. The man who held the Beretta was white. Pale. Likely local. Maybe a convert.

She knew that the Moroccan's rifle was old. A relic from the mujahideen, or any number of conflicts in Africa. Battered, chipped enamel. Probably killed dozens, if not hundreds. The Glock and the Beretta suggested scavenged weapons, acquired over the years, not an organized militia.

The car turned suddenly. "Shit, man. Look out," the white guy said.

"Cops." A deep, resonant voice with a thick accent. Had to be coming from inside a big chest. A big guy who wasn't Swedish. Another Somali?

"You drive like that and they are going to follow us."

"Road is closed."

"But you can get us there?"

"Sure."

"Put the radio on. Maybe we'll hear something." They were also talking in English.

The driver pushed a button and *Uptown Funk* pulsed out of the speakers.

"Put the news on, asshole."

Not friends then. The driver had probably only been hired for this job. Would know nothing, would only have met one contact until the operation started. He punched through a few stations, settling on one broadcasting live from the National Museum. A reporter was interviewing an eyewitness who was describing a heavy police presence and a calm response from the public. At least that's what Ingrid could make out. Her Swedish just wasn't good enough to catch every word.

"The time now is just coming up to one fifteen, and we'll be staying live with the developing story in and around Kungsholmen and the security situation at the National Museum, but right now let's catch up with the sport..."

One fifteen. Remember that. If they're handing over to the sport, then there couldn't be any casualties. They'd stay with the bomb if people had died. Ingrid wondered how long it would be before reporters made it to Republik and how much of a head start the SUV had over the police. There were eyewitnesses to her abduction. It wouldn't be long before they started to look for her. She felt the canisters inside her sleeves and hoped the head start was big enough: crooks would be easier to deal with than the cops.

They had been on the road for maybe ten or fifteen minutes when Ingrid remembered something that scared her more than the pistol digging into her shoulder: Skinny Boy had searched inside her backpack and he hadn't pulled out the third component. Now that she thought about it, he hadn't even seemed to be looking for it. The muscles in her jaw constricted: if they weren't after the circuit boards, what were they after?

Transcript from Riksdag Committee Hearing 23

December 14 2015

BILUNGS: Sergeant, please describe what you found when you got to Republik.
HOLM: Of course. Well, the paramedics were already on the scene, attending to Mr Linden, who they estimated had been dead for half an hour. Blotches on the skin, that sort of thing. And that is what the witnesses told us too, that Mr Linden had resisted handing over his valuables and there had been a quarrel with the man we now know is Aziz Abadi. No one had seen the assault, but a few people had heard Mr Linden fall and saw him hit his head. It is likely he knew very little about it. It would have been sudden, although possibly not painless.
BILUNGS: And you were the first police officer on the scene?
HOLM: No, that was Constable Larsson. And, um, I can't remember his name, Constable…
BILUNGS: [Looks at notes] Pedersen?
HOLM: Yes, that's it. But they had already left. Eyewitnesses, some of the hostages, had told them the direction they'd gone in—they left on foot, you already know this?
BILUNGS: Yes.
HOLM: So you already know they apprehended Abadi and the other gunman on one of the boats in the harbor.
BILUNGS: Yes, but three gunmen held up the Republik. What happened to the other man?
HOLM: Oh, him. Yes, he was arrested… we arrested him in an apartment in Husby later that day. You'd need to speak to Inspector Lundberg—have you done that?
BILUNGS: We will speak to everyone we need to.
HOLM: Oh, OK. But Lundberg will confirm, I think. He had removed the SIM cards from some of the iPhones he stole, but the GPS function still worked on the newer models, or maybe it was the older ones, I don't know, and, so, anyway, that's how

we found him. The cash, the credit cards, the jewelry… that had all been passed on.
BILUNGS: If we could return to the café. What time did you get there?
HOLM: [Refers to notes] Ah… five past one. And the first thing I did was call for more officers. Too many witnesses for me and Gunnarsson—that's Constable Oskar Gunnarsson—to interview on our own.
BILUNGS: How many people were there?
HOLM: [Pause] I would say around twenty, twenty-five. In addition to the four paramedics, there were fifteen people who had been part of the hold-up, and a few others who had entered the café after the gunmen had left.
BILUNGS: What did you do first?
HOLM: You must remember that I thought it unlikely that the minister had actually been taken. I had already spoken to her husband, Björn Friese. I had called him from the station.
BILUNGS: Yes, you've already testified to that. He told you that his wife was in a meeting in this very building, chairing [refers to notes]… the government's preparation for the climate talks in Paris.
HOLM: Even though Republik's was her favorite café in the neighborhood, Mr Friese thought it very unlikely, given the importance of her meeting, that the woman who had been taken was his wife. I mean, so certain that he remained completely calm.
BILUNGS: Did his certainty—
BORG: Sorry to interject, but before you continue I would like the witness to explain why her first response was to call Mr Friese and not proceed immediately to the Republik café.
BILUNGS: If you would like to answer, sergeant.
HOLM: Of course. I called Mr Friese first because my assumption was that—given his wife's prominence, and indeed his own prominence—he would be contacted and asked for a ransom. I needed to let him know, to let his secretary know, that he should not accept any calls from anyone he did not know unless and until one of the K&R team was with him.

BORG: K&R?
HOLM: Kidnap and ransom.
BILUNGS: Are you happy for me to continue, Mr Chairman?
[BORG nods]
BILUNGS: So you call a man to tell him his wife has been kidnapped?
HOLM: Yes.
BILUNGS: You don't visit him at his office, tell him in person?
HOLM: Normally, yes, it is the sort of news the Stockholm police would always want to give in person, but there was the bomb at the National Museum. There was no one of the right rank to go to Mr Friese's office. And as I say, when I spoke to him, he was certain there had been a mistake.
BILUNGS: Do you think his certainty affected the decisions you made when you got to Republik's?
HOLM: What do you mean?
BILUNGS: I am trying to ascertain if assumptions and preconceptions about what you would find when you got to the café had any bearing on the course of events in the hours and days to come.
HOLM: Well, um, [Pause] I had not yet had confirmation from colleagues at the Riksdag, sorry, here, that the minister was safe and out of harm's way, but I went to the café knowing that someone, a woman, had been kidnapped. And when I started speaking to the witnesses—
BILUNGS: Which witnesses, sergeant?
HOLM: The patrons in the café. Those people who had had their valuables stolen—
BILUNGS: But you were not able to speak to them all, were you?
HOLM: I believe you are referring to the fact that some of the victims have never come forward. There are two people known to have been at Republik's during the lockdown who fled before we arrived. We have not been able to trace either of them.
BILUNGS: Do you believe they were involved in the events we are discussing here today?

HOLM: I doubt it. It is more likely that they had some weed in their pocket or were wanted in connection with another offense.
BILUNGS: But you cannot rule out they were accomplices?
HOLM: I guess not, no.
BILUNGS: So, if you could please bring us to the point where you called the commissioner.
HOLM: Yes. Of course. But before I do that, it is important that you understand the café was now a crime scene. A murder scene, given what had happened to Mr Linden. It was my responsibility to preserve as much evidence as possible until the forensics teams could get there.
BILUNGS: And what did this involve?
HOLM: I made the decision to keep everyone in the back room of the café, the—
BILUNGS: This committee is now very familiar with the layout of Republik's.
HOLM: But unfortunately, this was extremely stressful for two of the witnesses, Mrs Dens and her daughter Mrs Nyborg, and they became extremely agitated. Screaming, that sort of thing, claiming that we were attempting to imprison them. [Pause.] I now understand that this particular setting was very traumatic for them to be restricted to. Um, so, you know, I assume, about the case they brought against me and Gunnarsson?
BILUNGS: A lawsuit for psychological trauma, we believe.
HOLM: [Nods] While I do not want to minimize the distress they experienced, their accusations have been very damaging to me. For several months until their case was rejected, I was portrayed as insensitive and incompetent—
BILUNGS: It makes no difference to your standing before this committee.
HOLM: That is good to know.
BILUNGS: I must ask you again. What led you to call the commissioner?
HOLM: Right. Of course. So when Gunnarsson and I spoke to the witnesses who were still on the premises, they were very sure that Anna Skyberg was indeed the victim. She was a

regular at Republik's and the staff there knew her well. The woman—the suspect—had even ordered the minister's regular poached egg. It seemed certain, no, likely, that Anna Skyberg had indeed been abducted.
BILUNGS: How likely?
HOLM: Looking back, I can see that maybe there were reasons that made it less likely—
BILUNGS: For instance?
HOLM: For instance, the clothes she was wearing. The witnesses said she looked like she had been for a run, she wasn't wearing make-up—
BILUNGS: Hardly the attire of a government minister chairing an important meeting.
HOLM: [Nodding] But, with the unfolding incident at the museum—which, of course, we had a good view of from the waterfront outside the café—I felt there was a risk a major attack was happening. We all think of Utøya. The bomb blast was a diversion, a ploy to get the largest number of police officers in the wrong place. There was already one man dead and I thought there was a chance Anna Skyberg would not be the only member of the government to be taken hostage.
BILUNGS: That's quite a leap, isn't it, sergeant?
HOLM: Maybe, but I was almost right, wasn't I?
BILUNGS: So you called the commissioner and recommended the shutdown?
HOLM: I called the commissioner's office and relayed my suspicion. I am only a sergeant, Mr Bilungs, I do not have any authority to affect such an outcome.
BILUNGS: [Reading from notes] 'Sergeant Sami Holm, who was the senior officer at the scene, recommended an immediate response.' Are you contradicting the commissioner?
HOLM: Even if I had made a recommendation, the commissioner would have been under no obligation to act on it.
BILUNGS: But act he did.
HOLM: Yes.

14

The car turned sharply and moved downhill. The street noise faded away. The radio crackled into static. An underground parking lot.

"Here," the white man said to the driver. "Right here."

Ingrid felt the Beretta jab a little harder into her shoulder as the car came to a halt. The driver did not kill the engine. She heard him climb out and the chilled underground air, redolent with gasoline, was sucked inside the car. She heard his footsteps as he walked round the SUV, then a clunk before he yanked open the rear door.

"Is this her?" A new voice, another man, speaking in English.

"I can take the hood off and show you," the white guy said.

"No." An accent. Not local. Didn't sound like the Somalis from the café.

The white man tapped the gun against her upper arm. "Get out now."

Ingrid was stiff from kneeling and rigid with dread.

"Get out of the car, lady. Do not take the hood off. You understand?"

Ingrid started to move her hands, to unball them, to spread her fingers against the clean leather seat. In other circumstances, she would have done all she could to leave a trace of herself in the car—pulled out a few hairs, dribbled on the upholstery—but apart from the fact that she would only have succeeded in making the cotton hood wet, she never wanted any investigator in any jurisdiction to know that an FBI agent had been taken hostage. Especially not one carrying weapons materials that could start a diplomatic incident. Or possibly even a military one.

She pushed herself up onto the seat, twisted round and sat down. In the background she could hear two men talking quietly. A jangling of keys.

"Get out of the car."

She edged toward the open door and reached out her right hand. It was quickly yanked and she was pulled upright. She could hear another engine running.

"I need my bag," she said. She was surprised how confident her voice sounded.

"No bag."

"I need Kotex." Damn. Not Kotex. Not American. "I have my period. I need Libresse."

She heard her bag being thrown from the car onto the concrete floor of the parking lot. Someone picked it up and shoved it at her. She clutched it to her chest like a comforter. A hand was placed on her shoulder, suggesting—firmly—that she should start walking forward.

"You can't put her in there." The white man's voice again. "It's minus fifteen. She'll die."

"There is blanket. Is only an hour. She no die."

"Don't be an idiot, man."

"She no die."

There was a pause. The keys stopped jangling. The background conversation ceased.

"OK, man. I shouldn't have said anything. I'm sorry."

Ingrid guessed the man whose hand was on her shoulder, whose thumb was pressing into her carotid artery, had just pulled a gun. A bigger gun than the Beretta. He grabbed the backpack out of her grasp and she heard a thud as it landed. It was a dull sound, not an echoing one: it had been thrown into another car. There was a screeching noise. No, it was more like a rip. She felt something press against her forearm: duct tape. Her legs buckled slightly as it was wound round and round her wrists, gripping them tightly together, pressing the bracelet deeper into her flesh.

"I need the bathroom," she said. "I have my period."

"What?"

Maybe she'd got the Swedish for 'period' wrong. "I am menstruating. I need to visit the bathroom." It was, for the time being, a lie but she figured it would be something that they hadn't factored into their plans. The FBI had a booklet called *Conduct After Capture*. She remembered something about trying to make your captors change tack as soon as possible. She couldn't recall why.

Two arms grabbed her from behind, lifting her off the ground. Someone else held her feet. She knew exactly what was happening. Her legs were placed in the trunk first, then her upper body.

Please, God, no.

"Keep your head down."

A rustling sound. Then a blanket—itchy, stinking— was thrown on top of her and the lid was slammed down. Seconds later, the sound of two doors pulled shut, a slight movement as the car was put into reverse, then a lurch as it moved backwards, turned quickly and revved away. Several more turns, an incline, and Ingrid could hear that she was back on the street.

Ingrid was lying in the fetal position, her cheek squashed against the carpet lining of the trunk, the components up her sleeves digging into her bound arms.

What the hell just happened?

She tried to work it out, to conjure up memories, but they all felt distant, unreliable, unconnected because nothing made sense. There had been gunmen. But before that there had been a bomb, or an explosion of some kind. Then… she struggled to remember. Everyone's wallets had been taken… She saw the blood seeping from the man's head. They were pieces of a puzzle scattered on the floor of her brain, pieces that she couldn't fit together.

Ingrid knew she should feel afraid but her overriding sensation was disbelief. A line from *Conduct After Capture* drifted through her thoughts: 'It is not uncommon for hostages to go through a period of denial after their capture. This period can last from a few hours to a few weeks.'

Weeks?

The car made several turns and, after a few minutes, they were in cruise mode. The freeway. There was no way to tell if they were heading north, south, east or west and the constant traffic noise meant there wouldn't be any church bells to listen out for, or muezzin calls, or playgrounds, but then none of that mattered: she hoped to God she would never be speaking to any investigating officer about this.

When the car had been traveling in a straight line, in the same gear, for what felt like ten minutes—it was probably only two—Ingrid reached up and pulled off the hood with her bound hands, and opened her eyes.

It wasn't completely dark. Daylight filtered in through the brake lights. As her eyes adjusted, she started to make out a few details. A tow rope. A chrome latch in the carpet. A rectangular sticker with rounded corners faintly visible on the inside of the lid.

Beneath her, Ingrid could feel the indentations marking the housing for the spare tire. She slowly stretched her legs—the fact that they hadn't bound her legs meant that at some point she would be made to walk—and felt what she presumed was her backpack.

Like the last car, it smelt new. Perhaps she had been abducted by professional car thieves. Or maybe someone who works for a car dealership. Or a garage. She listened, assuming that there had to be at least two men in the front of the car. It was possible it was just a driver, but until a conversation started she wouldn't be sure. She wanted them, or him, to be distracted before she attempted further movement in case she somehow jolted the car or made a noise.

What time would it be now? Two o'clock maybe? She didn't think it could be much later. Whoever was behind the operation was extremely organized. One team for the hold-up. Another to take her from the café. A third to take her out of the city. If the local cops had a lead on the first car, it would almost certainly be a day or two before they got a lead on the second. In her experience, it would come down to a member of the public reporting a suspicious vehicle, or responding to an appeal for information. Either way, no one was coming for her anytime soon. Which, given the nature of the articles she had stuffed up her sleeves, was probably a good thing.

A crackle of static, then a ringtone. Their cell was hooked into the stereo system.

Two rings, then an answer. "*Salaam?*" A metallic voice, like a robot speaking from inside a steel box.

The man in the car said something she couldn't make out. It might have been heavily accented Swedish, but more likely another language. If she had to guess, she'd go with Somali. She had no idea what they were talking about.

Then the phone line clicked. A flash of static. Followed by the sound of the engine and the wheels turning on the gritted road.

No.

Ingrid's chest felt like it was collapsing.

Please, no.

Suddenly her heart was pounding and her hands felt hot. She stopped shivering. Couldn't feel the cold. Didn't feel any damn thing at all apart from stupid. So incredibly stupid.

It was the phone. The goddamned Nokia. It was still in the café. She'd been so keen to make sure it didn't get stolen that she'd hidden it. She didn't know which was worse: that she would never know if her instructions had been changed, or that at some point a CSI team would find it and read her messages.

An old phone. A new SIM. Two messages sent. One received. Even a rookie on his first day in uniform would know what that meant.

15

There was still no conversation coming from the front of the vehicle. Either the driver was on his own or her abductors knew to talk quietly. She allowed herself a tiny smile: maybe, given that she was in Sweden, she was in the trunk of a well-made Volvo with sound insulation between the trunk and the main car.

Then another thought occurred to her, and this one hardened something inside her: the trunk had been deliberately soundproofed. There was a case in Megan's file. A pedophile in Nebraska who had lined the trunk of his Datsun with loft insulation to deaden the noise his abductees made as he transported them to their deaths. The memory created a vacuum inside Ingrid's chest.

She pulled the blanket tight around her, but it offered no comfort. It had been fifteen minutes, maybe twenty, and the trunk was colder than a refrigerator. The blanket smelt of wet dog. Odd: a spotlessly clean trunk and a dirty blanket.

She decided she couldn't wait any longer. They might reach their destination. Or her fingers might get so cold she wouldn't be able to use them. It was time to act. The duct tape around her wrists was over her jacket, which meant there was a little bit of give and it was just possible to move her hands.

In *Conduct After Capture* she'd read countless case histories of hostage situations. One of the clearest messages Ingrid had gotten from other people's experiences was that constantly planning an escape is key to surviving the ordeal without going crazy. The indentations from the spare tire beneath the trunk had given her an idea.

She felt for the chrome finger pull and tugged, lifting the carpet off the floor. She curled it upwards and grabbed it between her knees. She shuffled, positioning herself so she could reach down into the recess where the spare tire was stored. The canisters inside her sleeves pressed into her forearms as she stretched and twisted her bound arms around like a snake charmer, searching for something—anything—useful.

Bingo.

A hard plastic rectangle. An emergency tool kit. Or maybe first aid. She pressed her numb fingertips against the box, trying to grip it and pull it up toward her, but she just couldn't get the right angle, or move her arms far enough apart.

She repositioned herself onto all fours, gripping the folded carpet between her thighs, then tried again. Her hands were becoming useless in the cold and it didn't help that she could barely see. She ignored the pain she felt when the bracelet was forced harder into her wrist. She tried again and managed to push the box free from its molded plastic home. She grabbed at it, pressing her fingers hard against it, desperate not to drop it.

The trunk was suddenly illuminated and she dropped the case in shock. Then it was dark. Then light again. The indicators. They were turning. If they were leaving the freeway, Ingrid knew they could pull over at any moment. Her heart started beating harder, pounding painfully as she tried again, repositioning herself to get more leverage. She took a deep breath but her ribs felt constricted, as if encased in an iron mesh.

The indicators on the other side started to flash. Not turning, overtaking. She hadn't heard a gear change. They were still on the freeway. She exhaled: so long as they stayed on the freeway, she stayed alive.

She reached down again, felt for the plastic case and spread her fingers wide, pressing the box on each side, hoping to lift it up. Her hands were shaking. Her fingers were numb. Her heart was beating too hard. Her breathing was too shallow. This wasn't working.

She shuffled backwards, moving her knees away from the hard ridges of the spare tire and let her body collapse on top of her thighs, almost getting herself into child's pose. She pictured herself doing yoga in her apartment, the bright rectangles of sunlight stretching across the wooden floorboards. She smelt the rubber of her purple yoga mat and managed to slow her breathing by an increment. She heard the voice from the yoga app tell her to relax into the pose, to let her body release any tension.

Her apartment. Home. She imagined herself standing at the window, glass of Sauvignon Blanc in hand, looking out at the London skyline. The Eye, the Shard, the Gherkin, the Walkie-Talkie, the Cheesegrater—all the buildings she could name and all the ones she couldn't. The one in the distance that seemed to have three holes in the top. She traced the skyline in her mind from west to east and vowed that she would stand at the window again and watch the planes in their eternal formation, descending slowly over the city to Heathrow in the west. She would get home. Somehow.

There was a bottle of wine in her refrigerator. She could see the condensation clinging to its curves. She could anticipate the satisfying noise as she twisted off the cap, the sharp release of the first sip. She was damn well going to drink that wine. Whatever happened when the trunk was opened, she was going to survive this. This was not where she was going to die. Not like this. Not yet.

Ingrid tried to slow her breathing, to make her ribs widen, drawing in the freezing, gasoline-scented air. *And feel your ribs expand, let your tummy fall softly against your knees…* She had always hated the woman's voice.

She centered her thoughts on her sternum, just focusing on one bone, making it move, letting in the steel-cold air. The next breath was slightly deeper. She did it again. The cold hurt her lungs. And again. Her heart rate began to fall. She could do this.

She was going to survive. That's all you need to know, she told herself, that at some point this will be over and you will have survived.

The indicators flashed on again. No gear change. Only overtaking, not turning. Ingrid repositioned herself, hoping to get a good view of the plastic case as the lights blinked before trying to fish it out again. She shuffled forward, her knees making contact with the ridges of the tire casing, and she reached down, feeling the canisters inside her sleeves as she flared out her fingers and gripped the case. If she got this right, she would be rewarded with a secret weapon—a spanner maybe, or perhaps a small canister of antiseptic spray—something that could help her escape.

She couldn't get her fingers beneath the case. Her only option was to grip it hard, press her numb fingertips against it and lift it up. Her hands began to tremble—stress, cold, fear—but she held on to it and somehow dropped it onto the folded carpet in front of her. It was heavy and it clanked: definitely a tool kit. A shot of exhilaration burned through her body like tequila.

She felt for a clasp and flipped it open. Inside was a selection of ice-cold implements. It was a ratchet set, one large-handled tool with lots of interchangeable heads. Inside the lid, pressed into plastic grips, were different shapes. Thinner. Screwdrivers.

Perfect.

She pried one from its mooring, flipping it out onto the carpet where it promptly rolled into the void beneath her, clanking as it fell. She listened. No reaction from the driver. She pried out another one, taking more care this time, holding one end as she freed the other. It was small. Easier to conceal, but it would only inflict real damage if she rammed it into someone's eye socket. All the combat training she'd ever done had told her to aim for the eyes, but she'd never managed to do it. She'd always flinched at the last minute.

She wriggled onto her side and pushed the screwdriver inside the elasticated trim of her sock. A thick, three-season walking sock. Her ankle was so cold she could barely feel the metal against her skin. Ingrid closed the case, tossed it back into the void beside the tire and pushed the carpet back into place, the chrome clasp tinkling as it fell against the metal housing below.

She collapsed onto her side, her head falling heavily onto the stinking blanket, and closed her eyes. When she opened them, the indicator was flashing. A faint clunk, a gear change. They were slowing. They were turning. They were leaving the freeway.

16

The contact noise the tires made with the road changed as the car turned again. A smaller road with deeper snow. The faint light faded almost instantly. They were traveling through trees, cutting out the weak Arctic sun. What time was it now? Two thirty? Two forty-five? There wouldn't be much more than another hour of daylight this close to the winter solstice.

Ingrid felt around inside the trunk for the black cotton hood. She stretched out her bound arms as best she could, feeling for it with her numb hands. It had to be there. She patted the entire perimeter of the trunk but her frozen fingers did not find anything that felt like cotton.

The car slowed markedly, turned a sharp right and jolted as if going over a dip or ravine. Then it lurched from side to side as it rode over ruts and divots. A grinding of gears. Something snapping under the wheels. An unpaved road. She was being taken deep into the woods.

The canister inside her right sleeve pressed hard into her forearm as she felt around for the hood. She should move the components. If they made her take the jacket off, she risked losing two of them. She shook her arms, hoping to move the canisters close enough to the cuff that she could grab them with the opposite hand. If she could get one inside the other sock, then she'd have one in her jacket, one in the backpack, and one at her ankle, diminishing the chances that she would have to sacrifice all three when they finally got round to demanding them. It didn't matter what she tried: even if she hadn't been wearing the tracking bracelet, the duct tape was too tight to grab hold of them. Better to find the hood instead.

She thrashed about, desperate to have it back over her head before the trunk was opened. It must have got caught up inside the blanket. She flicked and tugged the blanket, patting it down, hoping her deadened fingers would be able to tell the difference between cotton and wool. Ingrid stopped the moment she realized why the car was traveling so slowly. The driver hadn't put the headlights on. If he had, there'd be a red glow from the taillights creeping through the trunk housing. And if the lights weren't on, it was because they didn't want anyone to notice the car. No witnesses reduced the chance of her being found. Given what was inside her sleeves, she thought, that might not be such a bad thing.

The car stopped and the driver put the handbrake on. He did not kill the engine before opening the door and stepping out. Another door opened. Both doors were slung shut simultaneously. So there had been two of them. Ingrid listened, hearing footsteps crunching across snow.

The hood.

She had to find the damn thing. She had to give the impression of being obedient. Of being dumb.

Voices.

Where was the hood? She grabbed frantically for it. Ingrid couldn't make out words over the thrum of the engine, but it sounded like they were speaking in English.

Come on! It had to be somewhere.

Footsteps. Approaching the car. Getting closer. Louder.

"No problems," she thought she heard one of them say. Maybe she could hear the name 'Mohammed' being repeated, but she wasn't sure. Her heart was pounding like a sprinter's as she searched, felt, probed. She grabbed at something soft. She rubbed it between her frozen palms. Her chest felt like it might implode. It was the hood. She started to breathe more heavily as she searched for the opening.

"You bring the boy?"

"I don't know." Their accents were so thick, and their voices so muffled, that Ingrid wasn't at all sure what she had heard.

A loud thud. She flinched and gasped for breath. Someone had knocked on the lid. "No problems," the voice said again.

"I hope you are right."

"And I hope it will be over soon."

Ingrid pulled the hood over her head and moved back into the fetal position.

"You have the key?"

A bleep. A clunk. A blast of even colder air. The lid made a faint whirr as it opened and Ingrid turned her head toward the dim light. She couldn't make out any detail through the cotton shroud.

"Good afternoon." A man's voice. Somehow, Ingrid knew he was smiling. "My name is Mohammed and I am going to be taking care of you thank you very much."

The wind surged through the trees and Ingrid could feel snowflakes landing on the hood. Her ankles were particularly cold. *Please, please, no.* She hadn't pulled her trouser legs down sufficiently well. Please don't let him see the screwdriver.

"I am not going to hurt you." He placed his hand on her shoulder and she winced. "Do not remove the hood. You understand?"

She nodded.

He helped her into a kneeling position and she inched forward, placing her hands on the iced metal rim of the trunk before climbing out.

"My bag," she said.

"No, no bag." The heaviness of Mohammed's accent suggested he had not been in Sweden long.

Another man—the driver?—said something she couldn't make out. Then there was a pause. A snigger.

"OK. You keep the bag. But I check it."

"I need the bathroom," Ingrid said as firmly as she was able.

"No bathroom." Mohammed still sounded as if he was smiling.

"I need the bathroom. I have my period."

"No bathroom." He said it in the same way he might say 'no problem'. "You come with me thank you very much."

He placed a hand on her shoulder and stood behind her. She felt something cold and metallic jab into the small of her back.

"You know what this is?"

She could guess.

"You do not run. You do not scream. Only do as I tell you. Understand?"

Ingrid nodded.

"OK then. Start walking."

17

"How much further?"

"Not far."

"How far?"

He jabbed the gun hard into the small of her back. "Just walk."

The tread of Ingrid's sneakers had become compacted with snow and her feet slid beneath her like a skater's. She held out her bound arms like a B-movie zombie and inched precariously forward. Her bare hands burned with the cold. In her jacket pocket she could feel the bulge of her thermal gloves and desperately wanted to be allowed to put them on.

The wind moved noisily through the trees, sending down flurries of snow, covering their footsteps and ensuring no one could follow. Ingrid's foot slipped and she stumbled, landing on her knees.

"You OK?" he asked.

"It would be easier," she said, "and faster, if I could take the hood off. I can't see where I'm walking."

"Not possible," he said, helping her up.

"But you've got a gun. If I look at you, you can shoot me."

"Walk."

After a few more steps, Ingrid fell again, deliberately, and landed awkwardly. She cried out, genuinely in pain.

"Get up," Mohammed said.

"I need a moment." Then she added: "I have hurt myself." Tears sprang from her eyes beneath the hood as the pain from her knee radiated up her thigh. Suddenly overwhelmed, she felt small, vulnerable. Her bravado had gone. Her training evaporated. The events of the preceding hours ripped through her brain. This wasn't a movie. This wasn't a training course. She really was sitting on the ice somewhere outside Stockholm with a bag over her head and a gunman for company. Her jaw began to tremble. Her teeth chattered and a silent sob rose up from deep within, escaping from her mouth with such force that her whole body shook.

"OK. You can take off the hood thank you. But you look down only. Only at your feet." So it wasn't that he didn't want her to see his face; he didn't want her to see the location. Ingrid held out her arms and he grabbed her wrists to yank her upright, his fingers brushing against the bracelet. "Only when I say, OK?"

He turned her round, faced her away from him and placed a hand on her head.

"You look up, you die. Understand?" His tone of voice lacked menace. He sounded rehearsed rather than sincere.

Ingrid nodded.

A moment later, his fingers grabbed at the hood, sliding it up over her face and off her head. Before she had opened her eyes, she felt the gun press against her waist. It was darker than she'd calculated, the snow almost blue in the deepening twilight. They were on a forester's path, a compacted strip of flattened snow ridged with tracks and the remnants of footprints. The path was too narrow for a car: the tracks belonged to a motorcycle or a snowmobile. Or maybe a wheelbarrow.

Where the hell is he taking me?

"Walk." Mohammed jabbed the gun into her, pushing her forward.

Ingrid looked down at her feet and was surprised to see how much snow was clinging to her jeans. The tears that had seeped from her eyes froze against her cheeks. She placed her feet where the snow lay a little deeper, bending her arms so her hands were by her chin. Her knee hurt when she put weight on it, but only a little.

"You have my bag?" she asked.

"Yes."

By four o'clock it would be pitch-dark and it would stay that way for sixteen hours. This was her best chance to escape. Just one kidnapper. If she could distract him, disarm him, get his gun, put a slug somewhere in his lower leg, disable him, she could run. She could get herself free.

From the angle the gun jabbed into her side and from the direction of his voice, Ingrid knew that Mohammed was tall. He also sounded young. Probably in his twenties. With her hands bound, the only way she could even the odds was by surprising him. But she'd have to be sure. There would be no second chances.

Her best bet was to trip him up, hope the gun fell from his grasp, grab it, use it if she had to, and then run. She just had to pick the right moment, to sense when he was already falling forward, leaning into her, and then stick out her leg. Her breathing got heavier just imagining it, the vapor condensing into white puffs as she labored through the snow.

"Where are you taking me?"

"Walk."

She changed her stride pattern to see how quickly he would bump into her, to gauge how close he kept. She started to move her arms, judging if she could get enough power to ram her joined fists up under his jaw. She didn't know how long she'd be on the path for. She had to take the first opportunity she got.

Either side of her were dark fir trees, rigid with snow, hemming them in. Keeping her head bowed, she looked left and right, but all she could see were trunks and snow-laden branches. It would be easy to get lost plus, she reasoned, it had to be twenty below. She was in sneakers and jeans: if she did manage to overpower Mohammed, she might not survive long. If she fell, hypothermia would kick in within minutes. She already sensed she was seizing up, shutting down. She was dressed for the city, not the wilderness.

Above their heads, Ingrid heard the buzz of a power cable, and drifting up from below was the deep moan of a freeway. Civilization wasn't far away. She could reach help, she knew she could. Then she remembered that she couldn't. She couldn't exactly knock on someone's door and say: "Hi, you don't know me, but I'm carrying some highly lethal weapons components and I need to deliver them to help stop the war in Syria. Will you let me use your phone?" She might as well rip up the *Conduct After Capture* booklet. Apart from hostages with Stockholm syndrome, she said to herself, she was one of the few people to be abducted who didn't want to get saved.

Stockholm syndrome. *In Stockholm*. What were the chances? She allowed herself a smile.

For her, there could be no rescue. No tearful reunion with loved ones. This never happened. She was never really here. Whether she survived this or not, no one could ever, *ever* know about it. She wiped the snow from her face and kept walking, listening to Mohammed's breathing.

"Stop," he said. "You stop here."

Ingrid could hear him fiddling with something so she risked looking up. The wide triangle of sky visible above the path was dark gray, like a steel door waiting to be slammed shut, and in the gloom, through the black trees fringed with white, stood a small dilapidated cabin.

"You put hood back on now."

Transcript from Riksdag Committee Hearing 23

December 15 2015

BILUNGS: For the record, please state your full name and rank.
FONSMARK: Birgitte Fonsmark. I don't have a rank. Technically, I am a civilian. I lead MAT, the Mobile Analysis Team within Police Sweden.
BILUNGS: And what is the role of the MAT?
FONSMARK: We track and monitor mobile and internet communications of persons under investigation.
BILUNGS: Only suspects?
FONSMARK: Yes. We have nothing to do with the intelligence services. We do not carry out general surveillance, only those individuals the police wish to pursue.
BILUNGS: And I presume you have been briefed on the purpose of these hearings?
FONSMARK: Yes.
BILUNGS: You understand that we are not here to apportion blame. This hearing is about discovering the true facts of the events of December 15 and 16th last year. Nothing you say here will have any bearing on your future career prospects and no one will be subject to sanction on the basis of anything they reveal to this committee.
FONSMARK: Yes, I understand that.
BILUNGS: So, we have already heard from Sergeant Holm that a cell phone was found at Republik. Perhaps if you could talk us through the significance of this phone.
FONSMARK: Significance?
BILUNGS: How it pertains to the events of December 15th last year.
FONSMARK: I think that is a question for an investigating officer. As I say, I am a civilian. A technician.
BILUNGS: Very well. Yesterday, Sergeant Holm testified to this committee that, around four o'clock, she was informed by the

CSI team inside Republik that they had found a phone—an old Nokia 3210—close to the table where the suspect had been having lunch. Sergeant Holm told us that it is very unusual these days to find a phone like this, and when they are used, it tends to be for criminal activity. Would you agree with everything I have said so far?

FONSMARK: Yes.

BILUNGS: When did you first become aware of the existence of this Nokia 3210?

FONSMARK: Me? I couldn't tell you. Sometime later that week, probably.

BILUNGS: Ah. [Refers to notes] It was my understanding—this committee's understanding—that you were sent the phone for analysis on the afternoon of the 15th. Is that not the case?

FONSMARK: I am the head of MAT. I do not log the deliveries.

BILUNGS: Of course. Do you know when your organization first became aware of the existence of this phone?

FONSMARK: [Refers to notes] A call was received from Sergeant Holm at four seventeen requesting immediate analysis. Once the CSI teams had taken swabs for DNA, it was sent to our laboratory. [Refers to notes] It was logged at five ten on the 15th.

BILUNGS: I am going to try and speed things up a little bit. Please interrupt me if I get anything wrong. [Pause] It was immediately discovered that the SIM card was brand-new, a good indicator that the phone had been used for criminal purposes.

FONSMARK: Yes.

BILUNGS: There was no record of any calls made by that SIM card, only three text messages. Two sent, one received.

FONSMARK: Yes.

BILUNGS: The first message, sent in English at twelve ten, read: 'ARE YOU HERE YET?' At twelve eighteen, the Nokia received a message, also in English, that said: 'STORTORGET CHRISTMAS MARKET. 9AM TOMORROW.' And at twelve twenty-nine, the Nokia sent a second text message that read: 'ARE YOU SURE? 9AM FOR THE CHRISTMAS MARKET

NOT 9PM? PLEASE CONFIRM.' Is that correct, Miss Fonsmark?
FONSMARK: Yes.
BILUNGS: Do you have a copy of the lab's report? Document AM/76TA?
FONSMARK: Yes.
BILUNGS: Could you please talk this committee through the findings on page eight?
FONSMARK: Yes. Sure. The records confirm that the two messages sent from the Nokia were sent from a location within a two hundred meter radius of the Republik café.
BILUNGS: You cannot be any more precise?
FONSMARK: The position is triangulated from three masts. With an iPhone, for example, there is usually other data—Wi-Fi connection, or Bluetooth positioning—that can narrow down the location, but with such an old phone, that is all the data can say with certainty. Smartphones send out GPS signals. They can be extremely accurate.
BILUNGS: We know the gunmen entered Republik at twelve twenty-eight. It is reasonable to think that the phone had to have been inside the café before then, therefore the message sent at twelve twenty-nine must have been sent from Republik.
FONSMARK: The data does not show that. It is supposition.
BILUNGS: But it is the only possible location for that text to have been sent from.
FONSMARK: I think your line of questioning would be better directed toward a police officer. I can only tell you what the data says.
BILUNGS: What does the data say about the phone that received the two messages sent from the Nokia?
FONSMARK: Well, OK, that I can tell you. Firstly, only one message was received. The second message, the one seeking confirmation, was never received. The only data we have for that SIM shows it received a message at twelve ten, and sent a message at twelve eighteen. We also know that SIM card was never used for any other communication, before or since.

BILUNGS: And do we know the location of that phone [refers to notes], the phone with the number ending in 6575?
FONSMARK: We can be less certain about its location when it received the first message—the system isn't entirely accurate for receiving data—but we know that the message it sent at twelve eighteen was sent from a location in Västerås. MAT passed on that information to Sergeant Holm at six fifteen.
BILUNGS: Could I ask you to talk the committee through the conclusion on page eleven, if you please?
FONSMARK: [Pause while she reads the relevant page] The conclusion is a straightforward one. When two SIM cards that have never previously been activated are used for the first time to communicate with each other, it is highly suspicious and frequently associated with criminal activity.
BILUNGS: Thank you.

18

"Bucket," Mohammed said, placing the metal pail inside the door. "No bathroom."

"I need water. To wash my hands."

He was wearing a hunter's hat, a scarf that covered his mouth and nose and an enormous coat that was far too big, even for him. The room was dimly lit by two oil lamps, so apart from his impressive height it was hard to make out anything about his appearance. Sub-Saharan African was all Ingrid could be sure of. He looked at her, a dusting of snowflakes clinging doggedly to his woolen coat. "OK."

Through the open door, Ingrid could see that it was now properly dark. What did that make it? Four thirty? Five? She had probably been there an hour. Mohammed left and locked the door behind him. Three sliding bolts and two padlocks. She heard his footsteps trudge away through the snow.

Ingrid hadn't gotten a good look at the cabin before Mohammed had put the hood back over her head, but from her brief glimpse it had looked abandoned. An old hunter's place. Maybe a holiday home, some place the children didn't want after their parents died. No electricity or running water. Too small to take a family. Impossible to get a car to. No good for a cosmopolitan twenty-first-century Swede. Probably hadn't been used for decades.

The cabin had an asymmetrical pitched roof and had been built, or had since been divided, into two unequal parts. She was in the smaller part, which would have once been the sauna. A wry smile curled her lips: her second sauna of the day. This one had thick walls—made of whole tree trunks—and no windows. About six feet by ten, lined down the long wall with a wooden bench. There was a burner, but it didn't look as if it had been lit in Ingrid's lifetime, and a broken thermometer on the wall. Had it been working, it would have registered a temperature that started with a minus. If she kept walking, pacing, circling her shoulders, she could stay warm enough. Unless she fell asleep, she wasn't going to die of hypothermia. At that moment, sleep seemed as preposterous as a hot cup of coffee and a pastry.

Don't think about food.

On the other side of the wall she could hear voices. Mohammed and one other. A man. She didn't think they were speaking either Swedish or English. They didn't speak often, and their conversations were short, usually ending in sounds of agreement. Either reassuring each other, or egging each other on, she couldn't tell. Ingrid paced the inside of the sauna, looking for anything that might help her escape, and made a mental list of everything else that was in her favor. Staying positive was one way hostages kept themselves alive.

Apart from the small bruise that was blooming on her right knee, she hadn't been injured… She had a weapon. The screwdriver might be small but, combined with the element of surprise, it had the potential to do harm… She was still in possession of all three components… They had taken the hood off… She hadn't been tied up and, if she needed to, she reckoned she could free herself from her duct tape bonds by removing her jacket. She wasn't going to attempt to do that unless she absolutely had to. So long as her kidnappers thought the tape was effective, they would be less tempted to restrict her further… She was less than an hour from Stockholm. If she could escape, she could still make the Christmas market in the morning… She was being held by Muslims. If they were devout, they would pray five times a day. That might just create five opportunities to escape.

She inspected the inside of the wood burner, hoping to find the kind of iron poker only used as a murder weapon in Agatha Christie spoofs, but the burner was empty aside from the fossilized remnants of a bird's nest that had fallen through the flue at some point in the twentieth century. The place was empty: no blankets, no rugs, just the bucket, the bench and the lanterns. She continued with her mental list.

The fact that she had told them she was menstruating—something that would be true within hours judging by the cramping in her abdomen—unsettled her captors. She was unclean. She didn't think sexual assault was an immediate threat… There was no electricity. Even if her captors had battery packs to recharge their devices, it wouldn't be long before their phones dried up. No communication, no Tetris, no Netflix or Al Jazeera: she wouldn't be the only one getting bored… Although the walls were thick and impenetrable without a chainsaw, Ingrid reckoned the roof was weak. She could feel a breeze every now and then. If there was a way out that wasn't through the barricaded door, it would be via the roof.

She stood on the bench, retrieved the screwdriver from her sock, reached up as best she could with her bound hands and poked a patch of ceiling where the wood was particularly soft. The screwdriver sank in, like pushing a spoon into cheesecake. She stared up at the black rotten wood and sighed: making a hole big enough to pull herself through would take days. And she didn't have days.

Footsteps. Mohammed was coming back.

She stepped down, pushed the screwdriver back inside her sock and felt the pouch against her leg. It was sodden, as were her jeans, but at least she still had some money. A couple of thousand euros. Something else in her favor.

The bolts rasped in their sheaths and the door rattled as Mohammed struggled with the padlocks. "Water," he said, placing a bucket of snow on the floor. A swirl of snowflakes spiraled in from the darkness outside. "Will be water soon."

"Thank you," Ingrid said. "How long will we be here?" Ingrid deliberately used 'we'. From chapter one, page one of *Conduct After Capture.*

Mohammed shrugged.

"Are we staying here tonight?"

Mohammed's eyes narrowed. "Depends."

"On what?"

He shrugged again.

"It is too cold to sleep here. I'll die if I stop moving."

He nodded. "Keep moving."

"For how long? How long are you keeping me here?"

He took a step back toward the door. "Until your husband says yes."

19

Husband? Ingrid didn't even have a boyfriend.

English wasn't his first language. Maybe he meant 'partner', as in business partner. Was he talking about Nick Angelis? It seemed unlikely. But words like 'unlikely' were acquiring new meaning.

She couldn't work out why they hadn't asked for the components. She hadn't even been frisked. The Skinny Boy in Republik had probably even felt one of them inside her backpack and not claimed it. So if they weren't holding her to nix the arms deal, why the hell had they taken her?

Ingrid didn't know enough about the factions in the Syrian war and their links to organizations like Al-Shabaab, but she could construct a scenario where they weren't trying to intercept the components, only to disrupt the handover. If they could make her miss the Christmas market in Stortorget, then maybe they could alter the balance of power at the Vienna negotiations? Was that why she was in a shed in the middle of a forest at twenty below?

Nothing made sense. A picture of her desk in the criminal division at the embassy forced itself into her head: case files, Post-it notes, the motorcycle helmet under her desk... *that's* where she was meant to be. The thought she might not make it back to her own life, to her real life, made her gasp.

She concentrated on her breath, pulling air in through her nose, expanding her chest and then letting the air out slowly through pursed lips, a vortex of steam evaporating in front of her. Repeat. The voice from her yoga app drifted through her thoughts... *become aware of your body, aware of the contact between your body and the floor...*

Ingrid realized she could no longer feel her feet. The bands of cold she had felt when she had disembarked from the ferry had spread from her ankles, sending tendrils of ice to her toes and upwards, encasing her calves. She picked up one of the two oil lamps and placed it beneath the bench, then sat down with her feet either side of it. She held her hands over the lamp and looked down at her gloves.

The gloves.

She had written the second phone number on the labels inside them. If she could find a phone, she could make contact with Magnus Jonsson, or whoever it was she was meeting in the morning. Her heart beat a little harder, warming her slightly: there was someone she could call, someone who didn't want the cops to find her either. Someone with the same goal. A possible ally. An option. It felt good to know her brain was still functioning, still alert to opportunities.

The warmth wasn't getting to her feet at all because they weren't just cold, they were wet. Wet feet, she knew, were potentially dangerous. Trench foot or gangrene or frostbite. She didn't know which. Couldn't remember. Couldn't concentrate. She bent forward and fumbled with her laces, eventually able to slip off her right sneaker. She peeled away the wet sock to reveal a puckered, white foot she barely recognized.

She limped over to her backpack, carried it back to the bench then felt around inside for her spare pair of socks. There were voices coming from the other side of the wall. It sounded like they were having a card game. Friendly. Relaxed. *Warm*. They had to have a source of heat in the other part of the cabin. She pulled on the socks and rubbed her feet as best she could with her taped-up arms, hoping to get some feeling back into her toes.

Ingrid examined the oil lamp. It was like something from a

period drama on TV but with an IKEA label on its base. It smelt slightly of lemons. More like a fake lemon-scented air freshener. She tipped it to one side to assess how much oil was in it, but as she had no idea how quickly it burned and no accurate means of keeping time, she had no way of knowing how long it would be before she was consigned to blackness.

Thoughts started to assemble themselves in order. A little regiment of clarity reported for duty inside Ingrid's head. She looked at the lamp, looked at the burner and down at the bench she was sitting on. She could make a fire. All she needed was some kindling. She glanced at her backpack and an eyebrow automatically rose up with satisfaction: the Libresse. They'd burn brilliantly.

Suddenly filled with energy, Ingrid tried the slats she was sitting on to see if any of them moved. She felt sure she'd be able to pry off one or two of them, but quickly realized that breaking them into pieces small enough to fit into the wood burner would be a different matter. They were two inches thick: it'd take more than a good, hard kick to break them. Her bubble of energy instantly burst and she slumped back down.

She wasn't sure if she should put her sneakers on. Dry socks inside wet shoes didn't make a lot of sense, but she had to be ready to run or fight if she was given the opportunity to do so. She bent forward and squeezed her dry feet into her sodden Nikes.

Through the wall, Ingrid could hear her captors walking and talking. One of them had a persistent cough. In these conditions it wouldn't be long before she did too. She started shaking her head. An involuntary action. A physical manifestation of disbelief. It still wasn't sinking in that this had happened, that this *was* happening. She'd wake up. She'd leave the movie theater. She'd snap out of whatever psychosis she was experiencing. She must have had a bang to the head.

Denial was another tool she'd read about. It allowed captives to function. Stopped them really going crazy. Denial gave you respite from dealing with the impossible present. It was probably evolutionary.

It took a while, but Ingrid slowly became aware of another sound. It sounded like a drip, but a drip would make a regular noise, like a metronome. This had a pattern, a rhythm. She pressed her ear against the log wall and almost instantly felt a vibration. A tap. Then another one. It was like a waltz. Quick, quick, slow. Tap, tap, tap. Tap, tap, tap.

She tapped back, the same pattern, performing an acoustic dance with whoever was on the other side of the wall. They stopped for a while, then tapped again. Ingrid replied, then tapped a rhythm of her own and waited.

A second later she got a reply. A perfect echo.

Someone on the other side of the wall wanted to talk to her.

Transcript from Riksdag Committee Hearing 23

December 15 2015

BILUNGS: Thank you for joining us today. If you would please formally state your name and occupation.
FRIESE: Björn Erik Friese. I am a lawyer.
BILUNGS: More specifically, you are a human rights lawyer, is that correct?
FRIESE: Yes.
BILUNGS: And you work for Osberg and Nyquist?
FRIESE: I do.
BILUNGS: Mr Friese, I will encourage you to speak freely. This is not an inquiry, you are not in court; we are only here to establish the facts of the events of December 15 and 16th last year. [Pause] Can you please tell the committee when you first heard of the situation unfolding in Stockholm on Monday the15th?
FRIESE: You mean the bomb at the National Museum?
BILUNGS: If you think that's relevant, but I suspect it would be more pertinent to start with the call from Sergeant Sami Holm.
FRIESE: Sure. I was at my office, in Osterlångg; I was having a video conference call with colleagues in London, an extradition matter. I felt my cell phone buzz in my pocket. Then it buzzed again. You know, it can take so long to set up these conference calls that I didn't want to interrupt it. But then my assistant Pia —do you need her full name?
BILUNGS: Please.
FRIESE: Pia Olin. She knocked on the door, indicated she needed to speak to me. She waited inside the conference room door, waving her phone at me... It became obvious that she had something important to tell me.
BILUNGS: And what did she say?

FRIESE: She suggested that I step out into the hallway and told me that she had a police officer on the phone for me. This is not so unusual, but I could tell from the expression on Pia's face that this was not a client who had absconded or something like that. She was scared. At least, that's how she looked. [Pause. BILUNGS indicates for FRIESE to continue] I took the phone from her hand, introduced myself and then Sergeant Holm apologized for not visiting me in person but in the circumstances she said she hoped I would understand.
BILUNGS: What did Sergeant Holm say to you?
FRIESE: She said that there were unconfirmed reports that my wife had been taken from the Republik café. I asked her what she meant by 'taken' and she said that eyewitnesses claimed they had seen Anna, my wife, being placed in a large black car, a Range Rover, possibly, by armed men and was then driven away at speed. I asked her if she was sure. [Pause] She said she could not confirm the reports, but if they were true she wanted to give me the chance to get Stefan, our son, to a place of safety—
BILUNGS: She knew you had a son?
FRIESE: Nodding. Though she may have said 'children' or 'family', something like that.
BILUNGS: She did not mention Stefan by name?
FRIESE: Not that I recall. I asked her if she had informed Sager House and she said that she hadn't—
BILUNGS: Just to be clear, Sergeant Holm called you before she called the Statsminister's office to inform them that—according to witnesses—the Minister for Climate and the Environment had been abducted at gunpoint?
FRIESE: That is what she said, yes.
BILUNGS: Did you think that was odd?
FRIESE: To be honest, I was only thinking about Stefan at that moment. I could not remember if he was with the child minder or if it was one of the days he was with his grandmother. That was my focus. In those moments. But very quickly, within a minute I would say, I realized that the police officer, Sergeant Holm, was mistaken.

BILUNGS: And you told her that?
FRIESE: [Nodding] Anna had a full day of meetings—she was preparing for the Paris climate talks—and there was simply no way she would be having lunch in the Republik, even though we like it there. We often ate there. We still do, despite everything. So, I called Anna, just to reassure myself, but her phone went straight to voicemail. I got Pia to call Anna's office, and Kasper, Anna's assistant, confirmed that Anna was here in the Riksdag. I think maybe even in the committee room right next door. Not sure why I would remember that.
BILUNGS: And Miss Skyberg's assistant, Kasper—this is Kasper Sjöberg?
FRIESE: Yes.
BILUNGS: Mr Sjöberg was sure Miss Skyberg was in a meeting next door?
FRIESE: Positive.
BILUNGS: And your son?
FRIESE: Pia checked the diary. He was with his grandmother, Anna's stepmother Sofia, and I called her and told her to expect that the police would probably knock on the door at some point. In fact, while we were on the phone, uniformed officers arrived. They stayed, parked outside, all day. I should like to say that, given the demands placed on the Stockholm police that day, they were very dedicated to the needs of my family and I should like their efforts to be recognized by this committee.
BILUNGS: But you were not able to reach your wife?
FRIESE: No, like me, she was also on a conference call, but her conference calls are a little more important than mine. Certainly at that time, and she was not contactable.
BILUNGS: But you were nonetheless sure that it was not your wife who had been abducted.
FRIESE: [Pause] Obviously, given the nature of Anna's work, and given what happened to Anna Lindh, and before her Olof Palme, there was always a small piece of me that feared that what Sergeant Holm was telling me was true. You know, the eco terrorists, some of them will do stupid things to make the

world pay attention. In the run-up to the Paris talks, I suppose I believed it was possible she really had been taken. And then, when the news reports started to come out… Well, you can imagine. TV4 is saying there are unconfirmed reports that Anna Skyberg has been kidnapped. And then, when those reports ceased, you started to think that possibly you had imagined it. I admit, it was a little hard to be sure they were mistaken until I had spoken to Anna.

BILUNGS: And when was that?

FRIESE: A little after two, I think. She left her meeting to be greeted by armed officers who explained to her she might be the target of a kidnap. She had already spoken to Sofia, her father's wife, at this point and was alarmed but reassured that Stefan was being protected. She had been told she would not be allowed to leave the Riksdag until the situation was under control. She wanted to know that I could rearrange my schedule to take care of Stefi.

BILUNGS: I would like to return to your phone call with Sergeant Holm. How did she seem to you?

FRIESE: In what way?

BILUNGS: I would just like to form an idea of your impression of her.

FRIESE: [Pause] I don't know what to say. It's not like she was standing in front of me. It was a short conversation.

BILUNGS: Did she seem anxious?

FRIESE: No, not especially. Nervous, perhaps.

BILUNGS: How do you mean?

FRIESE: She might have stuttered, stumbled over the odd word. I didn't think anything of it.

BILUNGS: And you didn't think it odd that she had called you first, that she knew you had a son?

FRIESE: Well, at the time, I was only thinking about whether or not there was any chance Anna could have been in the Republik.

BILUNGS: And thinking about it now—I mean, in your work, you must have many dealings with the police— do you think her actions were appropriate?

FRIESE: I have no comment to make about the actions of Sergeant Holm.
BILUNGS: Very well. If we could turn now to your first contact with the kidnappers.

20

Ingrid twisted round, pressing her ear into the log wall. She could hear men talking, but the tapping had stopped. Then she heard something unexpected: a bugle call. Images of shined buttons, peaked caps and parade grounds entered her head. It was a ringtone and when the call was answered one of the voices got louder. The only words she could make out were 'hello', 'yes' and 'fuck'. The rest was unintelligible.

The voice got louder. Angrier. There was a thud. A thump. Then another voice joined in. They were arguing. Another thud. Were they fighting too? Then the bugle sounded again.

"Hello?"

There was a long silence. Ingrid became aware of her own pulse as her ear pressed into the wood. De-dum, de-dum. She started to tap along.

"OK."

Then more voices, clamoring. It sounded like there were more than two of them. Had their instructions been changed? Was that what was happening? She pressed her ear as close as she could, hoping to make out what they were saying. She listened hard and tuned in to a sound that didn't appear to be made by a grown man. Singing. Tuneless singing. It sounded like a child.

Jesus, no.

A flash of Megan, a surge of anger. She could no longer feel the cold. Why would they keep the kid in with them? Why not put the kid in the same room as her? She didn't want to answer that question. She'd spent five years working in Violent Crimes Against Children. She knew why adults kept children against their will.

You goddamn fucking bastards.

Ingrid sucked down her rage. Just like all the times she'd walked into crime scenes and witnessed what the sickest minds are capable of. Children kept in closets, cellars. Feces, both animal and human, left for days on carpets that wriggled with maggots. Track marks in spindly arms, parents who actually inject their heroin into their nine-year-olds to make them feel better, or make them shut up. Ingrid knew how anger clouds your reactions, makes you miss things. You have to park it. Box it. Only open it up when the case gets cold and you need the rage to push you forwards. If you can't control your anger, an instructor at Quantico once told Ingrid, you'd better not work with kids. She breathed deep and hard.

Then she heard it. De-dum, de-dum. An echo to match her thundering heart. The kid was tapping on the wall when the men were arguing, when it was safe to make a noise. Ingrid's brain snowglobed with screwdrivers and lighting fires and fistfights with Mohammed, trying to figure out how she could get the kid out of there.

She tapped back, in the hope that knowing she was there and paying attention would offer some comfort. De-dum, de-dum. Then it hit her, like a fist to the face: the kid couldn't possibly have anything to do with the components.

She clenched her teeth, the muscles in her jaw tightening.

In the ten years—no, eleven—she had been in law enforcement, Ingrid had worked on over a dozen kidnappings. After Megan, they were the cases she muscled her way in on. In her experience, there were three reasons why people abducted children: sexual gratification, revenge and money.

If sexual gratification was their motive, why has she been taken? If you wanted to abuse a kid, you didn't want an adult hostage in the next room. Revenge was a possible motive, but in the cases she'd worked in VCAC that was usually only in custody cases. Again, if that was their reason, it didn't make sense for them to be holding her too. So that left money. They had to be holding the kid for ransom. Did that mean they were holding her for ransom too?

She shook her head, trying to loosen some sense from the facts that she knew. She thought about the gunmen in Republik. Two Somalis, one North African. They hadn't worn masks or disguised their identities. That usually meant they were preparing for martyrdom. But there had been no suicide-by-cop, just the taking of valuables and one single unidentifiable female.

Ingrid pictured her hand dropping her wallet containing over two thousand dollars and nothing else into the younger man's sack. Did that explain it? That they thought she was rich? There hadn't been any ID in the wallet, no driver's license, so if they were hoping to get a ransom for her, who the hell were they going to call?

Her husband.

They had taken everyone else's wallet too. Assuming an average of fifty dollars a wallet, they'd have maybe another grand to add to the money they'd gotten from her. Not exactly a raid on Fort Knox. Certainly not the kind of compensation for going to jail for decades for kidnap and firearms offenses. They'd probably get arrested for the murder of the man who hit his head too. That meant life behind bars. Why would they risk that?

She couldn't work it out. Maybe the cold or the hunger was impairing her thinking. It was more important to figure out a way of escaping. She thought about the screwdriver. A quick jab into the eye was the obvious choice. Ingrid imagined Mohammed coming into the room, the door open behind him, possibly bringing her something to eat… Unless she could take him out with a single hit, there would be a struggle. The other men in the room next door would hear. They would overpower her. But… It might give the kid a chance to escape. If she could make a big enough fuss, if she fought like a mustang, the kid could slip away.

But slip away into what? Twenty below? Middle of the forest.

She knew nothing about the kid. Didn't know what he or she was wearing. Most likely all that would happen was that she would end up tied hand and foot and the kid would simper in a corner and not even try to leave. Ingrid had seen that too: victims who had plenty of chances to escape but never took them because no one ever told them they could.

Ingrid pulled the screwdriver from her sock and realized just how tiny it was. Almost useless. Then a memory surfaced: a lazy night she'd spent at Ralph's—a name that no longer made her heart skip a beat—watching *Doctor Who*. Ralph had made her watch about five episodes back to back, hoping he could make her see why it was the best show on TV. One way or another, Ingrid had always attracted the nerds and the geeks. Ralph's attempt at conversion failed, but Ingrid had learnt that the Doctor's only weapon was a screwdriver. A sonic screwdriver, admittedly. All he had to do was point it at a problem and it immediately solved itself. Remembering how Ralph's long legs had entwined with hers on his couch, she pointed the tiny screwdriver at the door.

And a solution to her problem immediately presented itself.

21

Ingrid swiped one of the lamps and inspected the timber closely. The wood of the doorframe was almost as rotten as the roof. If she could dig out the rot around the hinges, the door would simply fall open.

Her bound arms started to hurt holding the flickering lamp at shoulder height, so she placed it at her feet while she thought things through. On the plus side, it wouldn't be too noisy. If the men were talking next door, and the wind was howling, she doubted her captors would notice her scraping away at the rot. Another bonus was that—unlike the roof option—it was achievable. Elation surged through her like fire: if she managed to open the door without attracting attention, it could be hours before they even realized she had gone. Her head started to nod in affirmation: this was it. This was her way out. She could raise the alarm, save the kid. Her thoughts swirled like snow outside an air vent, tumbling and falling, rising and darting.

She gripped her fingers around the handle of the screwdriver and started digging, flicking out splinters, taking control. She started with the top hinge, where the wood was so soft it felt like she was scooping out a pumpkin. After a few minutes, she pressed an index finger into the hole, digging out fibers with her nail, hoping to feel the metal of a screw. She wasn't even a knuckle deep.

Assuming each of the three hinges had three screws, that meant nine holes she'd have to make. A couple hours, tops. Perfectly doable. She'd need to be strategic, though. She couldn't do all three screws on one hinge in case the door shifted, started to stick, and alerted Mohammed to her plan. It'd have to be one screw from the top, one from the middle, then one from the bottom, then repeat.

Ingrid picked up the lantern and examined the hole she had made, hoping to see a glint of a screw shaft even though she knew they'd all be rusted dull. The hole looked even smaller than it had felt and her heart sank so fast and so hard that she almost heard it thud on the floor.

It's still a good plan, she told herself, it just might take a little longer.

"You'll find a way."

Ingrid looked up expecting to see someone, but she was completely alone in the sauna. She was talking to herself. She'd read about it in lots of hostage memoirs. It's normal, she told herself, just a survival mechanism. A way of keeping your spirits up.

Kneeling on the floor meant that the middle hinge was now at eye level and the lamp illuminated the area that needed to be scraped away. She gripped the screwdriver between her palms, and jammed it into the timber next to the hinge. The tip of the shaft did not sink into the rot. Ingrid tried again, putting a bit more force behind the movement. But the timber was solid. There was no rot. Ingrid tried a centimeter above, a centimeter below, but no matter where she prodded the screwdriver, there wasn't any rotten wood anywhere near the middle hinge.

She prodded again, just to make sure, but she already knew that her plan wasn't going to work. Perhaps if she had days to escape, she could do a little every day, but that was not a timescale she was willing to entertain. Not with the deadline to get to Stortorget. Ingrid dropped the screwdriver onto the floor and let her arms rest on her knees. A blade of freezing air forced its way under the door, knifing its way into her shins. She couldn't stay where she was. She scrambled to her feet, and pushed the screwdriver back into her sock. When she picked up the lantern, she noticed the confetti of rotten wood on the floor.

A naked flame. Wood shavings. A new plan started to emerge.

How long, she wondered, would it take to dry out the rotten wood splinters? Chipping out the rot was easy. Within five minutes she would have a handful of the stuff. She imagined shoving the splinters into a sock, drying them out over a lantern, then pushing the lantern over, letting the citron-scented oil engulf the splinters. Her brain flitted from thought to thought like a wasp in a jar. She could add the maxi pads…

Her mind pictured the fire she could start. She imagined it burning a hole in the side of the sauna and her jumping through the flames like a performing dog at a circus, and then laughed at herself. *Hostages who maintain a sense of humor and proportion tend to survive their ordeals with fewer psychological scars…*

Even if she was able to start a fire, the only means she had of controlling it was the slowly melting bucket of snow. She might as well tie a noose around her neck.

"You'll find a way. You always do."

Ingrid turned. "Who said that?"

The voice was familiar. American accent. She had to be talking to herself. She didn't know how long she'd been on her own for but she was losing it already. Textbook. All these years she'd been reading about hostage situations and here she was, following the template and going crazy. She hadn't known it could happen so quickly. Had the same thing happened to Megan, she wondered?

The TV reports of the house where Megan's remains had been found suddenly played in Ingrid's head. The shaky footage of the steps down into the basement. The 'House of Horrors' caption in a red band across the bottom of the screen. A whiff of cotton candy sneaked up inside Ingrid's nose and plunged into her brain.

Ingrid sat down on the bench and stared at the lantern, letting herself become mesmerized by the flame as her thoughts retraced their steps between Megan's abduction and her own. The more she stared at the lantern, the more she gradually became aware that it had started to flicker. Was it her imagination? Or was it running out of oil? She glanced over at the second lantern, then back to the first.

Then it occurred to her: she didn't need two lanterns. All she was doing was burning twice as much fuel as necessary. Fuel she could use when she'd worked out how to use fire as a weapon. She was acting like the lone survivor of a jungle expedition eating all the available food on the first day. She needed to ration her resources. She needed to be smarter.

Ingrid leaned over and blew out one of the lanterns and the sauna instantly darkened.

She sat back against the dividing wall, letting her ears tune in to the noises coming from the other side. Instinctively, she flicked something off her arm. But it was still there. Ingrid looked down at the sleeve of her jacket to see what it was.

In the darkness, a tiny beam of light was now catching the edge of the fabric. There was a gap between the logs.

Ingrid crouched down, put her eye up against the hole in the wall and peered through.

Transcript from Riksdag Committee Hearing 23

December 15 2015

BILUNGS: Thank you for coming here this morning. For our records, would you please clearly state your name.
BERING: Katarina Bering.
BILUNGS: And you work for TV4?
BERING: I do. I am the editor of the Nyheterna bulletin.
BILUNGS: But last winter you worked on the early evening news, is that right?
BERING: That is correct.
BILUNGS: You have been invited here today to talk specifically about the reporting of the alleged kidnapping of Anna Skyberg. Can you start by telling us when you first heard of her… I shall say 'disappearance' because obviously we do know that she was not the victim.
BERING: But we did not know that, what, almost exactly a year ago?
BILUNGS: It was December 15th. If you would, tell us how you heard about the kidnapping.
BERING: One of our producers, Nils Luft. The lockdown at the National Museum meant most of the team were out on the streets, but Nils had seen something come up on Twitter I think. He came straight over to my desk and asked to take a team down to Republik. He was out of the building within minutes. He phoned from outside the café less than fifteen minutes later. These situations are usually chaotic, there was no proper police cordon at that point, but he was prevented from entering the café. I told him to interview as many eye witnesses as possible. He was live on our sister station by twelve fifteen—
BILUNGS: Forgive me for interrupting, but I think it may be useful to play a recording of his report at this point. Paul, do you have the tape to play?

TRESOR: It's a file, not a tape. Right now?
BILUNGS: Please.

RECORDING:
[Luft] Thank you, Peter. I'm standing outside the Republik café on Skeppsbron in Gamla Stan, the scene of dramatic events here this morning. Three gunmen burst into the café a little over half an hour ago, held an estimated twenty people hostage for around twenty minutes, during which time one man was killed. After stealing the valuables of the hostages, the gunmen then left, taking a hostage with them. Peter, I have to tell you that the hostage has been named by witnesses as the Minister for Climate and the Environment, Anna Skyberg. [Presenter] Nils, what do we know about the gunmen? [Luft] There were three of them; they were armed with what one witness claimed was an AK-47 and a semi-automatic handgun. They have been described as being of African origin and they left the scene on foot. It is not known where they are now. [Presenter] Nils, what is the advice from the police at this time? [Luft] Peter, there is no official word, but if there is a chance that there are three gunmen at large, then I would imagine their advice would be to stay away from Gamla Stan. [Presenter] And any word on where Minister Skyberg has been taken to? [Luft] Peter, I don't have that information. [Presenter] And do we know if this incident is linked to what is happening at the National Museum? [Luft] Well, Peter, we can see the museum from here, but it would be speculation at this point to link the two events. As I speak to you, the police presence around this café is increasing, the armed response unit has just arrived as is standard with a terrorist incident of this nature. [Presenter] Nils, thank you. We're going to return now to our correspondent outside the National Museum—

BILUNGS: I think we can stop the tape now. Sorry, file. So, Miss Bering, when did you find out that the Minister for Climate and the Environment was not the victim of the kidnap?

BERING: I don't think I found that out until I got home. So, around ten o'clock that night. A colleague called to tell me.
BILUNGS: Oh. I thought you knew that Miss Skyberg was not involved much earlier in the day... [Refers to notes] Before the one o'clock news aired.
BERING: Ah. No.
BILUNGS: So why didn't you report the abduction of the minister on the lunchtime bulletin?
BERING: Um, well, we received a call from Tor Bronsen—
BILUNGS: The Statsminister's chief of staff?
BERING: [Nods]—and he basically told us that if we ran the story we would never get another interview with any member of the cabinet ever again.
BILUNGS: Did he give you a reason?
BERING: Only that it was a matter of national security. Obviously, we understand now that other kidnappings had taken place and they, the government, were clearly worried about panic spreading. But at the time he only mentioned national security and asked us to give him two hours before reporting the rumors.
BILUNGS: Rumors?
BERING: Possibly I use that word with hindsight. At the time we had every reason to think they were true. I told Bronsen that the story was already out, that Twitter was going bananas about it and that it was, you know, news and that we had a duty to our viewers to broadcast what we knew. It was at that point that the station's lawyer came into the newsroom: he had received the notice to desist from the Statsminister's office. Well, at that point we understood just how serious it was. I've been in the industry since university and I'd never received a notice to desist before. I was still on the phone to Bronsen and I said to him, "Now that you know I can't run the story will you tell me what's really going on?" And his answer was, "We may be at war." I'm fairly sure I laughed.
BILUNGS: Laughed?
BERING: I suppose I can almost understand it now. The National Museum—a symbol of the country—was under siege,

members of the cabinet were being abducted, the judiciary were being targeted… No, actually it was pretty far-fetched. The thing he said that did make sense, though, was that any media coverage of the Skyberg abduction could put the minister's life in danger. Probably, the notice to desist was unnecessary; I'm sure the major news outlets would have been persuaded to hold off for a couple of hours on the basis that someone's life was at risk. The trouble was that it was all over social media. Thankfully, the events at the National Museum meant we had plenty to report without the Skyberg story.

22

The gap in the log wall was long and thin like a scar. It was about three feet off the ground, making it awkward to peer through. Ingrid found the best vantage point on her knees, resting her forearms on the bench.

It was hard to make out much beyond the color of the pants the kidnappers were wearing. A tiny slice of blue denim jeans, a bead of red padded ski pants. No sign of a kid, just an old varnished table bearing two packs of Marlboro cigarettes, a packet of cookies and a five-liter bottle of water. A faint whiff of kerosene from their heater drifted through the gap.

The man in the ski pants was pacing methodically, like a surveyor measuring out yards with his stride. No one was talking and she could make out the tinny sounds of a game being played on a cell phone. She hoped it was a battery-draining app: a bored kid quickly starts to create problems.

The bugle call again.

"Uh-huh." Not Mohammed's voice. As he spoke his footsteps got faster and heavier and his voice grew louder. He wasn't speaking English, or Swedish. Possibly Arabic, but she couldn't be sure. "OK, OK."

It didn't sound OK at all.

"What did he say?" Definitely Mohammed speaking. In English.

"Problem. Big fucking problem."

Ingrid's heart began pounding harder. A problem for them was almost certainly a problem for her too. The furthest recesses of her brain noted that the kidnappers spoke to each other, and to her, in English.

Footsteps again, loud and echoey, followed by the noise of the door opening on the other side of the wall. The sound of winter boots thumping on the snowy ground followed by the rasp of bolts. A metallic fumbling as the padlock was unlocked. Ingrid braced herself. She staggered to her feet, aware of the pulse in her jaw pumping hard. The dread made her legs tremble. And then the door opened.

He was shorter than her, five six maybe, thickset and bulldog ugly. A sharp wind ruffled the fur trim of his hood. "What is your name?"

"I, er..." Ingrid couldn't think what to say. She tried to remember her cover story. Should she try to pretend to be Russian? Use her undercover ID? No.

"Your name?" he repeated, stepping inside the sauna.

Panicked, Ingrid said the first Swedish name that came into her head. "Anna."

"Anna what?"

She needed a quick lie. She didn't even know if she should be pretending to be Swedish. Having said her name was Anna, the surname that popped into her head was her cousin's married name, the one she used on Facebook. "Friese."

The instant the syllables left her mouth she screwed up her face. It was a stupid move. *How could I be so dumb?* If they Googled Anna Friese they would find the only person in Sweden who could be linked to her. Her stomach muscles contracted painfully.

"What did you say?"

He hadn't heard her properly. Her breaths were sharp and shallow as she tried not to gasp. Had she got away with it?

"What is your name?" He moved toward her, his hands remaining firmly in his pockets. The angle of his right wrist suggested he was gripping a handgun.

"I said it's none of your business."

"Tell me your name." The man was standing inches from her, looking up into her face. "Tell me."

Ingrid held his gaze and suppressed the urge to spit in his face. "No." She resisted the compulsion to look at the open door behind him in case it betrayed what she was planning. A swift uppercut with both fists, knock him out, and slip out into the forest. She felt heat in her cheeks. She knew she may never get a better chance. She feared what not taking the opportunity would do to her.

Ingrid tipped her head back an increment then snapped it forward, smashing her forehead into the man's skull, a flash of black obscuring her vision before she lifted her head. She clasped her hands together and raised them sharply, sending the components sliding down to her elbows, and smashed her fists into his jaw.

He staggered backward but did not fall. She took a step toward him, raising her arms above her head, ready to shove her weight down on his temple, but he sidestepped. She fell forward and her hands plowed through the air.

Ingrid turned to face him. He was clutching a Beretta. An M9. She glanced over him at the open door. Unless she got the gun off him it might as well be secured by deadbolts.

Her padded jacket made a scratching noise as her chest rose and fell with the exertion. Maybe fighting would garner her some respect. She tried to read his face, but in the lamplight his features—and intentions—were obscured. She focused on the gun. His hand wasn't trembling. A damn good sign he had no intention of using it.

"Your name," he said again. "Tell me your name."

Ingrid chose her silence carefully. There was no point in giving him a false identity. It wouldn't take long before he'd know she was lying. She shook her head. "Anna."

He raised the Beretta to shoulder height and placed his left hand over his right. A steadying stance. An assassin's stance. Of course the other reason people don't shake when aiming a gun, Ingrid said to herself, is because they're habituated killers.

"No name, no live," he said. "You give me your fucking name or I blow your brains out."

Ingrid swallowed hard, her gaze darting from the muzzle of the gun to his face. He took a step closer, bringing the Beretta to within a foot of her face. She could see his features more clearly now and she held eye contact with him. His mouth puckered in disgust at her defiance. A nostril flared. His head began to nod, incremental movements, each a visual clue to his thinking. Ingrid stood firm and maintained her stare.

"Anna."

He blinked, then turned his head sharply. He shoved the gun in his right-hand pocket and pulled an iPhone out of his left.

"Sit!" He pushed her backward onto the bench. He pressed the home button, swiped upwards then held it in front of her face.

The flash blinded her. As she pulled her face away, he took several more photos. Ingrid blinked and blinked, her retinas tortured by the LED assault. She heard a whoosh sound as he sent the photos. Email or text, she wasn't sure.

An image of a meeting room popped into her head. A case review session a few months down the line. A junior cop relaying the cell phone records for the vicinity to the senior investigator. What she didn't know was whether they were reviewing a case of kidnapping, or murder.

23

Ingrid sat with her legs apart and her elbows on her knees and tried to piece together what she'd just learnt.

The short, ugly guy almost certainly was not a killer.

It was not his intention to become one.

Her kidnappers didn't have a clue who she was.

Ingrid pulled off the beanie, her head suddenly hot, and rubbed her hair with her bound hands, noticing for the first time that her act of defiance had resulted in a bruise on her left thumb. Better than a gunshot, she told herself. She shook her head, disbelieving she had pushed it so far with a man holding a gun to her head. It was just the way he had started to nod, those micro-movements he wouldn't even have known he was making. She had read it as acceptance and acknowledgment that he wasn't going to follow through. She snorted at her stupidity: they could just as easily have been indications of a declaration, an affirmation that he was making peace with taking her life.

The cold air rushed into her mouth, her chest rising as her breaths got deeper, making the fibers of her jacket rub noisily against her neck. She kept filling and emptying her lungs: she was lucky to be alive.

When her breaths began to soften and her heart rate slowed, Ingrid tried to focus on one simple question: why on earth would anyone kidnap someone at gunpoint, in daylight, in the middle of a capital city, if they didn't know who they were? She hadn't been abducted by a sadistic loner, as Megan had been, who wanted her for sex or torture. And even though she had head-butted the man with the gun, he had not hit back: as far as she could tell, they had no intention of killing her. And the sounds from the other side of the wall told her they weren't intent on torturing and killing the kid either.

Was she being held for future sexual gratification? Had she been abducted by henchmen who were waiting for the linchpin of their twisted gang to arrive before raping and killing her in some sort of ritual? Unlikely: she had worked enough exploitation cases to know that neither she nor her abductors fitted the profile. In those sorts of killings, she flattered herself, the victims were not tall, muscular and in the habit of being complimented on their looks, but rather misfits with low self-esteem. Ingrid grimaced: Megan. Neither of them had had much confidence when they were fourteen, but Megan had undoubtedly fit the profile.

If sex and torture weren't the reasons for her abduction, that left revenge and ransom, but those options only made sense if the kidnappers knew who they were holding captive. She returned to the comment about her husband: who the hell did they think she was?

She jerked her head toward the door. One of the bolts had been slipped. Then the second. A fumble with a lock and then once again the door opened, the cold wind storming inside the cabin. Mohammed stepped inside but he did not look at her. His shoulders were drooping. The posture of a nervous man. Or an apologetic one. He reached into the pocket of his coat and pulled out an iPhone. He fumbled with it. The screen illuminated, lighting up his face. He seemed scared. He made no attempt to look at her before he pointed the phone's camera in her direction.

"OK," he said.

The short man strode into the sauna, his heavy-soled walking boots shaking the floorboards. He crossed the room in two strides and lunged at her.

"No, please, no." Ingrid knew what was coming and turned

her face.

His right fist hit the side of her jaw, sending her sideways into the log wall, scraping her cheek against the worn bark. Every instinct she had told her to raise her arms to protect her face, but the smuggled components kept her arms in her lap. The pain radiated across the top of her head.

His right fist rammed hard into her cheek, slicing the inside of her mouth against her molars. He grabbed her skull with his left hand and slammed his right into her eye socket. Ingrid yelped as the skin above her eyebrow split. Mohammed was over his shoulder, filming it all. Warmth ran down her face.

"Let me see," Mohammed said.

"Take the picture," the other man said.

"Yes, yes."

A camera flash, then another and another as her attacker gripped her jaw, making sure a record was made of her injuries.

"Look at me," he said.

Ingrid kept her gaze defiantly centered on her lap. She knew why they were taking photos and she wanted to make sure they didn't get a clean image of her.

"Look at me." He yanked her face and pulled her toward him, but he couldn't make her look at him. A hard, stinging slap landed on her right cheek.

He stood up straight. A retreat. If he could not make her look at him, he was going to pretend he hadn't asked her to. Mohammed moved toward the door and said something incomprehensible. Her assailant turned sharply and ran to the doorway. Ingrid wiped the blood out of her eye and watched as the two men peered out into the darkness. They could see something.

They pulled the door shut behind them and slid the bolts across. What was it? A rescue party and flashlights flickering through the trees? Flashing blue lights from the road below? Was she about to be found? She felt numb. Thoughts swirled inside her head like a wall of death rider, round and round, faster and faster, louder and louder. If a rescue party had located the cabin, there was no way she could escape.

"What are you going to do?" The voice again, and this time Ingrid recognized it and collapsed forward onto her knees. It was Megan's voice. She felt weak. Her best friend from childhood was talking to her. Her *dead* best friend. She knew it was just her brain playing tricks but she could not stop the tears from forming. The guilt of leaving Megan, of not looking back, would always have the capacity to overwhelm her.

A single word started to circle round in her head like a hawk, like a fin surfacing. Payback. If she hadn't run, Megan might still be alive. Payback. This was always going to happen. Abduction had been her destiny. Her penance.

"You'll find a way. You always do." She was summoning up Megan's voice from the deepest part of her.

Ingrid blinked back tears and looked around the sauna. There had to be something she'd missed, some rabbit just waiting to be yanked out of a hat. There had to be. There always was. She scanned the roof, the walls, the door, the bench and quickly found her eyes settling on the floor.

There was activity outside. A door slamming. A scratching sound. Perhaps the kid was talking loudly. What was going on? Heavy footsteps echoed under the floor. Were they leaving? Without her?

Ingrid was still staring at the floorboards, watching as blood from her cut dripped onto them. They wouldn't have taken the photos—hell, they wouldn't have beaten her—if they were planning to move venue. Whoever was approaching was unexpected. She hadn't heard helicopters or sirens, but her best guess was the cops. The kid was valuable, she wasn't. The kidnappers would take the kid and leave her.

Ingrid could not let herself be found. The repercussions—for the war in Syria, for diplomatic relations between the US and Sweden, for her career—were too great. She had to escape. Had to. She couldn't end up inside an interrogation room. Or a cell.

The short man was shouting. The kid was joining in. Undercutting it all was the thud, thud, thud of footsteps.

Footsteps.

That's why her eyes were focused on the floor. The footsteps were echoing because there was a void below. If there was a void, there was a way out, or at least somewhere to hide. Suddenly energized by the prospect of escape, Ingrid wiped the blood from her eye, dropped down onto her knees and pulled the screw-driver from her sock. She slid the metal shaft between the boards, pressing down hard on the plastic handle, trying to pry the end of one board free from the joist underneath.

She tried again. The wood moved slightly. A fever of excite-ment flushed her skin. She pushed the screwdriver between the adjacent gap, lifting the same board from the other side. It gave a little bit more. She repeated the maneuver until she could get her fingers underneath. Then she straddled the board and gripped one side of it and pulled hard. There was a squeak as nails that hadn't moved for a century were sucked out from their recesses.

"Yes! Come on!"

Elation surged through her limbs, warming her toes, forcing her to smile as the blood continued to drip down onto the floor.

All it would take to lift the entire length was a damn good pull, so Ingrid moved onto the adjacent board. The width of two floorboards would be enough for her to drop down below and hide or maybe even escape. She worked quickly, jimmying the flat end of the screwdriver under the wood, wiggling and shifting it till she felt the floorboard move. She didn't want to think about what she might find underneath.

She could hear voices but she didn't have time to stop and listen. She just needed a few more minutes, enough time to pry the first few nails free of the joist. Then it would just be two sharp tugs and she'd be out of sight. She glanced nervously round the room and made a mental note to take the lantern down with her as well as her bag.

The noise from outside was getting louder. It would take them a few minutes to get through the bolts; she didn't need to panic. She scrambled to her feet, swiped her bag and placed it close to the jimmied boards, ready to be thrown into the void. She worked the screwdriver under the wood again, pressing down on the handle with such force she risked breaking it.

A scraping sound. The bolts.

She pressed down hard again. She needed to free one more pair of nails. Her hands started to shake.

She glanced at the door, then back down to the floorboards.

"Shit."

There wasn't going to be enough time. Another bolt was pulled across.

Ingrid dropped the screwdriver and opted for brute strength, tugging hard on the floorboard. But with her arms bound she couldn't get as much leverage as she needed.

The bottom bolt screeched in its sleeve. A different voice. Swedish. Cops.

Ingrid yanked hard. The board creaked as she pulled but she couldn't free it. She needed to free more nails.

The padlock rattled. Her chest was pounding with pain. She could not let herself be taken into custody. There had to be another way. Her best shot was to barge past and outrun the lot of them. She concealed the screwdriver in her fist and the door opened.

She looked up and gasped.

No cops. Just Mohammed.

Ingrid sighed so deeply her ribcage collapsed forward.

"In here," Mohammed said to someone out of sight. "You will stay in here."

A trudging of footsteps in the snow, then a man with a hood over his head was pushed inside, stumbling with the force of Mohammed's shove.

"When the door closes, you take off the hood. Only then. Understood?"

The man nodded.

Mohammed looked at Ingrid: "If one of you escapes, we kill the other." The way he held eye contact made her think he meant it. The door slammed shut and she flinched.

The man pulled the hood down over his face. He had a black eye and a bleeding lip. He blinked several times before he saw Ingrid sitting on the floor.

"Oh my word," he said in Swedish. "It really is you."

24

Ingrid scrambled herself upright and moved toward him as he staggered, stumbling like a boxer in the tenth round. She guided him over to the bench and helped him sit down. His trousers—smart moleskin slacks—were sodden and his expensive leather shoes were puckered with the wet. He looked like he had been abducted during his lunch hour when he had popped out to buy a sandwich. He wasn't even wearing a jacket, just a woolen sweater that was now wet from the snow.

"You don't recognize me, do you?" he said. "I am Jens. Jens Luhrmann. We met once. A party in Södermalm." He was in his thirties, lean and compact—a martial arts build—with a prominent, cartoon chin. His accent was odd: perhaps he wasn't Swedish.

Ingrid shook her head. She knew it would be impossible to pretend to be whoever he thought she was, but she hadn't yet worked out a cover story. She tilted his head back and held the lantern over his cut lip. The bruised skin was taut and engorged. Blood oozed from a centimeter long split below his philtrum.

Ingrid grabbed her backpack and reached inside for the packet of maxi pads. Her fingers brushed against the cold Perspex canister as she pulled out one of the individually wrapped sanitary napkins. She got to her feet, tore off the wrapper and crossed the sauna to dip the pad into the slowly melting bucket of ice. Jens did not take his eyes off her as she knelt before him and wiped the dried blood from his chin.

"How long have you been here?" he asked. He was shivering, his legs twitching rhythmically and his hands trembling like poppy heads. Ingrid pulled out another sanitary pad and ripped off its cover. She handed it to him and indicated he should hold it against his wound.

"Three, four hours," she said in Swedish. There was just no way she could continue with the charade. Her language skills weren't up to the job, even if the gash above her eye sufficiently disguised her resemblance to a woman who had once been at a party in Södermalm. She studied him, trying to assess if her speaking voice had given the game away.

He spoke again. This time she did not understand him. She did not ask him to repeat it, but after a few seconds he did anyway. Again, Ingrid could not work out what he meant. It was possible he wasn't speaking Swedish. She remained crouching in front of him, staring hard into his bloodshot eyes.

Ingrid could feel her pulse beneath her right ear as she weighed up the wisdom of what she was about to do. Sucking the cold air deep into her lungs, she started to form the words. "We have not met before," she said in English. She spoke with a Russian accent, keen to disguise her true identity as much as possible.

Jens looked puzzled. He started to say something but his teeth were chattering so violently he could not get the words out.

"Tell me," Ingrid continued, "who you think I am."

"English?" he managed.

Ingrid nodded.

"You are not Anna?"

Anna? Had he said Anna? Ingrid felt a void open up beneath her solar plexus as her heart stalled. She nodded. That was, after all, the name she had given Mohammed. "My name is Anna," she said, a little uncertainly.

"But you are not Anna. I mean you are not Anna Skyberg. You are not Björn's wife?"

It was as if Ingrid's entire body had become hollow. Flesh, bone and blood had all transpired into air. Cold, freezing air. She shook her head as her thoughts returned like a bullet in flight to Republik. A café she had only known about because her cousin had mentioned it on Facebook. She had even ordered Anna's favorite item on the menu. A flash of the way the girl behind the counter had smiled at her surged through Ingrid's brain. *Dear God.*

"But it was on the news. The r-r-radio." Jens's hand dropped to his lap, unable to carry on holding the sanitary pad against his trembling lip. "You and the judge's son." His gaze became distant.

"Jens!" Ingrid placed her hand on his leg and squeezed hard. "Jens?"

He wrenched his gaze back toward her but now it seemed that he had never seen her before. "Anna?" His voice was faint, faltering.

"Jens? Jens!" Ingrid shook his knee hard. "It is really important that you tell me how you know Anna Skyberg. Jens?"

He nodded but his expression was blank. He was blacking out. Hypothermia.

"Jens!" Ingrid got to her feet. She grabbed his right hand and tugged him upwards. "Jens. Jens, you need to keep moving. Jens, get up! Jens!"

She tugged hard and got him upright. His hand was as cold as a corpse's.

"Walk with me. Come on now." Ingrid made him take a couple of steps but his body was shaking so violently that she had to hold him tight. "You gotta keep moving," she said before realizing she had let her accent slip. Chances were he wouldn't remember any of this anyway. "Come on. Just one foot in front of the other."

When you've lived through more than twenty Minnesota winters, hypothermia is something you know about, just like putting chains on tires and keeping a blanket in the trunk. Ingrid had experienced it herself many times and she knew the extreme shaking was Jens's body's last-ditch effort to maintain the correct temperature. If he lost any more body heat, the shaking would stop when the blood left his limbs to help preserve his core. Eventually, the blood would also leave his brain, sending him into a coma.

When Ingrid had worked for the sheriff's department she'd felt the symptoms of hypothermia overwhelm her on a stake-out. She'd radioed for backup but had no memories of being rescued, of being taken back to her apartment and placed in front of the gas fire and gently warmed back to consciousness.

"Jens, Jens, you need to tell me how you know Anna Skyberg. What's the connection between you? How do you know her? Jens!"

His eyes were swimming, he could barely focus. His shaking was uncontrollable. Ingrid knew the shaking was a good sign: it was when it stopped that he'd be in real danger.

"Can you put your arms round me? Can you try?" Ingrid placed his right arm over her right shoulder, then turned into him so that her back pressed into his chest. With her own hands bound, she couldn't grab his left hand and clutch him to her like a backpack in the hope her body heat would help keep him conscious. "Come on, Jens. Remember your left hand? Come on, throw it over my shoulder now. Come on. You can do it."

Somehow he managed to follow her instructions and his arm landed heavily around her neck. Grabbing both his hands in hers she started to walk.

"Walk with me. Come on, right foot, then the other. Come on, Jens."

With his body pressed against hers she could feel how lean he was. She remembered the classroom sniggers about her and Megan being the kids least likely to succumb to hypothermia. Jens, in contrast, felt like he had a BMI in single digits.

Hauling him like a sack, Ingrid walked Jens round the sauna, one heavy step at a time. With no fire, the only way she could stop him falling into a coma was to keep him moving. "OK, Jens, you're going to talk to me. We're going to walk and talk. That OK with you?"

He murmured something.

"Good." Even if she couldn't keep Jens's core temperature at the right level, the effort of carrying him was ensuring that she didn't succumb. "Now tell me about this party in Söder. Why were you at a party with Anna Skyberg?" It was only when she said her cousin's name out loud that Ingrid noticed she had been pronouncing it the American way. "I mean *Skoo*-berg."

He was trying to speak but Ingrid couldn't decipher his slur.

"What was that? Come on, Jens. Tell me again."

"Björn."

"Björn?" Anna's husband. "You know Björn?"

"*Ja*. Björn. Lise. Osberg. Osberg and Nyquist."

Some of those names were familiar, but Ingrid couldn't be sure where she'd heard them before. It was taking all her depleted energy to keep Jens on his feet, to keep him alive.

"Tell me about Björn. Tell me about Lise." He was like a dead weight on her back. "Come on, Jens. Who is Lise? Tell me."

He was murmuring something.

"What was that?" She lurched forward. Either she was getting tired or he was getting heavier. "Jens? Who is Lise? Tell me."

"*Frau*. My wife. She works with Björn."

Ingrid pulled on Jens's arms to prevent him from slumping. "Don't let go. Come on." She was trying to work out why kidnappers would target the relatives of three lawyers. Osberg and Nyquist was the name of Björn's firm. She had seen it on Facebook. A grudge? No, they'd just set fire to the place. Representation? Then why kidnap a judge's son too?

Her arms were starting to burn with the exertion. "Why are they holding us?"

His weight suddenly pressed down on her, forcing her to stagger. He mumbled something.

"What was that?"

He inhaled deeply. "Abdullah Saladdin." His voice was tremulous but belligerent, like a drunk's.

"Jens?"

He had suddenly become a dead weight. Ingrid felt herself

about to collapse under the pressure. "Jens? Who is Abdullah Saladdin?"

Jens slumped, pulling Ingrid to the floor with him. Ingrid wrestled herself from his heavy embrace and looked over at him. He had passed out.

25

Ingrid thumped hard on the dividing wall.

"Get in here," she yelled. "Now!"

All she could hear was the kid's voice. It sounded like he was mimicking her. The kidnappers were silent.

"Get in here. We need help."

She didn't have the strength to shout louder.

"Can you hear me? Get in here!"

Ingrid knelt down, the beam of light from the other side hitting her in the chest, and took Jens's wrist in her hand, her index and middle fingers pressing hard against his radial artery. The pulse was weak and slow. Too slow. It wouldn't be long before it was undetectable, before there was no blood left in his extremities at all. His lips were blue.

"Come on," she shouted. "Now! He's fucking dying in here."

There were sounds of movement from the other side of the wall. Footsteps, chatter, the opening and closing of cabinets, the boy's voice—she couldn't tell if he was talking to her or the kidnappers—followed by the sound of something metallic being dragged across the floor.

The floor.

Ingrid looked at the loosened floorboards. The jimmied ends protruded by an inch or two. If the kidnappers saw them, her chance to escape would dissolve like sugar in boiling water. She looked down at Jens, then back at the loosened boards. The best thing she could do for him was preserve her means of escape. She pushed herself to standing, took three steps over to the floorboards and stood on them, pressing the wrenched nails back into the joists below. She consoled herself with the knowledge that they'd be easier to loosen the next time.

The first bolt was scraped open, then the second. Ingrid returned to Jens, kneeling beside him.

"Hey, Jens, hang in there. I'm going to get you help."

He was unresponsive, his jaw falling slack as his head lolled to one side.

The door was pushed open and Ingrid flinched when a fierce wind knifed its way inside. She turned to see Mohammed and the short man, who was holding a semi-automatic carbine in front of his chest.

"What have you done to him?" Mohammed said.

"Shut the damned door. You have a heater next door, right?"

Both men looked confused. She repeated herself, slowly. "A heater?" She mimed rubbing her hands together.

The two men glanced at each other, clearly suspicious.

"Look at him!" she shouted. "He will die. You need to take him next door."

"Die?" Mohammed said.

Ingrid got to her feet and marched toward the door. The short man aimed the carbine at her chest.

"Then you close the damn door!" She knelt back down beside Jens and started to rub his arms. "You need to get him warm. He has hypothermia. Do you know what that is?"

The short man shook his head.

"Come here."

Neither of them moved.

"Come here!"

They shuffled over, the short man still keeping both hands on his weapon, and peered down at Jens.

"See his lips?" Ingrid asked. "They're blue." She wasn't sure if they understood everything she was saying. "You need to pick him up, take him next door. Get him warm." She forced her bound hands under Jens's right shoulder. "Help me!"

The men exchanged a look, both apparently seeking reassurance from the other that it was OK to do as she said.

"Mohammed! Help me."

Mohammed lumbered toward her and got down on his haunches.

"You understand what is happening?" Ingrid asked.

He shook his head.

"This man has hypothermia."

Mohammed's expression told her he did not know what she meant.

"He will die because he is cold. You will not get a ransom for a dead hostage, will you?"

Mohammed shook his head.

"He needs to be somewhere warmer. Next door. Hold his legs." She nodded at Jens's ankles, indicating that they needed to be lifted.

"You," she said to the short man. "I can't carry him." She showed him her bound hands. "You need to come here and pick him up."

He crouched down beside her, looked at Jens's face, then back up at her. He looked scared. Scared it was a trap? Scared Jens would die? Scared he'd suffer the consequences from whoever had ordered the kidnappings? Ingrid stared into his dark, undulating features: "He will die."

The man nodded. While maintaining eye contact with Ingrid, he laid down the carbine and reached inside his pocket. Ingrid stared at the weapon. Given how organized her kidnapping had been, there was little chance it wasn't loaded. The door was closed but not locked. She could grab the carbine, whack the man in the face with the butt, turn it round, aim at Mohammed…

Her head started to shake. With her hands tied, she wouldn't be able to pull the trigger. And even if she succeeded in knocking out the short guy, Mohammed was likely armed. Besides, she told herself, if she made an escape bid now Jens would almost certainly die. Air that had been trapped for many moments inside her mouth slowly escaped.

The short man pulled his fist out of his pocket, a Swiss army knife inside his curled fingers. He released a blade and thrust it toward Ingrid, making her flinch.

"Hands," he said. "You carry."

This wasn't what she wanted. She needed them to take Jens next door so she could lift the floorboards and make her escape. Reluctantly, Ingrid held out her wrists pulling them apart to make the tape taut. He sliced through it with one swipe and her arms instantly felt lighter.

The man snatched up the carbine, swiftly positioning his finger over the trigger as he stood up.

"Pick him up," he barked.

Ingrid nodded at him without making eye contact. "You got his legs?" she asked Mohammed.

"Yes, yes."

Ingrid tucked her feet under her knees and crouched beside Jens. She slipped her arms under his shoulders. "One. Two. Three."

Jens didn't make a sound as they lifted him up. Not a moan. Not even an involuntary gasp of air. He had slipped into a coma.

"You got him?" she asked.

He nodded.

They carried him toward the door, the short guy keeping the semi-automatic aimed at Ingrid the whole time, dropping the muzzle only briefly to open the door.

"You try to escape," he said, "I shoot you."

Ingrid ignored his threat, concentrating on not dropping Jens. Her arms were numb from being bound and she could barely feel her hands. She looked behind her at the floorboards, at her escape route, and let out a soft gasp.

Outside, the snow was falling thickly, tumbling out of the black sky like sugar from a sifter. The short man knocked on the door of the main cabin. Ingrid kept watch on Jens's face, hoping the breeze or the snowflakes would produce a neurological response.

A voice called out from inside. A man's voice. So there was a third kidnapper.

"Yes," the short man said.

There was the sound of a lock being turned, then a bolt being opened. The door opened slowly. Standing inside the illuminated cabin was a tall man. He had one hand over the boy's mouth. The other held the Beretta to the kid's temple.

Transcript from Riksdag Committee Hearing 23

December 15 2015

BILUNGS: Can I just check that you were offered a translator for this afternoon's proceedings?
LUHRMANN: I was. Thank you. But I believe my Swedish is almost fluent.
BILUNGS: It certainly seems that way. Now, this morning, you told this committee how you were abducted. This afternoon, I would like to talk to you about your captivity, if that's all right?
LUHRMANN: Sure.
BILUNGS: I appreciate that this is a difficult subject for you to discuss, so please take your time with your replies.
LUHRMANN: Sure.
BILUNGS: You have described being moved from Husby to the cabin near Järlåsa—
LUHRMANN: Though I did not know where it was then. I didn't find that out for a few days.
BILUNGS: Of course. Do you know what time you arrived at the cabin?
LUHRMANN: The blindfold wasn't completely successful, so I caught sight of the clock in the car, just above the gearshift, when I was lying on the back seat. It read 1:23, which I obviously knew was wrong as they had taken me from Östermalm around two thirty—
BILUNGS: [Refers to notes] There is something from the forensics team here... When the vehicle was recovered, it was estimated that the onboard clock was four hours and eight minutes behind CET. So that would make it, what, just after half past five when you saw the clock?
LUHRMANN: That sounds right. Probably I was in the car for another ten minutes after that, then the walk to the cabin... another fifteen minutes. So I would guess I got there a little before six in the evening.

BILUNGS: Did they tell you where they were taking you?
LUHRMANN: No, as I said this morning, they were... What is the word... In German we would say unruhig, unsettled, perhaps, spooked, maybe by the activity near the apartment in Husby, so they took me somewhere else.
BILUNGS: It hadn't been their intention to move you?
LUHRMANN: No, I don't think so. Nasim, one of the men who had taken me from the bank, I think he was panicking, sure he was about to get caught. The men at the cabin were much calmer, much more... how can I say this... intimidating.
BILUNGS: And there were three men?
LUHRMANN: Yes. And of course the boy was there, the judge's son. Not that I knew that at first. At first they put me in a room with the woman. It was dark in there. Just an oil lamp. But I recognized her straight away even though her face was cut. Bruised. I'd heard the radio reports earlier in the day. I'd seen Twitter. I felt like I was with a celebrity or something but, you know, obviously it wasn't her.
BILUNGS: Can you describe your fellow hostage?
LUHRMANN: If you can picture Anna Skyberg with blood running down her face, in casual clothes rather than a suit. You have to remember, I thought it was Anna Skyberg. I wasn't looking for, how you say... discrepancies.
BILUNGS: When did you discover that the other hostage was not the minister?
LUHRMANN: She told me, I think. But you know my memories from the cabin are not good. I wouldn't want you to rely on them.
BILUNGS: This is not a court, Mr Luhrmann, we only wish to reach a better understanding of what happened last year. What did she tell you about herself?
LUHRMANN: Well. Um. I think she said her name was also Anna, but that sounds like too much of a coincidence, so it is possible I am making that up. Not deliberately, you understand.
BILUNGS: Go on.

LUHRMANN: She spoke English with an accent. I would guess that she was Latvian, or Estonian. Some sort of Baltic—
BILUNGS: I thought you told the police you thought she was English? Have I got that wrong?
LUHRMANN: Um, I think... I think, no I don't think I ever said that but maybe, maybe you refer to something I believe—I'm not sure you understand, the hypothermia... by this stage, the doctors are surprised I remember anything at all—I think I remember something about her pronunciation of 'Skyberg'. I can't see why I would make it up, but she did say it the American way. Or the English way. Skye-berg, not Skoo-berg. The other things I remember the police were most interested in after... you know, when they came to interview me in hospital... it would have been the next day, maybe the day after that... they wanted to know about her injuries. There was a cut in her eyebrow, quite a lot of blood, but she was far more bothered about the blood on my face—
BILUNGS: It has been suggested that she had medical training?
LUHRMANN: Yes, I think Mohammed, Mohammed Al-Ghedi, the kidnapper, has spoken about this. He says she almost certainly saved my life. Apparently, she insisted that I was taken into the warmth. I have often wondered if she did what she did next to try and get me help. It was a big risk, but I think, or rather it is my suspicion, that her actions were altruistic, that she was attempting to make sure I got medical assistance. And, of course, the other thing about her was that she was strong.
BILUNGS: Your background, Mr Luhrmann, is in the military, is it not?
LUHRMANN: Yes, I served for twelve years with the 1st Panzer Division.
BILUNGS: And is it your opinion that the woman who was being held hostage was also from the military?
LUHRMANN: Yes. I would put money on it. How else do you explain how she was able to do what she did next?

26

Ingrid smiled at the kid and looked round the cabin for the heater. It was old and reminded her of something her dad had used on the farm to keep orphaned piglets warm.

"Close the door," she shouted to the short man. "Keep the heat in."

He kicked it shut, then turned the lock and pocketed the key.

Mohammed and Ingrid laid Jens down on the floor in front of the heater, the smell of kerosene prickling the inside of her nose. The boy started to wriggle in the tall man's grasp and was let go. He stared at Ingrid, raising his hand to his face, touching his eyebrow in just the place she was bleeding from.

"It doesn't hurt," she said, though probably the literal translation of her kindergarten Swedish was 'it no hurt'. She smiled again as she slipped off Jens's sodden shoes. There wasn't time to talk to the kid, to make sure he was being treated reasonably. Ingrid glanced up at the three hostage takers: who the hell kidnaps a kid? Was he taken from the school gate? From outside his house? With his parents watching? She winced at the thought then turned her attention back to Jens.

"What's wrong with him?" the boy asked. He was about ten, skinny, blond and oddly confident. There was something peculiar about him. Something she couldn't put her finger on.

"He's cold," she said. "Very cold." She needed to get Jens out of his wet clothes: she was never going to get him warm unless she could first get him dry. She started to unbuckle his belt.

"No!" the short man said. "*Nej.*"

"What?"

"No!"

"These are wet; we need to get him dry."

"No, you cannot."

"Why?" Ingrid moved on to the button of Jens's pants.

He stared at her, his eyes wide with outrage. "You are woman."

Ingrid exhaled in disbelief and let go of Jens's waistband. "Then you do it."

The short man placed the carbine on the floor then knelt between it and Jens. As he busied himself unzipping the pants, Ingrid plotted how many moves it would take her to pick up the weapon. One: get up. Two: step over Jens. Three: bend down. Four: get a blow to the head from Mohammed or the tall guy. No, she told herself, not worth the risk.

Ingrid looked round the cabin for blankets. There was a reindeer skin on the wall, but it was as old as the cabin and was so brittle it'd crumble like a cookie if it was moved. There was nothing of comfort in the cabin at all. No mattresses. No cushions. Scanning the room, Ingrid's gaze crept upwards: the entire ceiling was lined with foil-covered insulation boards. Before her brain could start to process the significance of the foil, she had to concentrate on Jens. She needed something warm. Anything.

"Your coat," she said to the tall guy. "He needs your coat."

He looked at her blankly and coughed.

She patted her own jacket. "Your coat," she said firmly.

He shook his head.

Ingrid stood up. "Give me your damn coat!"

Still he shook his head. Behind her, the short man said something and instantly the tall guy shrugged, loosening his arms from the sleeves. He refused to hand the full-length sheepskin coat to her, instead pushing past her and taking it over to Jens. He laid it on top of him.

"No," Ingrid said. "You need to wrap him in it. Like a sleeping bag."

The short man understood and crouched down. He rolled Jens's limp body over, expertly getting him on top of the coat, then covering him in it. He had to be ex-military. Or militia. Either that or a hospital orderly. Only someone with training, someone used to moving dead weights—or dead bodies—could roll an unresponsive patient so easily. She took it as a good indication that he would also know exactly how to use a semi-automatic weapon.

Mohammed started to move the kerosene heater closer to Jens.

"No," Ingrid said. "Not too close." Hypothermia patients needed to be warmed slowly, away from direct heat. As the lack of blood in their veins made them susceptible to burns. "Socks," Ingrid said. "One of you needs to put your socks on him."

Mohammed nodded and while he unlaced his boots, a cell phone vibrated on the table. The short man got to his feet, picked up the carbine and snatched up the phone. Ingrid watched his face closely as he scanned the message. A slight narrowing of the nostrils told her it wasn't good news. He looked up from the screen and over to her then sucked his teeth. She imagined that the photos of her beaten face had failed to persuade her 'husband' to pay the ransom.

Mohammed put his socks on Jens's feet. "What else?" he asked.

Ingrid made deliberate eye contact with him. "More layers."

He looked confused.

"More clothing. As much as possible. But you really need to get him to a hospital."

He shook his head. "Thank you but I do not think so."

"Then keep talking to him, you never know what he can hear, what signals his brain will tune in to. And when he wakes up, he'll need fluids. Water. You understand?"

She needed to get back into the sauna, lift the floorboards and escape. Short of dialing nine-one-one, or somehow grabbing a gun and overpowering three captors, escaping was the best thing she could do for Jens. She looked over to the boy, who was staring at her as if she were a chocolate bar he wasn't allowed to eat until after he'd finished his supper.

Food? What the hell were they going to eat?

She smiled again at the boy, who stuck out his tongue at her. He did not seem in any way distressed. Nor did he seem drugged. Ingrid wondered if he suffered from some form of autism.

The short man tipped a Marlboro out onto the table and placed it between his lips. He struck a match and held it to the tip of his cigarette. Ingrid watched as the tobacco glowed and smoke drifted out of his mouth. Two more weapons, she thought. A box of matches and a lit cigarette. She couldn't remember the last time she had seen someone smoke indoors.

She looked down at Jens. On a battlefield he would be mistaken for a corpse. His lips were still blue, but the lack of blood at least meant his cut had stopped bleeding. She pressed her index and middle fingers into his neck, searching for a pulse. His skin felt like damp clay.

"Come on," she said under her breath. "Come on, Jens." The only pulse she could feel was her own. His jaw was loose, his body limp.

"He will live, yes?" Mohammed said.

Ingrid pushed her fingers harder against his throat, feeling the gristle of his windpipe under her touch. Nothing. She pushed her hand inside the coat, placing her palm directly above Jens's lean muscular chest. She kept it there for many moments, hoping that through the layers of clothing she would detect a heartbeat.

"Yes?" Mohammed repeated.

No heartbeat, just the gentle expansion of his ribs as his body drew in a breath. He was alive. Ingrid caught the eye of the boy, who was still staring at her.

"I think so," she said to Mohammed, "but he really needs to be in a hospital." She looked up at the short man, who held the cigarette between his fingers in the same way Rita Hayworth might. "One phone call would save his life."

"You," the short man said, smoke curling out of his lips as he spoke. "You will save his life."

"There is nothing else I can do for him. I'm not a doctor. He needs to be in hospital."

He expelled a thick toxic plume of smoke in her direction. "No."

Jens's breathing was shallow but regular. She took off her beanie and carefully stretched it over his head. Even if they saved his life, these minutes without blood in his brain could cause irreparable damage. Someone needed to call the emergency services and if the short guy wasn't going to do it, she had to get back into the sauna. She had to lift those floorboards and find a way out.

27

"No, you stay with him."

"There's nothing else I can do." Ingrid stood up defiantly, the Perspex tubes shifting inside her padded sleeves as she did so. "We just have to wait." *Or, you know, call an ambulance and get him to hospital.* She went over to the boy, who was perched on a large wooden chest.

"Hej," she said. *"Mitt namn är..."* She was about to say 'Ingrid' but stopped herself. "Anna."

"My name," he said in Swedish, "is Magnus. I am ten years old. I live in Stockholm."

"Nice to meet you," she said and extended her hand. He took it and shook it theatrically. Maybe it wasn't autism, but the kid's confident demeanor suggested some kind of personality disorder. It was only when she sat down next to him that she registered what he had just said. The pronunciation in Swedish is so different. Like Mao-ness. *Magnus.* She felt a tremor in her jaw. Was this who she had been sent to meet? Was she supposed to give the components to a child?

"How old are you?" the boy asked. His intonation was slow, mannered, like he was reciting his multiplication tables.

"Um. I am thirty-three," Ingrid said, remembering her basic Swedish. The boy was almost impossibly blond, with curls like a golden retriever's framing an angular face. His alert blue eyes barely blinked. Ingrid took a deep breath and spoke quietly: "What is your *full* name, Magnus?"

The boy was staring at Jens. "Will he die?"

"Ah—" She didn't know what to say. Her Swedish wasn't good enough to convey the complexities of Jens's condition. "Um, I hope not. He just needs to get warm." She just wanted him to tell her what his surname was.

The boy nodded. "Do you like Candy Crush?"

"I, er, I don't play it."

"I play it very well." He turned away from her and picked up a new-looking Samsung.

"Are you hungry, Magnus?"

He remained completely still as he considered her question then shook his head enthusiastically. He was like a toddler.

"We feed him," the short man said.

With what, she wanted to ask. All she could see was the packet of cookies. There were no cooking facilities, and nowhere comfortable for the boy to sleep. "What time is it?" she asked.

The short man tapped the screen of his phone. "Twenty-two eighteen."

Later than she'd thought.

"Shouldn't the boy, shouldn't Magnus, be in bed by now?"

He scrunched the remains of his cigarette into an ashtray on the table. There were as many as twenty butts in it. Ingrid suddenly saw it as a way to measure time: if your kidnapper smokes at a rate of one cigarette every forty minutes, how long have you been held captive?

Without looking up from the Samsung, the boy asked: "Does your face hurt?"

Ingrid glowered at the short man who, sensing the weight of her stare, looked up from his phone and met her eye. "Yes, a bit."

The short man sucked in his cheeks. His expression told her he'd do it again if he had to. Mohammed's face, by contrast, displayed a mix of apology and fear. The kid, head down, thumbs skating over the screen, had a face that was utterly unreadable. Ingrid had worked with enough children to know that, just because a kid can't express his emotions, it doesn't mean he's not feeling them. She put an arm out to comfort him, but he pulled sharply away. Could he really be the person she was supposed to hand the components to?

"Magnus?"

The boy didn't answer.

"Magnus. What is your full name? Your family name?" The muscle in her jaw twitched.

The boy continued playing with his game, furiously obliterating boiled sweets from the screen. The battery on the Samsung, she noted, was at twenty-three per cent. It wouldn't be too many hours before the boy's entertainment died. She looked around the cabin. There was no obvious means of recharging any of their phones, and the only sustenance she could see was the cookies. What was going to happen when their batteries died, or when the Marlboro or the kerosene ran out? Nothing indicated they planned to hold them for very long.

Ingrid stood up and all three men stiffened in response. They watched her as she walked slowly over to the table and poured some water into a plastic cup. They didn't attempt to stop her. She lifted a cookie out of the open packet and ate it: she was asserting her autonomy and they weren't cracking down. It was a good sign.

She started to pace around the cabin, a space that was maybe twelve by twenty feet. She walked slowly, watching the men as intently as they watched her. She could tell now that the tall man was Mohammed's brother. It wasn't simply that the two were so similar in build; their body language suggested a bond that predated their current confines. When the brother coughed, Mohammed's expression was of concern rather than irritation.

Her captors, she realized, had no more freedom than she did. No more access to food or water or escape. She checked on Jens as she passed him, waiting to see his chest rise before walking on. Her foot pressed down on a squeaking floorboard: somehow she had to get back to the other side of the wall. The floor under her sneakers was strewn with sawdust that must have come from the installation of the foil panels. Other than the ceiling, the cabin appeared to have been untouched for a century: hard wooden furniture, small shuttered windows and a stove with a broken flue. There was nothing in the place that suggested they had planned for a lengthy stay.

Something must have gone wrong with their plans. Her abduction from the café, timed to coincide with the bomb, her transfer from one vehicle to another, it had all been so professional. But now Jens was close to death, and she had been taken instead of her cousin, and their plan—whatever that was—appeared to be falling apart.

She didn't have time for their plan to crumble slowly; she needed to blow it apart. As quickly as possible.

"Who is Abdullah Saladdin?" she asked.

The three men looked at each other, each wondering if one of the others would answer. Mohammed smiled and leaned forward. His lips parted as he worked out how to respond, but just as he was about to speak, he looked up at the ceiling. A flash of panic jolted across the short man's features. A helicopter. Cops. All three of them stood up and grabbed their guns.

Shivers ran over Ingrid's scalp. Cops might mean medical assistance for Jens, but it signaled hours in detention for her. Hours she needed to spend getting to Stortorget.

The men checked their weapons and pocketed boxes of ammunition as the sound of the rotors deepened and pulsed. The foil panels on the ceiling had clearly failed to fool the thermal imaging cameras: the helicopter was circling.

Magnus suddenly started clapping like a toddler being presented with a birthday cake and they all turned to look at his beaming, smiling face. "Daddy," he said. "My daddy is coming to get me."

28

"Your daddy is in the helicopter?" Ingrid asked

He nodded vigorously.

Ingrid tried to remember the Swedish word for pilot, but failed. "He flies helicopters?" she asked. Jens had said that the boy's father was a judge.

Magnus moved his head from side to side, shaking his curls like a shampoo model. The boy's English was probably better than her Swedish. "Why is your daddy in a helicopter, Magnus?" she asked in English, but his fixation had already switched to the short man, who was shouting in Arabic at his cell phone, furious because a flurry of messages arrived while he was trying to dial out. The brothers talked frantically to each other in their mother tongue, panic raising their voices an octave. Ingrid switched back to Magnus, who appeared more intrigued than scared.

"Why is your daddy in the helicopter?" she asked again in English.

This time he turned his head toward her and pursed his mouth in concentration. "It's a secret," he said, then giggled.

Ingrid's eyes widened in surprise: the kid knew how to say 'secret' in English. She took a step toward him. "What secret? What's the secret, Magnus?"

The boy stared hard at Mohammed, who had started to mumble. A prayer perhaps? Was he preparing for martyrdom? A muscle in Ingrid's jaw began to twitch. She crouched down in front of the kid. "What secret? Magnus, tell me your secret."

The boy glanced at her quickly, then stared over her shoulder to the short man, who was ranting into his phone.

"Magnus," she said softly, "why is it a secret?"

He looked down at her, his expression almost one of surprise that she was still there. He pulled an exasperated face, as if he was annoyed that she hadn't answered her own question.

"I can't tell you!" He laughed and clapped again, like a seal at a circus.

She pushed herself to standing and, as she did so, the cuff of her jacket rubbed against the tagging bracelet. It took a moment for the dots to join in her head, but when they did her mouth fell open: what if it wasn't the cops? What if the helicopter had been dispatched by whoever was monitoring the bracelet?

She felt dizzy at the thought and staggered slightly, reaching out to the wall for support. She tried to remember what the Australian woman in the sauna had said. That they would come for her if she didn't make the drop. Her head started to shake from side to side. No, it couldn't have anything to do with the bracelet. The drop wasn't until nine in the morning. They wouldn't be coming for her yet, would they?

Ingrid faced the wall and furtively pushed her cuff up to expose the bracelet. It was smaller than the ankle tags she'd seen on felons released from prison, but she wondered if it nevertheless had additional functionality built in. She examined it surreptitiously, looking for a microphone or a camera. If there wasn't just a GPS transmitter, but a means of real-time surveillance, was it possible that the arms dealers would know what had happened to her as well as where she was?

Nervously, she fingered the edges of the bracelet, but couldn't feel any perforations or indents that suggested it was also a listening device. Apart from the hinge and the edge where the two halves locked, it felt perfectly smooth. Nothing. She pulled her cuff back over the bracelet and turned round.

The kidnappers were huddled together, arguing urgently. Mohammed looked scared and his brother kept hitting him on the back as if to bolster and encourage him, but his expression remained that of a man on the verge of vomiting. Magnus was transfixed by the three of them, observing them with curiosity, as he might animals in a zoo. The gunmen had probably made the same calculation that she had: if a helicopter had spotted them, it wouldn't take more than ten minutes for a ground team to be deployed.

She was screwed. She was completely trapped and her only means of escape was back on the other side of the wall she was leaning against. A vision of what would happen if she didn't escape ran through her head. An interrogation suite, an interpreter on her left, a lawyer on her right, and a couple of cops opposite asking the same questions over and over again: who are you really and why were you found in possession of a large quantity of cash and illegal weapons components? How long would it be before they found out who she really was? Maybe her cousin would inadvertently identify her. Her heart tightened painfully at the thought. The Bureau and the State Department would have to be involved. And then there were the peace negotiations.

Ingrid didn't know how many laws she had broken in which territories, or what sentence she would serve in which country. And that assumed she survived the coming hour. She ran her fingers through her hair, not quite believing what a train wreck her life had become.

A wreck that was about to get worse. Panicked kidnappers who want to be martyrs. Gung-ho police who don't have to worry about neighbors becoming collateral damage. A shootout was inevitable, wasn't it? What was that line from Bonnie Tyler's big hit in the eighties? We're living in a powder keg and we're giving off sparks? Ingrid suddenly felt like human kindling. She placed her hand on Magnus's shoulder but he stiffened under her touch.

"Sorry." She withdrew her hand.

The rotors of the helicopter pulsed overhead, making the entire cabin vibrate. Mohammed's brother opened a case and pulled out several more rounds of ammunition, stuffing his pockets before shoving a vintage handgun into his waistband and handing another to Mohammed.

The kidnappers were shouting at each other, and over each other, incessantly and their phones didn't stop ringing. Their callers were immediately berated and their demeanor spiraled from panic to fear. Pressure formed at the base of Ingrid's neck as her body absorbed the enormity of what was happening. It took a few moments for her to register that something had changed. The men were fighting so much that at first they didn't notice either: the sound of the rotors was dimming.

Ingrid had to make her move if she was going to get out before there was a knock at the door. Could she join forces with her kidnappers and help them fight their way out? She knew a better plan was encouraging them to run, but it would be useless if they were seeking martyrdom over freedom. The men finally noticed the drop in decibels and their shouting downgraded into an intense debate about why the helicopter had flown off. It was time for Ingrid to act.

"Hey," she said.

The short man turned and glowered. He sniffed sharply, his nostrils briefly flaring like a cobra's hood. He did not speak.

"I need to go next door," she said, pointing toward the dividing wall. "I need something from my bag."

The three of them looked at each other, deciding between them whether they should accede to her request.

The short man shook his head. "No."

Ingrid pictured the cops finding her backpack and discovering the component: her kidnappers had no idea she could add arms smuggling to their rap sheet. "I have my period," she said. They looked at her blankly. A suspicion snuck up on Ingrid that she was about to enjoy the next few sentences that came out of her mouth. "I need sanitary protection."

Their expressions did not change.

"Kotex? Tampax?" Making men uncomfortable about menstruation was just too easy. "I am bleeding." She held her hands in front of her crotch.

Slowly, incrementally, their faces drooped with disgust.

"Now," she said. "I need to go now. I need the Kotex that are in my bag."

The three men did not move. Her demand appeared to scare them more than the threat posed by the helicopter. She pictured the two pried floorboards slightly proud of their neighbors.

"Now," she reiterated. "I need to go now."

It was Mohammed who moved first. An almost imperceptible bow of the head, followed by a formal nod. "I will get your bag."

"No," his brother said, then added something else in what she presumed was Somali. He pulled the gun from his waistband, a beaten-up SIG 1911. His hand gestures indicated he didn't want to open the door. He thought the cops were outside, taking up positions.

Ingrid needed to keep the pressure on while they were unsettled. "I don't just need the contents of the bag," she said, "I need to use them. Do you understand?" She wondered if she should mime removing a tampon and embarrass them into capitulation. "Now."

Mohammed said something to his brother.

"What are you saying?" the short man demanded to know. He obviously didn't speak the brothers' language.

"I will take her," Mohammed said. He turned to Ingrid: "You try to escape, I shoot you. OK?"

No, not OK. Ingrid nodded.

"Then you bring her back," the short man said. "She has to look after him." He pointed to Jens, who was still motionless on the floor.

Ingrid consented. She checked Jens, who didn't show any signs of either improvement or deterioration, then pulled her gloves from her pockets. She looked at her hat on Jens's head. She wanted to take that too, but knew it would arouse suspicions that she intended going further than the six feet to the sauna next door.

The boy was staring at her.

"I won't be long," she said. Somehow, she never minded lying when she knew she was being untruthful nearly as much as when she unintentionally broke a promise.

Magnus nodded. "OK, Anna."

He was the calmest ten-year-old she had ever met. The perfect hostage.

"Ready?" Mohammed asked.

Ingrid stepped forward, expecting Mohammed to stand behind her, place one hand over her mouth and hold a gun to her temple with the other.

"You stand here." He indicated a spot just in front of the door.

Ingrid stood where she was told as his brother took up a position to her right, the SIG leveled at her head. The short man turned the key in the lock and slowly pulled open the door.

A dark rectangle of night, a swirl of snow and a blast of ice, but no flashlights from the cops, no gunfire, no instructions from a bullhorn.

"OK," Mohammed said, raising his *Dirty Harry* Smith & Wesson. "Walk."

Ingrid pulled on her gloves, still reveling in the fact that her hands were no longer bound, and edged out into the night, the brother's steady aim following her as she moved. Mohammed walked behind her. She heard him cock the safety of his revolver, something he had presumably learnt from Clint Eastwood.

"Stop."

She did, feeling the snow settle briefly on her face before melting. She turned her head through a one-eighty, but her eyes had not adapted to the dark and all she could see was the falling snow and the elongated rectangle of illuminated ground at her feet.

"OK, walk."

Ingrid turned and took the few yards to the sauna door, her sneakers slipping underneath her. The door to the cabin was closed and locked, plunging them into darkness. Her exposed ears burned in the wind. Mohammed made a rustling noise behind her. It sounded like he was searching for something. Checking his pockets. Ingrid knew that, at that precise moment, he couldn't possibly be aiming his gun at her.

• • •

Transcript from Riksdag Committee Hearing 23
December 16 2015

BILUNGS: Thank you for joining us this morning. I appreciate that you probably know everyone in this committee room, but for the official record if you wouldn't mind stating your full name.

BILDEBURG: Sofie Bildeburg.

BILUNGS: Thank you, Mrs Bildeburg. Can you please start by telling us when it was on Monday December 15th 2014 that you discovered that your son had been captured?

BILDEBURG: Captured? I'm not sure I can answer that. Missing, though, somewhere between six and seven o'clock.

BILUNGS: The police reports suggest he had been abducted around lunchtime.

BILDEBURG: Yes, but I did not know that. It was only when he didn't come home from school that I had started to have suspicions. But, of course, with all the road closures and the chaos in the city that day, I tried to reassure myself that the school bus was stuck in traffic, or that maybe I had forgotten he had a judo class or something like that. You know how it is, you think the worst and then try and find all the reasons why you are being an idiot.

BILUNGS: Mrs Bildeburg, I'm sorry, I obviously have the wrong information, but it had been my understanding that you had known much earlier in the day that Magnus had gone missing. I thought that he had some kind of tracking device. Am I wrong about that?

BILDEBURG: No, no, you are quite right. Magnus is autistic, he doesn't—didn't—assess danger in the same way most of us do. When he was a toddler he would always wander off. He didn't develop attachments… I'm sorry.

BILUNGS: Do not apologize. I hope we all understand that this must be painful for you. We can take this at your own pace, Mrs Bildeburg. Do not feel you have to rush.

BILDEBURG: Thank you, but I think I would really rather… if I am able, you know, to just, well, to get this over with.

BILUNGS: As I say, at your own pace.

BILDEBURG: Magnus didn't form attachments in the same way

most children do. If I took him shopping he would always wander off and he would never reach that point where he would wonder where I was, or where he was. He had an incredibly high pain threshold too. He fell off his bike once, a gash from hip to ankle, and he didn't even seem to notice. When he was tiny… people would see a young boy on his own and would often help him find his mother, or his father, but it was always us who were distressed by his disappearance. But as he got older, people didn't look twice at a seven-year-old walking alone, and so he ended up further and further away. We had heard about electronic tags for prisoners, and we wondered if there was something similar for Magnus. Anyway, we found this little device that clipped onto his belt, and we made sure he wore it every day.

BILUNGS: It would be helpful if you could tell us a bit more about the device and how this led to the discovery near Järlåsa.

BILDEBURG: It seems quite old-fashioned now, but one of the officers who liaised with us told us that if we had used a mobile phone, a smartphone, the kidnappers would have turned it off or thrown it away. They had probably never seen a tracking device and maybe thought it was an MP3 player or something, that's even if they noticed it at all. It was no bigger than a box of matches, a black plastic box of matches. [Pause] Yes, sorry, you wanted to know how it worked, didn't you? We paid a subscription to a monitoring service, and that service has a website, and whenever Magnus disappeared, we would log onto their website and a little red dot would flash on a map and one of us would go and find him. When we got iPhones, obviously we could track him on our phones. We no longer had to be, you know, one of us at the computer giving directions to the other.

BILUNGS: Thank you. So on December 15th last year, at what point did you become aware that Magnus was not where you expected him to be?

BILDEBURG: Not, as I say, until about seven o'clock in the evening. My husband was in court, though the kidnappers had called his office about four in the afternoon. I believe they refused to talk to anyone except my husband, but obviously he couldn't be interrupted. It had been a long day in court and he did not go back to his office after they adjourned for the day, though he did pick up his messages from his secretary and he was told then that someone had been trying to contact him for the past few hours and that they had refused to leave a message. It's not uncommon, when you're a judge. Witnesses, usually those who haven't been called, want to pass something on. No one thought anything of it. Anyway, Magnus had been due to take part—as I think I said—in a judo competition after school that day, so I did not expect him home until after six. At seven o'clock, I called his teacher, the one taking him to the competition, and he told me that Magnus hadn't been on the bus. They assumed he was ill and we had collected him [Begins to sob]

BILUNGS: Take your time. We can take a recess if you need one.

BILDEBURG: [Shakes head] I just need a moment… So, I logged onto the website, I think my husband came home at about the same time, and when we saw that Magnus was in Järlåsa we thought there had to be a mistake. I mean, what is it? Seventy miles outside the city? He couldn't possibly have walked that far. He didn't really like getting on buses. My first thought was that it was a mistake, a glitch. But then when you factored in that he hadn't been seen since lunchtime, well, we talked about it and called the police.

BILUNGS: And what was their response?

BILDEBURG: They were very busy that day, obviously. As we all know. And their response, their advice, was that they would send round an officer to take a statement, but that if we were really worried we should probably drive over to Järlåsa ourselves. They had manpower issues.

BILUNGS: Really, a ten-year-old boy has been missing all day, you have a location for him and they do nothing?

BILDEBURG: They did send an officer over. Sigmund, my husband, met with the officer. I had driven out to Järlåsa—it wasn't in Järlåsa, you understand, about five or six miles north of the town. There was nothing there. Just the forest. There were no houses, no lights. I told myself—again—that there was a glitch. Of course, I know now that I was just a few hundred yards from Magnus. [Sobs] So, when Sigmund—who you have to remember had been in court all day, who really hadn't known the details of what had gone on except for the bomb at the National Museum—when he was talking to the police officer who probably arrived a little after nine… It was only when the police officer mentioned that Jens Luhrmann had also been kidnapped but that they were sure Anna Friese, sorry, Anna Skyberg was not a victim that Sigmund made the connection.

BILUNGS: The Abdullah Saladdin case?

BILDEBURG: Exactly. After that, things started to happen very quickly.

29

Ingrid turned quickly and took a step toward Mohammed, whose head was bowed as he searched for the sauna key. She brought her left arm up sharply, snapping his head upwards. He grunted, too stunned to shout. Ingrid kicked the revolver from his hand and brought her knee up hard into his crotch. He exhaled explosively but could not speak. With him doubled over, clutching his balls, Ingrid threw her right fist into his temple, making hard contact with his skull, knocking him sideways. She bent down, grabbed the gun and turned.

Her body was cold and stiff but she powered down through her legs, driving her heels into the ankle deep snow, pushing up onto her toes. She had covered twenty or thirty yards before Mohammed shouted. She would be another thirty yards away before the cabin door was unlocked, before they tried to come after her. Deep into the darkness. Free. She knew she should slow down—falling and freezing was a far greater threat than a shot on target—but the instinct to flee was too great. It was also the only way she had of keeping warm.

The sound of her breath, of the sleeves of her jacket as she powered her arms up and down and her sneakers crushing into the snow, felt amplified, as if she was leaving a sonic trail for her kidnappers to follow. An eerie whale song of distant trucks emanated from the road in the valley below.

Then a single crack splitting the cold night. A gunshot.

Sucking down the freezing air deeper into her lungs, Ingrid ran faster. She knew she was too far away. She told herself it was dark and they couldn't see her, that they were just wasting ammunition. Her grip on the Smith & Wesson tightened. She risked a glance backwards but couldn't see anything. No silhouetted figure standing in front of the open door, taking aim.

Another shot.

Was this one louder? Closer? Something about the acoustics meant it didn't sound like it had come from the cabin. Ingrid powered on down the path as it curved through the pine trees, her ankles turning on the ridges of compacted ice under the freshly fallen snow.

She was leaving footprints. A trail. A case study from her training for the sheriff's department thrust itself into her thoughts: the world's dumbest bank robber… caught by deputies who followed his footprints through the snow. She had to get off the path and pick her way through the trees and down toward the road.

The snow either side of the path was knee deep. Impossible to run through. She checked over her shoulder but it was too dark to tell if anyone was following her, so she stopped and listened. For a moment the forest was silent apart from her labored breathing, the icy air stabbing like a blade as she filled her lungs.

A shout. A flash of light. A millisecond later she heard the third gunshot. She was sure it hadn't come from the cabin, but in the darkness it was possible she'd become disoriented. She looked down and made out footprints leading in both directions: maybe she'd turned round somehow? A breeze torqued through the trees, releasing a flurry of snow from the dark branches.

More shouting. Men's voices.

The footprints had been made by several different shoes, and as the snow was falling quickly, they were recent: they couldn't have been left by the kidnappers. Someone else was in the forest. She gasped: and that someone was firing at her. She looked at the revolver in her hand. A vintage Smith & Wesson 29. She pulled off a glove with her teeth and checked the chamber. Five bullets. She tucked it into her waistband and started to run.

The snow either side of the path curved upwards in folds like unbaked meringue. Parts of it looked waist deep so she stayed on the path and kept running.

But running toward what? The road was the obvious choice, but was that too obvious? Would that send her straight into the path of the cops? But what other choice did she have? Deeper into the woods? She kept to the path that inclined down toward the bottom of the valley.

Ingrid felt something warm on her face: blood. Running had reopened her wound. She had lost count of the number of times she'd interviewed witnesses who only remembered that the woman was pregnant or the man was six five: people only recall your most striking feature. A bloody gash might mean no one noticed she looked like her cousin. It might buy her a few seconds of anonymity.

Her feet started to slip and she slowed down, making her aware how deep her breathing had become. Her chest was heaving, steam billowing from her lips like cigarette smoke. Up ahead was a pinprick of light. No, it was more of a beam of light. There was someone on the path below her, scanning the trees with a flashlight.

Ingrid stilled her breath.

They were about a hundred yards away, moving slowly and deliberately, sweeping the path in front of them with the flashlight. They were looking for something. Or someone. Ingrid heard a bark: they had a dog with them.

Ingrid frantically looked around for an escape route. If she continued downhill she'd encounter them. Leaving the path would be like drawing an arrow in the snow and shouting 'follow me'. Retracing her steps would take her toward angry men with guns.

The flashlight owner was only fifty or sixty yards away. She had to make a decision. Left or right? Forwards or backwards?

"Or upwards?" It was Megan's voice.

Ingrid looked up and smiled. The idea that Mega Megan would ever have suggested climbing a tree was preposterous. Almost as unthinkable as Ingrid Fatberg doing it. Ingrid took a deep breath and reached up, her gloved hands grasping an overhanging branch above her head, dumping a thud of snow onto the ground in the process.

The dog started barking immediately. The flashlight holder shouted and yanked on its leash, but the animal did not stop howling. Ingrid hauled herself onto the branch, making the most of the fact that the dog owner wouldn't hear her movements over the barking. She scrambled toward the tree trunk, then shuffled around onto the opposite branch and climbed up.

"Polisen!"

Polisen. The police. Ingrid puffed out her cheeks. *When am I going to catch a break here?* Ingrid was covered in snow. Every layer down to her bra would be soaked through within minutes. Either she was going to get shot or she was going to freeze to death in a goddamn pine tree and wouldn't be discovered till the spring when the snow melted. *Great suggestion, Meg.*

The dog kept barking as it strained against its leash. Ingrid looked around her. The trees were close together, like legionaries in formation, but jumping to the nearest one was impossible. Up was her best bet: further from the path, further from the dog's nose. Ingrid reached up, pulled herself onto the branch above and clung to the trunk, her teeth chattering like a wind-up toy from the prank shop. She hoped she was the only one who could hear them.

The police officer called out again. This time Ingrid could make out it was a woman's voice. Then the crackle of a police radio. The dog was snarling, its guttural noise vibrating the air between the branches. They were only twenty feet away.

Ingrid adjusted the position of her feet to avoid losing her balance and sent another slump of snow down onto the ground. She could hear the crunch of the officer's footsteps and the panting of the dog. She dared not look at their approach and instead faced into the blackness of the forest. She could see the beam trace its way across the ground beneath her. In a few moments, in just a few steps, they would come to the pile of snow she had dumped. Her pulse rushed through her ears, obliterating every other sound. Ingrid held her breath. Her stomach muscles tightened. She waited.

30

Ingrid resisted the urge to wipe the falling snow from her face as she listened to the footsteps draw nearer. The police officer said something softly to the dog, as if she too could sense Ingrid's presence. Ingrid swallowed hard, suppressing the desire to gasp.

The footsteps stopped. They were directly below her. She could hear the dog sniffing and the noise its tail made as it beat excitedly against its handler's leg. A whimper. Then a bark. Then a howl.

"*Polisen,*" the officer said again. Presumably the next few words were 'if there's anyone there' but Ingrid was too anxious to tune in and translate. The beam from the flashlight flickered through the trees as it bounced between the serried tree trunks.

"Shhh." But the dog did not quieten. If anything its howl became a snarl, and the officer yanked on the leash, squeezing the dog's windpipe. "Down," she said. "Lie down. I need to listen."

Ingrid heard the dog paw at the ground, accompanied by the soft shuffle of snow being clawed and redistributed. The officer said something quietly to the dog. Under less stress, Ingrid told herself, she'd understand at least fifty per cent more of what she was saying. Under less stress, she also reckoned she might make better decisions than to hide in a goddamn tree.

"It's nothing. Come on."

The dog whined as the officer pulled on the leash.

"Now," she said firmly. "This way."

The dog yelped. Then the trudge of feet moving through crisp snow.

"Come on."

Ingrid waited till they were ten feet away before daring to draw breath. She clung to the trunk, grateful and amazed that she hadn't pissed all over herself or shaken so violently with the cold that she'd lost her footing. She tracked the flashlight through the trees and listened to the receding staccato static of the police radio.

When she could no longer hear their footsteps she climbed down to the branch below. She waited and listened again, then dropped down to the ground, landing in over two feet of virgin snow. She'd had worse landings.

She was shivering so violently she was reminded of Jens: she had to keep moving. She stepped onto the path, checked up the hill in the direction the cop had gone and decided to follow the path downhill. It was too dangerous to walk through the trees, and with any luck she had already encountered the greatest threat she would meet on the path.

Ingrid started to jog, shaking the snow from her head as she ran, the components jiggling inside her sleeves with each footfall.

In the distance she could hear yelling. It was the cop but she couldn't make out what was being said, and she wasn't going to wait to find out if the cop was shouting at her. The low snarl of the dog trembled through the night.

Gunfire. A semi-automatic. The carbine. Ingrid glanced toward the rat-a-tat-tat, bright flashes tracing through the darkness. The dog barked ferociously, seething like a beast from a horror movie. And then it stopped, the silence beckoning through the trees: it must have been shot. Ingrid couldn't hear the cop either.

She hammered down the path toward the road as quickly as her frozen limbs would carry her. Her knees jarred each time her sneakers thudded into the compacted snow, her lungs burned as they drew down the icy air. Her ears were filled with her pulse, her breathing, the shish-shish of her jacket, her feet as they slid on the path beneath her.

Another crack of gunfire. Ingrid reached under her jacket and pulled the revolver from her waistband. Her hands were so numb she could barely feel it. She wasn't sure if her frozen fingers would be able to pull the trigger.

The closer she got to the road, the more she realized she didn't know what she would do when she got there. A helicopter and a beat patrol had already identified the location. It wouldn't be long before the entire area would be lit up with flashing blue lights. She stopped running. She needed to think. She needed a plan. She didn't even know which direction to head in.

Ingrid bent over, resting her hands on her knees, and tried to catch her breath. She watched as puffs of steam dissipated into the night. Her priority, she decided, had to be getting out of the area as quickly as possible, in any direction. And then she absolutely definitely had to get dry. She would die if she didn't.

Was that a better option than getting caught, she wondered, an unmarked grave versus decades in jail? Was that preferable to the hell that would be unleashed if she cracked in an interrogation suite? Ingrid shook her head. She'd lost too many people too young to think like that. It was always better to stay alive. Always. She owed Megan that much. She started walking and thought about what she'd do when she made it to the road. She had a couple thousand sodden euros strapped to her leg and a vintage pistol in her hand, both of which could persuade someone to hand over their car. Then there was hitching. Trucks stopped in Sweden, especially in the cold. She pictured a middle-aged trucker with food stains down a sweatshirt stretched tight over his belly, taking one look at the gun and offering to take her anywhere she wanted to go. But then he'd probably have had the news on all day, maybe even scanned the police channels on his CB radio. Hitching was too risky.

"Something will come up." Megan's voice. "It always does."

The Smith & Wesson shook wildly as her convulsions deepened. She needed to get the blood circulating, so she forced herself to scissor her arms and willed her legs to carry her more quickly. Her limbs were slow and her movements jerky. She felt like a robot from a 1950s sci-fi film.

"Come on!"

She staggered down the path, lurching and stumbling until something made her stop. A new noise. It was a low hum. A car engine, ticking over. A car driver, lying in wait. It felt as though the air in her lungs had been sucked out, as if her ribs were about to snap as her chest caved in. She stumbled forward, lumbering like Frankenstein's monster, and after another bend in the path she saw them. Lights. Flashing blue lights. It was the cop's car.

31

The Swedes, like Minnesotans, often kept their engines running in winter to stop them seizing up. Throughout her childhood, the good folks of Jackson County had left their vehicles spewing exhaust fumes outside 7-Elevens while they bought beer and pretzels. It was only after she'd joined the sheriff's department that Ingrid found it remarkable that none of them ever got stolen, though once Mrs O'Hagan had run out of gas, she'd spent so long gossiping.

Ingrid hid behind a tree, scooped up a handful of snow and threw it at the car. When no one got out, she crept toward it and peered through the rear nearside window. Her breath was short and shallow. She brushed the snow from her face then wiped the window: the back seat was empty. Nervously, she moved to the front seats: the car was empty. Exhale.

Ingrid checked over her shoulder toward the path before opening the passenger door. The warmth from the car's interior felt like a blast from a fan heater. The light from the bulb above the rearview mirror beckoned to her like a camp fire. Another glance up the path: no footsteps, no flashlight. On the passenger seat was a bar of Marabou chocolate. The taste of family. Of childhood. Ingrid grabbed it, pulled off her glove with her teeth and attempted to tear the wrapper, but her hands were convulsing so violently that it took several attempts. She shoved the chocolate into her mouth and was shocked at how sweet it was. She hoped the sugar would help reduce the shivering.

Ingrid stood for several moments, leaning on the roof of the car, hoping the warm air would soothe her. The police call handlers on the radio were busy. Calm and efficient voices, repeating messages, seeking clarification. There was something reassuring about the one-sided dispatch reports, something familiar, even if she could only understand a quarter of what was being said.

One phrase kept being repeated: '*Nationalmuseum*', and her thoughts zeroed in on the road closures and cordons that should have told her something bad was about to happen. Could that really be the same day? Her eyes drifted to the back seat where she spotted a blanket. Her frozen brain was slow to process information, but she started to wonder if she should take her wet layers off and wrap herself in it.

Idiot!

Why the hell was she letting the heat escape? She shook her head in fury and slammed the door. The blanket wasn't going to save her: the goddamned car was. The fact she hadn't realized straight away showed how poor her cognitive function had become.

But it makes sense, doesn't it?

Not just getting in, but taking it. Stealing the car was the sensible choice, the logical one. Wasn't it? Ingrid looked up as a truck passed down the road, its engine noise muffled by the shroud of snow that hugged the valley, its tires drifting snowflakes across the gritted road surface in its wake. She'd gotten used to British snow, the wet kind. She'd forgotten about the hard, brittle snow of home, the kind that billows like sand. She became mesmerized by the waft of snowflakes and watched as the truck's taillights disappeared into the murk. She shook her head: *you should at least sit in it.* Ingrid had already broken so many laws that her taking a car seemed like a misdemeanor.

She staggered round to the driver's side, her wet clothes weighing her down like a diver's suit. She reached out for the door handle. Her right hand was shivering so jerkily it took three attempts to grab it. The door felt heavy, as if made of bronze, and required more effort than expected to pull it open. Her movements were slow and labored, and everything took vast quantities of concentration and application. The only exception was the frenetic chattering of her jaw.

Ingrid sank onto the driver's seat, took a few deep breaths, then hauled the door shut. She searched the instrument panel for the heating controls, turned the fan to maximum and pulled off her other glove. She barely had the strength to hold her hands in front of the vents. They were too cold to feel anything anyway, so she let them drop down onto her knees. Her jeans were soaked through. A twinge of period cramps radiated across her abdomen.

Damn.

She let out a sigh as she realized her backpack and the maxi pads were still in the cabin. She smacked the heel of her hand into the steering wheel, making the component inside her sleeve slide up and down.

Ingrid felt her body weaken, her muscles slacken, and she slumped over the steering wheel. She remembered bending under the table in Republik and sliding the third component inside her backpack. Her stomach gripped like a fist, forcing the partially digested chocolate bar back up her esophagus and into her mouth. She swallowed.

There was no way she could go back for it. Not through the snow, not toward the men with guns and the cop. All that effort, all that endeavor, and she had left one of the components behind. She couldn't believe it.

"Put it behind you."

She couldn't. She was cross. Riled. Furious. All she could see was the crumpled Russell Athletic logo of the open backpack, the Libresse just visible through the zipper.

"I told you to put it behind you."

Ingrid smiled, but not at Megan's cheesy advice. A new picture had formed in her head, that of a CSI officer explaining the contents of the backpack to a detective.

"One pair of underwear, you say?"

"Yes. Calvin Klein."

"A toothbrush?"

"Uh-huh."

"A packet of Libresse. Opened. Two napkins used, both found inside the cabin, both with the blood of the male hostage on them?"

"Yes."

"And this, this... what did you call it?"

"A component..."

Ingrid wondered what it was really called. Maybe it had been invented by someone who had lent it his name—it almost certainly was a man— or maybe it was one of those scientific things that had been given a joke name that had stuck, like the planet the nerds still called Xena.

She wondered what kind of DNA profile they'd get from her bag. There were bound to be stray hairs and skin cells. They'd find something for sure but, as far as she knew, she wasn't on a DNA database in London. Even if there was a reciprocal arrangement between European labs, the Swedish police shouldn't be able to trace her.

Unless they caught her.

Ingrid looked down at her hands. They seemed to be shaking less. And she could now feel the warmth of the heated seat coming through her wet jeans. She looked in the direction of the path. There was nothing but darkness. She reached behind for the safety belt, strapped herself in and put the car into gear. Slowly, she maneuvered the vehicle, turning it to face the road, then eased it down the slipway and onto the highway, grinding the unfamiliar gears as she did so. Ingrid didn't know which direction she was going in, but would follow any signs she saw for Stockholm. The dashboard clock read 23:11: she had ten hours to get to Stortorget. Easy.

A short convoy of cars sped toward her but slowed when they saw the flashing lights. Ingrid kept her eyes peeled, looking for a road sign that would tell her where the hell she was.

A new voice crackled over the car radio. Not a dispatcher. Someone in the field, speaking quietly.

The dispatcher asked the officer to repeat themselves.

Ingrid made out the word 'cabin'. Then the word for 'helicopter'. Then 'hostage'. Her mouth fell open. She forgot to breathe. Fear poured through her like molten metal.

Her fractured brain could only make out the odd word and phrase. The dog was dead. Gunfire. Request for backup. The word 'location' was repeated several times. And the word 'car'.

Dear God, no. No!

"OK. Will do. Tracing the car now."

Ingrid was driving a very efficient, and extremely visible, tracking device.

Transcript from Riksdag Committee Hearing 23
December 16 2015

BILUNGS: For the record, would you please state clearly your name and rank.

RASMUSSEN: Ilse Rasmussen. I am a sergeant with the Uppsala County police department.

BILUNGS: Thank you. I would like to take you straight to the night of December 15th last year. Can you tell the committee what you found when you arrived at the cabin in Järlåsa?

RASMUSSEN: Certainly. We had received a call from a local resident—in fact, we had received several: the entire population of Sweden was looking out for unusual activity that day—saying that an old cabin had been visited by men of, as he described them, 'African descent' in recent weeks and that there had been a lot of cars pulling up and driving away throughout the afternoon—

BILUNGS: Excuse me. [To clerk] Has this witness been called? [Clerk shakes head] Will this witness be called? Seems he has valuable information. [Clerk refers to notes]

RASMUSSEN: Um, sir, there will be a good reason why the witness has not been called. He was the man killed that day. Anders Möven.

BILUNGS: Yes, of course. I'm sorry. So it was Mr Möven who called you?

RASMUSSEN: Well, he called one-one-two. If he had called the station it is possible we may have responded sooner. The dispatch center had so many calls to allocate that day.

BILUNGS: So when did you receive the information?

RASMUSSEN: It came through to us just after 9pm. There is a shift change at 10pm, and so the day crew left it for me to investigate when I clocked on. I took Tug—that was my dog—and arrived at the cabin shortly after ten thirty-five. As you probably all know by now, I left the engine running—it did not occur to me that anyone would be stupid enough to steal a police car—and Tug and I set off through the woods to the old Eriksson place.

BILUNGS: The Eriksson place?

RASMUSSEN: Sorry, that's the cabin. Owned by the Eriksson family.

BILUNGS: I see.

RASMUSSEN: It's famous—locally—for being the cheapest building on the most expensive piece of land. There's an old dispute... Sorry, did you want to say something?

BILUNGS: I don't mean to be rude; I simply want to guide you back toward the events of December 15th.

RASMUSSEN: Yes, of course. Sorry. I tend to talk a lot when I am nervous.

BILUNGS: Relax, Miss Rasmussen.

RASMUSSEN: Sergeant Rasmussen.

BILUNGS: Sergeant Rasmussen, indeed. So, you were on the path? When did you hear the first gunshot?

RASMUSSEN: Um, I am not sure. I was very close to the cabin. Maybe around ten forty-five.

BILUNGS: So you did not hear the shots fired by Anders Möven?

RASMUSSEN: No. When we interviewed his wife, she said he had opened fire on a fugitive in the woods around ten thirty-five. I must have still been in the car at that time. Certainly I did not hear his shots. Obviously I would not have entered the woods without backup if I had. No, I did not know anyone was in the woods until shots were fired at me when I approached the cabin. But, if I may, I think it is relevant that—

before then—while Tug and I were walking along the path, Tug clearly picked up the scent of someone, or something, and given that Anders Möven told his wife he saw someone in the woods, I think it is likely it was a person. Tug was barking, he wanted to run into the woods, but I could not see anything. You know, I only had a flashlight, and the trees are pretty dense up there, but I couldn't see anything. And you have to remember that, at this point, there was no report of gunfire, and I wasn't really expecting to find anyone at the Eriksson place. All I wanted to do was get to the cabin, rule it out, and get back to the car.

BILUNGS: Are you suggesting that your dog was barking at the female hostage?

RASMUSSEN: Yes. Well, probably. We know she was there, the DNA evidence from the Russell Athletic bag confirmed that, as did Mohammed Ali Ghedi. And the photos sent to Björn Friese, of course. It's fairly remote up there. Not a place for a casual hike at ten thirty at night when it's minus twenty.

BILUNGS: Quite. But you couldn't see anything?

RASMUSSEN: No.

BILUNGS: To be clear, you did not see the suspect?

RASMUSSEN: You mean the hostage?

BILUNGS: [Pause] Does it seem wrong to call her a suspect?

RASMUSSEN: Um, I guess not. No.

BILUNGS: Please, continue.

RASMUSSEN: So, yeah, sure. So Tug and I continued up toward the cabin. When we were about a hundred yards away, he pulled on his leash so hard I had to let him go. We know now that he had found Anders Möven, who forensics say had received a gunshot wound to the leg from the Beretta we later recovered. Of course, the fatal shots, those from the semi-automatic rifle, the carbine, were fired at Tug, you know, to silence him I guess, and Möven received a direct hit to the head, probably because he was leaning over, trying to soothe the dog. Obviously, when Tug stopped barking I knew he had been killed. I did not know about Möven until the next day.

BILUNGS: But you did not radio for backup?

RASMUSSEN: No, quite the opposite. I switched my radio off. It was clear to me that I had found the cabin where the hostages were being held. I knew that a police helicopter had already surveilled the area and that back-up would not be too far away. I considered that, should my radio be heard, should I make a sound, then I too could be the recipient of a round of automatic fire.

BILUNGS: Were you armed?

RASMUSSEN: Of course. But I was not about to start a gunfight with someone holding a semi-automatic weapon. I took cover behind a tree.

BILUNGS: And that is when you saw the kidnappers?

RASMUSSEN: Yes. There were three of them. Once they knew they had shot the dog—they must have done because Tug had stopped barking—and possibly they knew they had also killed Möven as he had also stopped firing, they started arguing. I could not hear exactly what they were saying, but they were extremely agitated. Wild, almost. It was clear to me that they were panicking. I assume they must have been aware of the helicopter surveillance. They had, as you know, made an attempt to insulate the roof of the cabin, but the aerial team got a strong thermal reading anyway, not that I knew that then, but I did know the helicopter had been in the area and guessed that it was likely they'd seen something. I calculated that it wouldn't be long before the aerial team requested a ground approach so… Sorry, I, um, so I guess what I'm trying to say is that I figured help would come soon. Which is why I decided that if I made my presence known, I risked provoking more gunfire and endangering the lives of the hostages. At the time, we assumed they were holding three of them: the Bildeburg boy, the woman and Jens Luhrmann. It was only after I was sure the gunmen had fled into the woods that I approached the cabin. That's when I found Mr Luhrmann and requested backup.

BILUNGS: And the boy? Where was Magnus Bildeburg?

RASMUSSEN: I do not know. I did not see him leave. If he was taken by the kidnappers he did not make a noise. I mean, given where we found his body, it looks very much as if he simply walked out the door after the kidnappers had run off. He must have fallen. If he hadn't been wearing the tracking device, it might have been days before we found his body. There was heavy snowfall that night.

32

Ingrid kept looking in the rearview mirror, expecting to see flashing blue lights. She stopped listening to the police radio. It required too much concentration. If they were coming for her, they were coming for her. She needed to prepare.

The snow was getting heavier. In between the forceful swipes of the wiper blades, Ingrid stared at the road. It was a major highway, the sort of long-distance freeway that would be six or eight lanes in the US, but Sweden's sparse population meant it was only a one lane expressway. Up ahead she saw a sign with a list of destinations and distances. Ingrid looked at it hard, then back at the road, then at the sign again: Stockholm wasn't on the list. She needed to turn around, only not in the car she was driving.

In rural Sweden on the day of a major incident, she had no idea what kind of response the local cops would be able to mount to the theft of one of their own cars. One unit? Two? Was a whole convoy about to descend on her while the helicopter was summoned back to the area? She knew she didn't have more than a couple of minutes to ditch the car.

The illuminated sign of an ICA supermarket loomed into view. When she got closer, Ingrid also spotted the golden 'M' of a McDonald's drive-thru and the logos of various furniture and pet supply retailers. She swung sharply into the parking lot, the revolver tucked inside her waistband digging a little harder into her back as she did so.

It was almost entirely empty, with just a few vehicles parked near the McDonald's. Everywhere was closed. Ingrid pulled up round the back of the restaurant and instinctively turned off the engine. She immediately turned it back on—just in case—then got out of the car and climbed out into the cold. She walked toward the parked vehicles, the snow stinging her face, her sneakers sliding beneath her on the icy ground. None of the cars had lights on. More importantly, none of them had been left with the engine running.

The retailers' colored signage threw a sickly hue over the deserted and silent parking lot. It felt post-apocalyptic, abandoned, as if all human life had been wiped out by a mysterious virus before the store employees had had the chance to turn off the power.

There was a clattering noise behind her. She turned quickly. A man, head bowed, let the lid of a large plastic dumpster fall as the rear door of McDonald's swung shut. He raised his vision, saw her, and carried on walking in her direction. One of the cars had to be his. He was forty yards away: she had about seven seconds to make a decision.

Ingrid pulled off her gloves and shoved them in her pocket and watched the man approach. He was young, under thirty, tallish and skinnyish, though under so many snow layers it was hard to form an accurate picture. Her heart rate quickened. He reached into his pocket and she reached behind her, slipping her hand inside her waistband. He looked up again and paid her a moment's attention, trying to work out if he knew her, if she was someone's girlfriend or a co-worker's ride home. She made eye contact with him and he smiled before looking down and pulling his car keys out of his pocket. Ingrid clasped her trembling hand around the Smith & Wesson.

"Drop the keys."

He stopped walking. Ingrid checked over his shoulder to make sure no one was following. A distorted wail of a police siren drifted through the valley.

"Drop them." She spoke in English and made no attempt to disguise her accent. She gestured with the revolver, making sure he understood his only option was to comply. But his face remained blank. Either he was numb with fear or he did not understand English.

"Keys," she demanded in Swedish. "Now."

His head dipped and there was a jangle as he let the keys drop from his grasp.

"Good," Ingrid said. "Now go."

Was it possible she was sweating? In these temperatures?

"I told you to go."

But he did not budge. He seemed willing but incapable. The metallic, scraping noise of chained tires grinding over icy roads mingled with the siren. It sounded like a convoy.

"Now."

He suddenly looked younger, as if he was far more scared of telling his father he'd given away the keys to the family Volvo than he was of the woman with a gash on her face and a gun in her hand. He also looked incapable of moving.

Oh, Jesus. I'm really going to have to do it.

Ingrid aimed the gun at the ground and pulled on the trigger. The shot split the air in two, the sound expanding through the night and creating pressure in her ears. Her numb, frozen hands could barely deal with the recoil. The man did not even look at her; he just turned and ran back toward the McDonald's.

Ingrid scooped up the keys, her trembling fingers shoveling up snow as she did so. She aimed the key at the cars and pressed the button. The indicator lights of a station wagon flashed under a luminous crust of snow. A clunking noise told her the doors had unlocked.

She ran the few steps to the car, yanked the door open, and jumped in. She put the key in the ignition and turned it, holding her breath as she did so. The engine started and she exhaled a deep and grateful sigh. She checked over the instrument panel, looking for the light controls. When she looked up, she realized she couldn't see a damn thing through the snow. She flicked both levers behind the steering wheel, turning on the indicators and the wipers. She didn't have time to get out and clear the snow from the windshield. She just had to go.

Ingrid slammed the door. Its loud reassuring clunk was swiftly followed by a soft slumping sound as a covering of snow slid to the ground. She put the car into first and pulled away, the wheels spinning over the ice.

She headed for the exit, bunny-hopping the car as she moved through the gears and turned back onto the highway. A cluster of silhouetted figures against McDonald's open door watched her drive off. They would have already called the cops.

She accelerated down the highway in the opposite direction to the way she had come. In the distance, right in the crevice of the valley, was the flashing blue light she'd been expecting.

Good. The cops were a minute from the parking lot; they'd be waylaid by the McDonald's employees, distracted by looking for the bullet. It might be two or three minutes before they called in the registration of the car she was driving. She almost smiled: a four-minute head start was all she needed.

33

Ingrid tried to figure out how the FBI would deal with her. The helicopter would be in the air, following the car. Road-blocks would be set up a few miles down the road; two or three cars would follow, with more approaching from the other direction. It was possible the Swedes would also call in a specialist firearms unit because they didn't know she only had four bullets.

She checked the mirror, forgetting the rear window was still covered in snow. She found the lever for the rear wiper and flicked, instantly sweeping away a semi-circle of snow. No one was following. Ingrid put her foot to the floor, putting as much distance as she could between her and the inevitable tail.

She listed the information the police would have on her. They knew she had stolen two cars and that she had a gun. They would also know where she had stolen the first car from, which meant they would probably assume that she was one of the kidnappers and not one of the hostages.

Dear God, no.

Up ahead was a blue flashing light. There was nowhere to pull off. It was just a long curving highway with no intersection in sight. She was trapped like a cowboy in a black-and-white movie, just waiting for the Indian arrows to rain down.

After another five hundred yards or so, Ingrid could see a

cluster of lights. She swallowed hard: a roadblock. She had to make a U-turn. She checked her mirrors then saw there was a truck coming in the opposite direction. It was too close for her to attempt the maneuver. She slowed down, the seconds dragging as she waited for the truck to pass. She changed down the gears, checked behind, then checked the road ahead. She was just about to make the turn when she saw that it wasn't a roadblock: she was passing the cabin. Two police cars and an ambulance. She collapsed against the seat, overwhelmed with relief. The paramedics would be with Jens. With luck, he would survive.

She drove on. Ninety kilometers an hour. Far too fast for the conditions. The snow was falling so thickly she couldn't see more than a couple of hundred yards. But she had to plow on. She had to make progress. She had to escape.

She checked the fuel gauge. A quarter of a tank. It was enough to get to Stockholm, but there was no way the cops would let her get that far without intercepting her. She hoped a sign for a bus station or a train station would hove into view, but then that was such an obvious move for a fugitive there'd probably be officers waiting for her.

Ingrid slowed slightly to read a road sign. An arrow indicated the turn for Stockholm was up ahead. She knew it was a risk to head back to the city. More cops. More surveillance. More witnesses. But, she told herself, there were also more means of escape. Ingrid took the turn.

She found herself on an off-ramp that turned sharply through the trees. When it straightened, she could see she was about to join the main freeway into the city. Three lanes of traffic in both directions. Street lighting. And people. Ingrid had just bought herself a few more minutes.

Setting up a roadblock on a freeway took coordination, several units working in concert. There still wasn't a police car following her, and as far as she could tell there wasn't a helicopter overhead. It was possible, she thought, that the increase in snowfall had grounded the air surveillance. Maybe it had also caused some accidents, or delayed police officers starting their shifts: maybe the snow was her friend.

Ingrid passed a factory, an outlet mall, a gas station and several other indicators she was much closer to Stockholm than she'd realized. After another mile, the street lights stopped and once again the highway was flanked on either side by dark swathes of forest. She kept looking for signs she was being followed, but the only other vehicles on the road were trucks and domestic cars. She considered whether she could risk driving all the way into the city, into obscurity. She quickly banished such thoughts: there was simply no way the cops wouldn't come for her. No way.

There was a cluster of taillights in the distance. An accident, or a roadblock. Ingrid looked around for a turning, an exit of any kind. But there wasn't one. The median strip meant she could not do a one-eighty. Her only option was to keep going. She took a hand off the steering wheel and ran it nervously through her hair. Her fingers caught on the knots and tugs in her wet hair, releasing a waft of the essential oil from the steam room. *Was that really just this morning?*

After another half a mile, Ingrid made out the cause of the backup: cars were slowing down for another intersection. There was a trail of red taillights of cars on the on-ramp waiting to join the freeway. She signaled to pull off.

She reached the top of the slip road and immediately discovered the cause of the traffic. A roadhouse. The kind of place that in the States would serve steaks with pitchers of beer while a YouTube sensation blasted out country classics from the stage. Ingrid turned the car onto the forecourt, slowly passing the nose-to-tail cars waiting to exit. She checked her mirrors: there were no flashing blue lights behind her.

The parking lot of the Freedom Hall was maybe a quarter full. She parked in between two other vehicles and looked at the signage on the marquee entrance. The headline act was called River Sticks and, judging by their disregard for spelling and the clothes of their fans, they were some kind of heavy metal band.

Ingrid kept the motor running and considered her next move. Now that the car was off the road, it would take the cops a little longer to find it, but not much longer. She was surprised that no one had followed her. And then she realized why: they hadn't needed to follow her in a car because they were tailing her electronically. She pictured a red dot on an illuminated map on a computer screen. She looked down at the glove box and feared what was inside it.

No. Please no.

She took a deep breath, reached over and opened it. Just a packet of tissues and some chocolate wrappers. She almost gasped with relief: no cell phone for the police to put a trace on.

Ingrid watched the black-clad music fans trudge through the snow to their cars and made a list of her assets: a couple thousand sodden euros strapped to her ankle, a vintage Smith & Wesson in full working order and… the list stopped there.

She was fatigued, hungry and so burned out on adrenaline she couldn't trust her judgment. She didn't have a clue how the next few hours—or minutes—would play out, but she did know one thing for sure: even if the cops weren't tracking her remotely, it wouldn't be long before they found the car. She needed to get out of the car.

34

Ingrid killed the engine and opened the door. As she got out, she felt the revolver brush against the seat. She pulled it out of her waistband and looked at it. Was it an asset or a liability? Might she need it again, or was it better if the police found it when they discovered the vehicle?

All that mattered was evading capture, and knowing she wasn't armed might move her down their priority list. She threw the gun onto the seat, closed the door and walked through the soft falling snow toward the smokers outside the Freedom Hall. They ignored her—maybe the cut on her head didn't look so bad—so she pushed through the double doors and found herself inside a crowded ticket hall. It smelt of wheat beer and sweat.

She stopped dead. There were so many people. Too many people. Jens had said something about Anna Skyberg's capture being on the news. It only took one person to think they recognized her.

She looked at the patrons lining up at the coat check. Many of the women had dyed black hair, excessive amounts of kohl eyeliner and facial piercings. The men mostly wore jeans and tee-shirts emblazoned with logos of the band, video games or retro brands. The best way to get out of the Freedom Hall that didn't involve handcuffs was to look like one of them. She could either hide in the restrooms and hope to swipe some unclaimed gear from the coat check later in the night, or she could make a purchase from the merchandise stall.

She crossed the lobby to examine the array of River Sticks tee-shirts, caps, and sweatshirts. No pants. No shoes. But a change of outfit nonetheless. The girls running the stall were just packing up.

"*Hej*."

"*Hej*." One of them looked up, an expression of concern on her face. She said something Ingrid did not understand.

"My Swedish not so good," Ingrid said in English with a heavy Russian accent. She hoped changing her voice would deter the girl from thinking she could be Anna Skyberg.

"Um," the girl's face scrunched up as she computed a translation. "Who did that to you?"

Ingrid raised her hand to her eyebrow. "Boyfriend."

"You want me to call the police?"

That's the last thing I want. "No, *tack*. It's OK."

The other girl emerged from underneath a trestle table. "Oh, honey, that doesn't look good." She had a shaved head and a tattoo of rose thorns emerging from her neckline.

"You are American?" Ingrid asked.

"Minnesota."

You have got to be kidding me.

"Grand Rapids. You probably never heard of it. Only people who have are Judy Garland fans."

Ingrid had been there several times.

"She was born there."

"Oh."

"You should dump him, you know. Any guy who does that to you. Is he here? Because I can get the boys to have a word, if you know what I mean."

Ingrid shook her head. She didn't know what to say. This was the longest conversation she'd had with anyone since she'd ordered brunch in Republik. She needed not to be so memorable. "How much?" she asked. "For the sweatshirt?"

"Eighteen hundred kronor."

Ingrid had no idea how much money that was. "You take euros?"

The two women looked at each other. "Sure. We're playing in Denmark the day after tomorrow anyway."

"And tee-shirt. And a cap. And… what else you have?"

The girl with the shaved head looked at her quizzically. "You sure you want all of it?"

"Please," Ingrid said. "I need. He is looking for me." Ingrid hoped her face was pathetic enough to convince them. "Please. I need to get out of here without him knowing. He cannot find me. I need…"

"OK, honey." The American reached out a hand, her nails shiny and black, and placed it on Ingrid's forearm, almost touching the Perspex tube. "You can have the lot for, what, I dunno, two fifty euros."

Ingrid nodded and placed her own hand on top of the girl's. She made deliberate eye contact with her: "What I really want…"

"Yes?"

Ingrid pointed to her head. "Is that."

"What?"

"Your hair." Her accent was holding steady.

"You want to shave your head?"

Ingrid nodded.

"Well, all you need are some clippers. You can do it yourself. Save a fortune at the salon."

Ingrid shook her head. "No, I want now. He must not find me."

"Now? You want to shave your head? Here?"

Ingrid nodded. A change of clothes, a change of style, and she could slip out unnoticed. Might even be able to hitch a ride into the city with some of the stragglers, or wangle an invite to an afterparty somewhere. She could disappear for a few hours. A plan had emerged. An exit had opened up.

"You sure?"

Ingrid was very sure. "And some of… what you call this?" She pointed to her own eye.

"Make-up?"

"Yes. I want to look like you."

Her eyes widened. "Right now?"

"Yes. I will pay. He is looking for me." Ingrid pointed to her wound. "He cannot find me."

The girl pursed her lips in a display of concern, her eyes checking Ingrid's to make sure she wasn't a fruitcake. She turned to her friend. "You OK to pack up, Marta?"

"*Ja*. Sure."

"OK then, honey, let's do this thing." She beamed at Ingrid, pushed an armful of merchandise at her and grabbed her hand. "Darling, you are soaked through. Let's get you out of those things." She led her through the lobby into the dark and empty auditorium toward the backstage area. Her name, she said, was Mary Jane, though everyone called her Mare. "As in nightmare." In the space of less than two hundred yards Ingrid had Mare's entire life story. She'd had evangelical parents who were too damn easy to shock and, although they'd threatened to disown her when she got her first tattoo, they still came to the wedding when she married the bassist in the band. Ingrid missed out on some of the details as she was too busy clocking the emergency exits and possible hiding places. She kept expecting to hear sirens.

"So where're you from?" Mare pushed open a dressing-room door.

"Russia."

"Really? Whereabouts? Because, I'm pretty sure we've got some dates lined up in Moscow."

"St Petersburg."

"I thought that was Florida."

Ingrid smiled at her and stepped into the dressing room, where three people were engrossed by their cell phones, all slumped in various stages of exhaustion.

"Hi everyone, this is..."

Ingrid had to think quickly. "Katja."

"And this is Andy, my husband. Say hi, honey."

"Hi."

"And Lizzie and Mustang. Guitar and drums."

They both nodded.

Ingrid knew she needed to act like a fan. "I cannot believe this," she said, looking at Lizzie. "So cool." She cracked the biggest, dopiest smile she could manage.

"What happened to your face?" Mustang asked in a slow Texan drawl.

"Boyfriend," Mare replied. "Where's Antonio?"

Lizzie, without looking up from her phone, said: "Groupies."

"The other dressing room?"

"Guess so."

Mare turned to Ingrid. "Then we'll take the restroom. Let me grab my stuff. Any of you know when the bus leaves?"

Andy shrugged. "Stef said we'd push off at midnight. He wants to be in Malmö for the morning. Hey, you want me to get Martin to have a word with… with your boyfriend?"

Ingrid shook her head, then looked away nervously, trying to behave like a starstruck fan. She had no idea how big a band River Sticks were. Maybe they played stadia in the States. Maybe they were big in Japan. Or maybe they'd just had some randomly successful YouTube hit in Scandinavia. She hoped they didn't ask what her favorite track was.

"So Malmö's next, then Copenhagen. We're going to Russia, right? Katja here just told me she is from St Petersburg."

Lizzie looked up, her make-up not quite removed, leaving dark circles under her eyes: "Think we're gonna be there next week. Maybe you could show us around?"

This was more contact with potential witnesses than Ingrid had anticipated. It was all taking too long. She needed to be less memorable.

"I live in Stockholm." She turned to Mare. "Please, hurry."

Mare looked surprised. "What's the rush, kiddo?"

Kiddo? Did she call her kiddo? Ingrid had to be a decade older than her. "Just, please."

Mare nodded. Ingrid hated how easily she was manipulating this woman. She was the kind of girl—she couldn't be more than twenty-five—that Ingrid had interviewed too many times, the kind who'd wound up at the wrong party, or delivering drugs, or stealing a car because her boyfriend had suggested she would do it if she really loved him. "Sure."

Mare swiped a bag of cosmetics off the counter, grabbed Ingrid by the wrist and dragged her out into the hallway. At the end of the corridor were the women's restrooms, a brightly lit space featuring a Formica vanity unit with three inset basins, and five cubicles, two of which were occupied. The women inside them were talking to each other, while a third fixed her make-up in the mirror. She looked at Mare, gave her a nod of approval as if to say how cool she thought she looked, then returned to her reflection.

Ingrid caught a glimpse of herself. She looked almost feral. "I need…" Ingrid pointed to the cubicles. She didn't need the bathroom at all—she had barely eaten or drunk anything for over twenty-four hours—but she needed not to be scrutinized by another potential witness. It was only when she got into the cubicle that she discovered her period had finally started.

"Damn."

"You OK?" Mare asked.

Ingrid looked around for her backpack, then groaned when she remembered where it was. "You don't have tampon, do you?"

Transcript from Riksdag Committee Hearing 23

December 16 2015

BILUNGS: Thank you for coming here today. I say this to all our witnesses. You are not on trial, we are not here to apportion blame, merely to reach an understanding of what happened on December 15th and 16th last year.
FIGES: I understand.
BILUNGS: If you would please give us your full name and your rank. Thank you.
FIGES: I am Paul Figes. I am the Director of the Stockholm City Police.
BILUNGS: And were you on duty on the night of December 15th?
FIGES: Yes. Of course.
BILUNGS: And can you explain to the committee what your priorities were that night?
FIGES: [Pause] I suppose there were three main areas of operation. One was to recover as much forensic material as possible from the crime scenes, so that would be the explosion at the National Museum, the Republik café in Gamla Stan, the abandoned Volvo in Husby that Magnus Bildeburg had been abducted in, and the bank in Mårtensdal where Jens Luhrmann had been seized. And obviously getting witness reports—
BILUNGS: This was still going on, late at night?
FIGES: The forensics, yes. The witnesses, not so much. After those initial few hours, we relied on the hotline. If members of the public contacted us, then obviously we would take their statements, but no, by the evening we were following up the lines of inquiry we already had. Which leads me to the second area of operation that night… trying to find the hostages.
BILUNGS: Were you aware of the events unfolding at Järlåsa? The cabin?
FIGES: Of course. Not in real time, but I received regular

updates, you know, every fifteen minutes or so. Sometimes, the other constabularies are a little, how shall I put this, leery of sharing information with their colleagues in the city, but we had good channels of communication that night. With all police forces around the country. The entire nation was on alert.
BILUNGS: Yes, I think we all have very clear memories of that night. But... Director, one of the, um, one of the reasons you have been asked to testify here today is to explain to the committee the significance of the operation at the Freedom Music Hall.
FIGES: Sure. Of course. I mean, it is something we all wish we had handled differently. I'm sure the Uppsala force in particular would like to have that night over. Mistakes were made, obviously. But then again...
BILUNGS: Director?
FIGES: Well, they are only mistakes in hindsight. At the time... you need to understand that some officers had been on shift for almost twenty-four hours by that point. And the Freedom Hall? Well, it is right on the boundary between the city's jurisdiction and the county's. It is common to seek approval before carrying out such a major operation on the other's patch. Obviously, on this occasion, I can see why the public would think that waiting for consent was... unwise. But that is protocol. That is how we work. We are a hierarchical organization. We always refer up.
BILUNGS: But that doesn't explain all of the mistakes—
FIGES: You know as well as I that the officers who let the fugitive escape are deeply embarrassed, especially as we now know she drove right past them. But once the weapon had been recovered, I think they made an appropriate call. She was no longer, as far as we knew, posing a threat to the public, and to put all those resources into finding someone who had stolen and abandoned—without crashing or causing an accident—two cars would have been, well, questionable when there were so many other things to be focusing on. The beat officers blockaded the venue, questioned everyone inside, but no one had

seen a woman meeting the description they were given. Those witnesses—primarily the members of the River Sticks band—who now say they did meet her that night, were asked if they had seen a blonde woman in her thirties. They all said they had seen a much younger woman, whose hair was wet and appeared dark, and whose most obvious feature was a cut in her eyebrow. This was a rapidly moving investigation. My officers were working with partial information.

BILUNGS: If we can turn to the WP-638.

FIGES: The missile component? [BILUNGS nods] With all due respect, we did not know about that for several more days, or at least until the following day. But I think you wanted me to tell you about our operational priorities that night?

BILUNGS: Yes, but I—we—appreciate your perspective on what might have gone wrong. If we could just stay with the WP-638 for a moment. There is quite a discrepancy between whether you knew about it the following day or several days later. Which was it?

FIGES: Oh, right. The Uppsala County officers obviously retrieved the suspect's bag late on the 15th, the Monday night—

BILUNGS: This is the Russell Athletic backpack?

FIGES: Yes. The contents were looked at but not thoroughly examined—that would require a specialist forensics team—that night, and it's clear from the initial reports that they did not know what the WP-638 was. I think it was later in the week when they shared it with academics at the university, Uppsala University, that it was first suggested it might be a military component. [Sighs] Of course, once we knew that, it changed everything. Turned everything upside down. All assumptions were thrown out the window.

BILUNGS: Yes, and we'll get to that. You mentioned you had three priorities on the night of Monday 15th. You've told us about two of them—the collection of forensic evidence and locating the hostages. What was the third?

FIGES: That would be setting up the observation points at the Christmas market in Stortorget. As you presumably know, we had recovered the burner phone from Republik, the place where the woman, the suspect, had been abducted from. We did not know then that the phone was definitely connected to her, but it had been found near the table where several witnesses said she had been sitting. It wasn't locked or, you know, password protected or anything. It was too old, I think, to even have those features. And the fact that it only had one message on it, and that it was so, um, antiquated made us strongly suspect criminal activity. That single message said '9am, Stortorget' or something like that. We had to assume that, even if she did not turn up there, we would intercept some kind of criminal activity, you know, given the profile of the phone.

BILUNGS: And at the time did you think this was also related to the Abdullah Saladdin case?

FIGES: Initially, no. We did not make the connection to Saladdin until the middle of the afternoon when we identified the link between the abductees, with the caveat, of course, that Anna Skyberg was not actually abducted. It would be understandable if—as would appear to be the case—the officers on the scene assumed, initially, that the phone belonged to one of the kidnappers, rather than one of the hostages. Especially as, at that time, we assumed the woman was the minister. So, yes, we thought the phone was linked to the perpetrators of the crime, not one of the potential victims.

BILUNGS: What did you think the message on the phone meant?

FIGES: We had an open mind but my main concern was, obviously, that this wasn't to be the location of a second explosion in as many days. We started the surveillance almost immediately—it is only a short walk from Republik so we already had officers in the vicinity—and, over the course of the day, we made sure we had plain-clothes officers in all the buildings overlooking the square; we had several posing as stallholders, several more as shoppers and diners. A huge uniformed presence too.

BILUNGS: And there was also an armed response?

FIGES: Yes, the firearms teams were deployed, as was the dog

unit. Snipers at the windows with the best vantage points, armed officers working on the crepe stall, that sort of thing. And, of course, we installed cameras too. We were ready for whatever would eventuate.
BILUNGS: I'd like to pick up on something you just said, Director. You just referred to the abducted woman as a, er, I believe you said she was a 'potential victim'. By the following morning, by the time everything was in place in Stortorget, you were referring to her as a 'suspect', is that correct?

35

A hand bearing two applicator tampons appeared from under the cubicle wall.

"Here you go."

"*Tack*. Thank you." Ingrid gratefully took them from the anonymous woman's grasp.

"No problem," she said. Yet again Ingrid marveled at how readily, and fluently, Swedes spoke English then suddenly remembered Nick Angelis' instructions to only speak Russian or Italian. In the privacy of the cubicle, Ingrid allowed herself a tiny smile: given how disastrously the mission was panning out, her linguistic failings seemed minor.

"Katja, you want to get changed in there?" It was Mare's voice. "I can hand you the sweatshirt."

"Thank you. That would be..." Ingrid struggled to stop herself from saying 'great' in case it was too American, "...very nice."

The girl in the next cubicle unlocked the door, shared a brief conversation with her friend at the mirror and then shouted out a goodbye.

"Thanks again," Ingrid said as she pulled up her sodden jeans over her pruned thighs. She slid the bolt on the cubicle door and opened it a crack.

"Guess it ain't your day, huh?" Mare said, handing her a tee-shirt and a sweatshirt still in their clear plastic sheaths.

You don't know the half of it. "No, guess not." Ingrid closed the door and unzipped her padded jacket. She carefully peeled it off, tugging gently on the cuffs, desperate to keep the Perspex tubes inside their hiding places. Changing her sweater for something with the band's logo—a three-headed dog and a crossed pair of drumsticks—wasn't nearly as helpful as a change of jacket. "You don't sell jackets?"

"Wow, you really are a fan, ain't you?" Mare said from the other side of the door. Ingrid heard a buzz as she tested the clippers. "We had a few tour jackets made, but we don't have any left. You might be able to order them from the website."

Ingrid's sweater and thermal under layer had survived her ordeal well. Apart from being a little wet around the neckline, they were the items of clothing she did not need to change. She pulled the hoodie on over her sweater. At least now she could cover her head; protection from both the elements and cameras. Her jeans were soaked from mid-thigh to the hem. She bent down and peeled the left leg up and pulled out a few hundred euros from her ankle pouch. She shoved the wet cash into her jeans pocket then picked up her jacket from the floor, carefully grabbing the elasticated wrists. She slid her left arm in, navigating past the Perspex tube, then twisted to get her right arm into the sleeve, but when she let go of the cuff, the component slipped out, clattering on the tiled floor.

"*Govno!*" Swearing in Russian came naturally. She dropped to her knees and reached a hand under the cubicle wall.

"What was that?" Mare said. "Everything all right?"

"I, uh," Ingrid's heart pounded so hard it hurt. "I dropped something."

"Can I help?"

Ingrid watched as the tube rolled out of view. She bent forward, pressing her wet hair against the wet floor and looked toward the component. It hadn't cracked. It hadn't fallen out of its case.

"No, thank you." Ingrid stretched out and her fingers touched the Perspex, but she couldn't grasp it.

A footstep. A brightening of the light as Mare opened the adjacent cubicle door. "I got it."

"No! Really."

Ingrid felt her jaw crumple as she watched the black fingernails of Mare's right hand grip hold of the component. Ingrid's breath stalled in her chest.

"Here you go." Mare rolled it back toward her, and Ingrid snatched at it, immediately pushing it up inside her sleeve. Exhaling, she stood up, one arm pressing against the cubicle wall to stop her from falling. When she finally got her breath back, Ingrid opened the cubicle door. She almost didn't recognize herself in the mirror opposite.

"What do you think?" Mare asked. "The merch?"

"Sorry?"

"The hoodie?"

"Oh, yes," Ingrid said, distracted by her appearance. "Very nice."

Ingrid leaned against the sink unit and peered into the mirror. Her hair was matted and wet. It looked dirty. Maybe it was dust from the rotten wood? Maybe there was blood in it.

"Does it hurt?"

The cut in Ingrid's eyebrow wasn't as dramatic as she'd feared, but her right eye was bloodshot. She raised a hand to touch her face and felt just how sore and tender her cheek was. It would be badly bruised in a day or two.

"Not so bad." She ran the faucet and washed her face. Mare handed her a fistful of blue paper hand towels and she dabbed her face dry.

"So your boyfriend's still here?" Mare asked.

It took Ingrid a second to work out why she would ask such a thing. She nodded. "He is, how you say, controlling."

"He's done this before?"

"Yah. Once or twice." Ingrid made sure her accent was still screwed on properly.

"I gotta ask, honey, why do you stay with a guy like that?"

Ingrid shrugged. "This time I leave him."

"You don't sound convincing."

Domestic violence victims rarely did. "Yes, I get out, go back to Russia."

Mare tilted her head in sympathy.

"But, you know, first I must escape tonight." Ingrid pointed to the clippers.

"You sure about this?"

"Yes." She knew she sounded a little hesitant. She'd actually thought about shaving her head many times, mostly whenever she took her helmet off and couldn't do anything with her flattened mop. It would take some explaining in London. But if she was fielding questions from co-workers about her buzz cut that meant she had survived or ended up in jail. "I want to look like you."

There was a rumble of noise out in the corridor. Doors opening and closing. Heavy footsteps. Ingrid shivered. She had taken too long. She should have been on her way by now. She dived back into the cubicle just as the restroom door flung open.

"There you are." A man's voice. American accent. Exhale.

"What is it?" Mare asked. "Andy?"

He was panting heavily. "The cops are here. The place is on lockdown."

Ingrid pressed herself against the cubicle wall and silently screamed.

"Why?" Mare asked.

"Don't know. Just wanted to check where you were." There was a pause. "You still with that girl?"A faint rustling of clothes and the quietest of whispers. "Oh, OK."

Before he closed the door, Ingrid heard shouting in the corridor. She swallowed hard.

"You OK in there?"

She swallowed again. "I… Yes. I guess."

"It was just Andy. Did you think it was your fella?"

Ingrid unlocked the door, made deliberate and extended eye contact with Mare and nodded.

"Oh, wow, you're really scared of him, ain't you?"

Ingrid nodded again, a little alarmed at how fluent she was at role play. "You will help me, yes?"

Mare waved the clippers through the air. "If you're sure?"

Ingrid stared at herself and pictured striding into a meeting at the embassy with a shaved head. "Yes. Sure."

Ingrid was taller than Mare, so the best way to do it was for her to bend forward over a basin. She was a little disappointed she wouldn't get to see her hair fall off like a military conscript at the beginning of a Vietnam movie, but there was a plus side: her hair would fall into the basin and not onto the floor. Easier to dispose of. She knew she couldn't hide anything from a forensics team, but so long as it wasn't obvious to the patrol cops that she'd shaved her head, they wouldn't know she'd changed her appearance. She felt the metal of the clippers against her neck.

"Ready?"

"Yes."

The buzzing was accompanied by a vibration. Ingrid gripped the side of the vanity unit as Mare moved the clippers in short back-and-forth movements over the back of her head. She'd expected long, sweeping strokes like a lawnmower moving through tall grass.

"OK?" Mare asked.

"Yes, OK."

"So are you going to tell me what really happened to you tonight?"

Ingrid gripped the chipped Formica edge of the unit a little tighter, her face pressed against the ceramic basin.

"I mean, you come to a gig with your boyfriend, who beats you up, now you want to change your appearance…" she tailed off. "Plus," Mare took the clippers off Ingrid's scalp and held them in mid-air, "you're not carrying any Swedish money."

Ingrid raised her head and stared at Mare in the mirror. She looked at herself. Her hair was like one of those school projects where kids grow cress out of an eggshell. Then she looked back at Mare, whose hand held the clippers aloft, buzzing.

"Because, your story ain't adding up, honey. Either you tell me what's really going on, or you're going home looking like a desk-toy troll."

36

"So, let me get this straight. You come up from the city with your boyfriend. He's a big fan of the Sticks, but you're really just here because he asked. Or maybe insisted. How am I doing so far?"

Ingrid nodded.

"He's this big controlling bully, doesn't let you even have your own money, he gets a bit drunk, then he sees you talking to another guy, sees more than is really going on, and decides to teach you a lesson. He hits you. The other guy looks like tomatoes on toast, and you finally decide that tonight is the night you leave him. You run off, hide outside in the cold, see him prowl about the place, and you know he won't leave without you. Am I still getting it?"

"Yes."

"So you think, I know, I'll change my appearance, maybe hitch a ride back into town with someone else. Am I still right?"

Ingrid nodded again.

"And you didn't call the cops? You didn't try and report the assault?"

"No," she said timidly.

"Well, with any luck the cops have scared him off and you can walk out of here a free woman." She turned to face the mirror, an eyeliner stick in her right hand. "Take a look. What do you think?"

Ingrid was so stunned by her reflection that she took a sharp intake of air. She kept running her hand over her head, ridiculously pleased at how it felt to stroke her shorn scalp. But now Mare had added dark kohl around her eyes. She looked like a punk Cleopatra.

"Oh, wow. Wow."

It kind of suited her. It certainly suited her needs right now: no one was looking for a shaven-headed goth. Mare had done a good job covering up her wound. She looked at her reflection, then at Mare's. There was something missing.

"You like it?"

"Yes, yes I do." Ingrid leaned in over the sink to get closer to the mirror.

"What is it?" Mare asked.

Ingrid reached up to her left earlobe and unhooked the small silver hoop earring she was wearing. She looked at Mare in the mirror.

"I think…" She held the earring against her nostril. "For here? No?"

"Are you crazy?"

Ingrid shook her head.

"Well, I think I have some peroxide or something back in the dressing room. You don't want to get an infection."

"Surely I can just—"

"Wait! I'll be two ticks."

Mare left the bathroom, noise from the corridor briefly echoing its way into the tiled restroom before the door swung shut. Ingrid placed the earring on the countertop and looked at herself again, momentarily mesmerized. *If my mother could see me now.* In fact, she couldn't wait to send her mom a picture. Shocking Svetlana Skyberg was a pleasure that was showing no signs of diminishing with age. Then she thought about striding into her boss's office in the embassy just so she could see his disapproving face. But for that to happen she had to find a way of getting back to London.

She scooped up the hair from the basin—there was less of it than she'd imagined—and tossed a handful down one of the toilets and pressed the flush. She then flushed another handful down one of the other toilets, keen not to create a blockage that would red-flag her change of appearance. She winced as she remembered how her DC colleagues had been called in on a murder investigation: the super in an apartment building had been clearing a drainpipe and discovered several toes.

Ingrid grabbed a paper towel and wiped out the last of the hair from the basin. She tossed it in the trash can then picked up the earring and shoved it in her pocket. There was no point in waiting for Mare to come back. She needed to find a way back to the city. She looked at herself one more time; she made sure the hood of the sweatshirt was outside her jacket and pulled the zipper apart to ensure the band's logo was visible. If she got the chance, she'd sneak into the coat check and swap her jacket for another. Just so long as it had elasticated cuffs.

More footsteps in the corridor. Ingrid turned sharply as the door opened. It wasn't Mare. It was a man. Dark clothes. Uniform. A cop. Ingrid's jaw fell open.

"*Förlåt*," he said. Sorry.

He barged in, checked the cubicles and ran out as quickly as he'd entered. It was only when the door clanged behind him that Ingrid felt the thunder in her chest. Her ribcage bellowed in and out.

Was that it?

She panted hard. He had looked right at her. In the eye. Had he only seen the scalp and the make-up? Ingrid looked at herself in the mirror and smiled: it had worked. Her smile was short-lived. What if the other cops asked Mare if she'd seen a woman matching her description? What if Mare said something? Or was about to say something? Ingrid needed to get to her before they did.

She yanked open the door to find six or seven uniformed police officers in the corridor. Most of them were huddled, swapping notes; two more were checking behind the other doors. Ingrid quickly shut the door and puffed out her cheeks: they wouldn't all be as dumb as the cop who had just looked her in the eye. She couldn't leave. She was trapped.

There were no windows in the restroom, no obvious means of escape. Just in case real life was like the movies, she looked above to see if there were loose ceiling tiles or a ventilation shaft she could escape through. Nothing. The only way out was into the corridor.

Ingrid took a deep, centering breath and tried to put herself in the mind of the officer leading the search for her.

Focus. Come on!

She reasoned that they had come to the music hall because they'd traced the car. And if they had found the car, then they had found the gun. Immediately that would de-escalate the operation, wouldn't it? And if they had searched the premises and not found someone meeting the description the man from McDonald's would have given them, they'd move on, wouldn't they? They might keep a couple of uniforms on site, but that would be it. The danger, she sensed, would eventually pass.

The feelings of panic did not subside because another thought entered her head: CCTV. It wouldn't be long before the cops would view the footage, see her approach the merchandise store and release an APB for a woman in a River Sticks hoodie. How long, that was the question. If they were smart, the venue obliging and the surveillance was digital, then maybe less than an hour. But if the venue hated the cops—certainly, when she'd worked in the sheriff's department the Jackson Astoria had never appreciated a visit from uniformed officers—and they recorded onto tape, or the investigating officers were dim-witted and exhausted, then maybe she would get back to Riga before they joined the dots.

Right now, the only thing she felt sure of was that the one place the police weren't looking for a woman in her thirties, five ten, slim build and wearing a River Sticks hoodie was in the ladies' restrooms of the Freedom Music Hall. For the first time since she'd gotten off the ferry, Ingrid was exactly where she needed to be.

Ingrid decided to make good use of the facilities. She

unzipped her jeans, squelched out of her sneakers and struggled to peel the denim off her cold, wet skin. By the time Mare returned, she had almost dried one leg under the hand dryer.

"What are you doing?" she asked, surprised to find Ingrid bare-legged. "Oh, yeah, makes sense." Then she looked a little closer. "What's that on your leg?"

Ingrid gulped hard and looked down. She was relieved to realize Mare had only spotted her ankle pouch. Thank God she couldn't see the bracelet on her wrist.

"For money, you know?"

"Like runners have?"

Ingrid nodded. "I need to pay you. For this." She grabbed at the sweater.

"Like a fanny pack for your leg."

Ingrid hadn't heard anyone say 'fanny pack' for a long while. It meant something different in England. "Two fifty, OK?"

Mare tipped a bottle of hydrogen peroxide onto a cotton pad. Judging by her contorted facial expression she was attempting mental arithmetic. "Do you know why the police are here?"

Ingrid shrugged. "How much?"

"Two fifty is fine." She held out the cotton pad for Ingrid. "Sorry I can't give you a discount. The stuff is actually really quite expensive. Antonio won't let anything get made cheaply. Says it'll damage the brand."

Ingrid put the jeans on the countertop and held the cotton pad up to her face. "Which side?" she asked.

It was a question Mare took her time to answer. "Left. I think. Guess they must be looking for drugs. Doesn't seem to matter where we tour, cops have never heard of straight edge. And when we tell them they never believe us."

Ingrid wiped the pad over her nostril, then pulled the earring out of her pocket along with the crumpled euros. She put some notes on the countertop then wiped over the earring.

"I might have to give you change in kronor, if that's OK?"

That would be perfect.

"Like this?" Ingrid asked, inserting one end of the hoop inside her nostril.

"Uh-huh. The thing you need to be careful of, the thing you need to make sure of…"

"Yes?"

"Is you only want to do it once, you know. Quick and hard. I mean, just shove it. Get it over and done—"

"Aah." Ingrid's eyes immediately watered. It felt like a wasp had flown up inside her nostril and stung her repeatedly. *"Govno!"*

"Yup, like that I guess. Let me look."

Ingrid couldn't open her eyes. She screwed her face up tightly to try and contain the pain.

"It's not bleeding. That's good."

Ingrid could feel something running down inside her nostril. Blinked-back tears.

"It looks good," Mare said. "You should open your eyes."

Ingrid gripped the edge of the countertop, blinked several times and then stared at her almost unrecognizable reflection. She'd be fine if she ever needed to go into witness protection.

The door flew open and they both turned.

"You better come." It was Andy. Breathless, anxious. He looked down, saw that Ingrid was bare-legged and was suddenly bashful. "They're, um, they're evacuating the building."

TRANSCRIPT

Transcript from Riksdag Committee Hearing 23

December 16 2015

BILUNGS: Are you comfortable? [Translated]
GHEDI: [Via translator] Yes. Yes.
BILUNGS: If at any time you do not understand what I am asking you, please say so and I will attempt to rephrase my questions. Is that OK?
GHEDI: [Via translator] Yes.
BILUNGS: Would you please state your full name.
GHEDI: [Via translator] Mohammed Ali Ghedi. Thank you.
BILUNGS: I would like to summarize for the committee, but please do correct me if my information is inaccurate.
GHEDI: [Via translator] OK.
BILUNGS: You have pleaded guilty to your involvement in the events of December 15th and 16th last year, and as such have been sentenced to ten years' detention after which you will be deported to Somalia. Is that correct?
GHEDI: [Via translator] Yes. Yes.
BILUNGS: You were convicted on charges of kidnap and holding persons against their will. Can you tell us how you

came to be involved in this... this operation. Perhaps you would like to start with your association with Abdullah Saladdin?

GHEDI: [Via translator] Yes, yes. OK. Abdullah Saladdin worked at the community center in Husby. He has been very helpful to me when I first arrived. A beautiful man. A peaceful man. He has suffered so much in his country. When I show him my scars, he show me his. But I was a soldier, he was a teacher. A teacher should not have scars like his. And yet, still, he was the kindest man. A man who helps so many people. You must understand, we only want to help him, because by helping him, we help others.

BILUNGS: Go on.

GHEDI: [Via translator] He was to be deported, back to Eritrea, and I was asked if I help him stay in Sweden. We knew what happen to him if he deported. We want to stop that.

BILUNGS: How did you think you were helping him?

GHEDI: [Via translator] His lawyer... [Stops, consults with translator] OK, OK. Yes, I understand. We hear Osberg and Nyquist are best immigration lawyers in Sweden, but they refuse his case. We look for way to make them represent him.

BILUNGS: By kidnapping the loved ones of employees of the firm?

GHEDI: [Consults with translator. Via translator] Um, yes. We did not ask for money. We thought they would say yes very quickly. Abdullah is good man. We thought they help him.

BILUNGS: At what point were you recruited to the plan to kidnap the relatives of employees of Osberg and Nyquist?

GHEDI: [Via translator] I do not understand the question.

BILUNGS: Forgive me. The kidnappings took place on December 15th last year. When did you first learn of the plan?

GHEDI: [Via translator] I do not know. Maybe beginning of December.

BILUNGS: And how far advanced was the plan at that point? Had the targets already been identified, for example?

GHEDI: [Via translator] Yes.

BILUNGS: Were there other targets?

GHEDI: [Via translator] No.
BILUNGS: So you hoped that by kidnapping the wife of Björn Friese, the husband of Elise Blomquist and the son of Judge Bildeburg you would persuade the firm to take on Saladdin's case and the judge would overturn the deportation order, is that it?
GHEDI: [Via translator] I… Yes, that was the plan. Thank you.
BILUNGS: It was a very elaborate operation. The kidnappings, the bomb at the National Museum… [Refers to notes] The police have arrested and charged twenty-two men in relation to the events last year. Three teams responsible for the abductions, the men who were responsible for the events at the Republik café, who will also be tried for murder, others for procuring vehicles, firearms offenses… let me see. Then there is you and your brother at the cabin in Järlåsa, Samir Mustafa, who has pleaded guilty to the shooting of Anders Möven… the teams who drove the hostages between the locations, the couple who operated the safe house in Husby… Nazim Khan, the bomber… it goes on. It's an extensive list of accomplices, Mr Ghedi. It seems there was no shortage of people willing to bring the entire country to a halt that day. It all seems, how shall I put this, a little over the top to get one man legal representation in a deportation case. [Pause] There is a suspicion, both in the country as a whole and I suspect in the minds of several people in this room, that you did not all care that much about the fate of Abdullah Saladdin. What was your real motivation?
GHEDI: [Confers with translator. Via translator] Yes, yes, of course. Sir, for myself, I only wanted to help Mr Abdullah. Thank you.
BILUNGS: It had no bearing on your actions, none at all, that if you were convicted of crimes in relation to the events last year you would serve time in a Swedish prison. The consequence of that, I put it to you, was that it would delay your own deportation.
GHEDI: [Via translator] It is true I do not want to go back to Somalia, and yes it is true that many would prefer to live in a

Swedish prison. In prison we do not starve, we do not get beaten, but for myself I only want to help Abdullah Saladdin. He is a great man.
BILUNGS: Very well, if we accept that was your motivation, will you accept that some of your… accomplices were motivated by the certainty that—should they be convicted—they would delay their own deportation by several years. Does that explain, partially at least, why so many people were so keen to take part in the crimes committed last December?
GHEDI: [Nods. Via translator] It is possible, yes.
BILUNGS: Thank you. Now, I would like to turn to the WP-638, the component for the Haze missile. Your fingerprints were found on the casing of the component, yet you told the investigating officers that you had no idea what it was. When did you first see the WP-638?
GHEDI: [Confers with translator. Via translator] Do you mean see? Because it was dark.
BILUNGS: Yes, I mean see.
GHEDI: [Via translator] Then I have never seen it. I touch it when I search the lady's bag.
BILUNGS: This was after, as you claim, she overpowered you and escaped?
GHEDI: [Via translator] Yes.
BILUNGS: What were you looking for in her bag?
GHEDI: [Via translator] Food, money maybe.
BILUNGS: And you still maintain, despite your involvement in these crimes, the conspiracy to bomb a national monument, to bring the government of the nation to a standstill, that you had nothing to do with the procurement or distribution of the WP-638?
GHEDI: [Via translator] I did not. It was already in her bag.
BILUNGS: [Pause. Reads from documents] Please tell us about the woman you held hostage. Describe your interaction with her.
GHEDI: [Via translator] All I know is her name. Anna. And she was not Swedish. American, I think.

BILUNGS: What makes you think she was American? Other witnesses have thought she was Russian, possibly Latvian.
GHEDI: [Via translator] I do not know. But when she was shouting. When the man was dying, when we thought he might die—
BILUNGS: You mean Jens Luhrmann?
GHEDI: [Via translator] Yes. When she shout, she sound maybe a little American.
BILUNGS: Thank you.

37

The cold wind made Ingrid's damp jeans feel like ice. Seven or eight police cars were parked outside the Freedom Hall, all with their lights flashing, most with their engines running. None of the officers were paying her any attention at all. That would change as soon as they checked the CCTV footage.

Ingrid shivered and pulled her new baseball cap tight over her newly shorn head. Already it had a crust of snow forming on the peak. "You're sure?"

"Just get on, will you!" Mare said.

"Before he finds you," Andy added.

Ingrid held onto the handrail and pulled herself up the stairs into the bus.

It smelt of upholstery cleaner and air fresheners. Behind the driver's pit were several rows of seats, after which the bus started to look like a motor home. Cabinets with countertops and fruit hanging in hammocks. No doubt there was a supply of herbal tea somewhere. Beyond the kitchen was a stack of curtained bunks.

The coach was busy. Young, white Americans mostly talking loudly, shouting across one another.

"They've got guns," one woman said, her hands cupped around her eyes as she surveyed the parking lot.

"I saw dogs earlier."

"We gotta get outta this place."

"If it's the last thing we ever do."

Ingrid stared through the tinted windows. There were maybe forty or fifty cars still in the parking lot as the last of the remaining fans were shepherded off the premises. Many stood with their phones out, filming the police as they scurried around, taking up positions and shouting to each other. A small crew of grimacing roadies trudged heavy flight cases from the venue to the bus.

Ingrid raised her hand to her mouth to stifle a yawn. It had to be close to midnight. She didn't know where she was going to sleep, but Mare had promised they could drop her off close to a railway station. Maybe she could just ride the transit system all night. She watched through the tinted windows as a couple of police officers broke away from a conversation and started walking toward Mare and Andy. All it would take was one careful officer, one guy who had just started his shift, and it was all over. Ingrid couldn't take her eyes off them as they approached the open door of the bus.

"You seen this shit?"

Ingrid slowly turned her head. A man in his thirties in a window seat was showing her his illuminated iPad.

"I mean, what the hell's going on? Bombs, government lock-down. Twitter's crazy with some hostage thing that the networks are refusing to report, apparently." He looked up at her again. "And now this, whatever this is. Jamie says it'll be good publicity. Says we'll sell out in Malmö now. You with Antonio?"

"No. Um, Mare." Ingrid turned her attention back to the police officers, worried that Mare and Andy were in the process of consenting to the police checking the bus before departure. She looked at the man with the iPad again. Thirties, extremely pale skin, a tee-shirt that read 'I Want To Believe', a mop of tousled mid-brown hair. Her type. She smiled at him.

"Dominic," he said, indicating with his chin that she should sit down next to him.

Ingrid instantaneously flushed with panic: what name had

she given Mare? Anna? No, no, she'd used something else. "Katja." She hoped that was right.

"Where are you from, Katja. You don't sound Swedish."

"Um, Russia. St Petersburg."

"You don't recognize me without the make-up, do you?"

Ingrid sat down next to him and pulled off her gloves. "No, sorry."

He mimed playing the keyboards. "I know, you've only got eyes for Antonio. You're not the only one. As soon as they can pry him off the girls in whichever janitorial supplies closet they're holed up in, we'll be on our way."

There was a thud, and the coach shook.

"Don't look so scared."

She hadn't known she was that jumpy.

"It's just the roadies opening up the luggage hold."

She pictured the cops inspecting the flight cases for a stowaway. She swallowed hard.

"May I look? Please?" Ingrid pointed to Dominic's iPad. He had a CNN article open. The headline read: 'Terror In The Heart Of Stockholm'.

"Been a crazy day. Amazing not more people have been killed," he said. "Everyone's mom is calling and making sure we're all OK. Kinda glad tomorrow night is our last night in Sweden."

Ingrid couldn't listen to Dominic and take in everything she was reading. A bomb at the National Museum. Government offices on lockdown: no one going out, no one going in. Police had sealed off an entire block in Hammarby. A hold-up at a café in Gamla Stan that had left one man dead. Judge Bildeburg's son Magnus was missing. She scanned the article quickly but didn't see any mention of a woman being taken hostage. There wasn't one. Her insides constricted: why wasn't there one?

Ingrid pulled off the stiff baseball cap to run her fingers through her hair, only to remember she no longer had any. She stared at the open door, expecting cops to board the bus. Beyond the tinted windows, there was the constant sound of sirens as more and more police vehicles arrived. Why were they sending more officers? Had they viewed the CCTV already?

A new thought rose up inside her like a dagger, like bile: if they bring dogs, it's over. Over. They would absolutely have her scent by now.

"Where the fuck is Antonio?"

Ingrid turned abruptly toward the back of the bus. A large woman with a luxurious Afro haircut and a New York City accent padded down the aisle. She looked like she had just walked out of Studio 54 in the late 1970s. "I swear the next time we is all back in the States we is holding auditions for a new lead singer. He—"

"Hey." It was a voice from the back of the bus. "Dusty, I'm here already."

"Well lookey at that. And what's your name, honey?" Dusty said to the groupie whose head was poking out of the curtain concealing one of the bunks. The girl looked embarrassed. "It don't matter anyways." The loud woman turned her attention back to Antonio. "Are we taking this one with us?"

Antonio clearly wasn't sure.

"Well, you got about two minutes to figure that out. Now where's that Andy? They're saying five inches of snow in the next three hours, so I want this bus to start moving, ya hear me?" Dusty lumbered to the open door of the bus. "Now what the hell —" She was stopped mid-flow by a uniformed officer stepping on board.

"Good evening. I wish to speak to the person in charge," he said.

"You're looking at her. Dusty Prentiss. I manage this sorry ass bunch. We will be on our way very shortly, let me assure you of that."

"We need to check the coach."

"You ain't gonna find any drugs."

"We are not looking for drugs."

The cop—a trim, tall man in his fifties—stepped up into the gangway, followed by an equally tall female colleague.

Ingrid tried not to look, sure they were about to haul her off the bus and straight into an interrogation suite. She looked at the seat pocket in front of her and thought about dumping the components. Pointless. They'd link them to her anyway. Her hands were trembling, but not with the cold. She kept swallowing, her mouth painfully dry.

"Um," Dominic said, smiling. "It's not usually this interesting."

Ingrid smiled back at him, glad of the distraction.

"People think being in a band must be really exciting, but mostly it's just buses and motels. Unless you're Antonio, in which case it also involves laundry closets and fire escapes. Though maybe not in this weather."

Ingrid's brain was in panic mode, rattling through options and scenarios, none of which made sense. Then out of her mental chaos came one clear thought. She couldn't quite believe what she was about to do. There were other skills she'd rather rely on. She knew she wasn't going to be proud of herself but she reached across and put her hand on Dominic's knee. "I don't know. I always thought keyboard players were, how do you say, sexier."

He beamed. "Really?"

"Oh, sure. I mean, it's what you do with your hands that counts, right?" She was cringing inside, but the bashful smile on Dominic's face told her her plan was working. His eyes were drawn from her face to the officers making their way up the aisle. Ingrid's heart shook her entire ribcage.

"Good evening," the male cop said to someone in the front row of seats. There was enough stubble on his chin to suggest he'd been working a very long shift.

Ingrid wrenched her attention back to Dominic and moved her hand to cover his.

"Hey, you're cold," he said.

She grabbed his hand and placed it on her thigh.

"Really cold." His palm pressed into the damp denim. She looked into his eyes as his hand started to gently rub her thigh. It was a protective gesture, not a sexual one, but she needed him to start realizing he was onto a sure thing.

The cops were less than ten feet away, checking under the seats, asking Dusty who everyone was.

Ingrid raised her other hand to Dominic's face. "You can warm me up, no?"

"Well, um—"

She leaned in. A kiss would be too forward, too aggressive. She pressed her nose into his jaw, a demonstration of affection rather than lust.

The cops moved forward another row. She felt their footsteps like a giant's in a fairytale. Boom, boom, boom. Or maybe that was her heartbeat. She raised her face, gently placed her lips against Dominic's stubbled jaw, and with her hand turned his face toward hers. He pulled away so he could look at her, his eyes examining her face intently. Why couldn't she have found a guy like Antonio? She was throwing herself at him but he was too much of a gentleman.

"I am getting little bit warmer." Ingrid was a useless coquette. Her usual way of flirting with a guy was to beat him in a five-mile run. She smiled at Dominic, picked up his iPad from his lap and placed it in the seat pocket. "Kiss me."

"I, ah—"

Ingrid didn't give him a chance. She held his jaw firmly and planted her lips on his. Then she grabbed his hand and moved it onto her waistband.

"Your pants are—"

"Shhh."

She carried on kissing him, but her elevated temperature and quickening pulse had nothing to do with passion and everything to do with the police officers in the aisle. He started to kiss her back, and she leaned further across him so that only the back of her shorn scalp would be visible to the cops.

"Yes, sir," Ingrid heard Dusty say, "he's one of ours too. Say, Dom, who's the chick?"

Ingrid's entire body was shaking with fear. Dominic withdrew slightly from her kiss, so she nuzzled into him, faking embarrassment, making sure her face was buried in his neck.

"Um, hi." She felt him swallow hard. "This is, ah..." he had forgotten her name.

"Katja," she whispered.

"Katja," he said. "She's ah, she's um, well, a bit shy."

"Don't look that way to me, sunshine," Dusty said. "Looks like you're the one who's blushing."

Ingrid cupped her hand over his jaw and pulled him into another kiss. He tasted salty, earthy, his skin smelt of soap. He must have showered after coming off stage.

"Say," he pulled back from her, "you're really trembling."

She stared hard into his eyes. "You better warm me up."

He put an arm around her shoulders and pulled her close. "Well, um, er—"

She kissed him again, pushing her tongue against his lips, forcing him to part his as the cops moved on to the seats behind them. She breathed heavily, though Dominic mistook her relief for something else and started kissing her back, his hand moving further up her thigh. Ingrid began to warm up and, as the threat of discovery diminished, her body started to relax.

She didn't remember the cops leaving the bus. She didn't remember the bus pulling out of the parking lot. But when she woke up, Dominic's arm was still around her shoulders and the watch on his wrist said it was five past six in the morning.

38

Ingrid leaned over Dominic and peered out of the darkened windows. A freeway. No road signs. She shook her head slowly: how the hell had she let that happen? She slumped back against the seat and realized what had woken her up: period cramps. She needed to find the restroom.

She patted her jacket pockets and was relieved to find she still had the second tampon. She staggered down the aisle toward the onboard toilet. Almost everyone was asleep or dozing with headphones in.

Locked inside the lavatory, Ingrid stared at her shocking reflection and considered what her next move should be. The kohl eyeliner had smudged halfway down her cheeks and her nostril was slightly red around the new piercing. She kept shaking her head, unable to comprehend how deep a hole she was in.

How was she supposed to get back to the Christmas market in Stockholm for nine o'clock when she didn't know where she was? She presumed she was somewhere south of the capital heading for Malmö, but she really didn't know. The only thing she was sure of was that she had just three hours to get to her… She didn't even know what to call it. Appointment? Rendezvous? Drop?

Three hours. Her head would not stop shaking.

When the clock ran down on a case, Ingrid always focused on the things she knew rather than the things she didn't, so she decided to make a mental list of everything she knew for sure—one: she looked like a freak show; two: she was bleeding heavily and had period cramps; three: she probably had the entire nation's police force looking for her; and four: Mare never gave her change and she didn't have any local currency or a phone. But as her mother would say when she was feeling particularly maternal: you've still got your arms and your legs, haven't you?

Ingrid changed the tampon and washed her hands, then returned to staring at her unfamiliar face, gripping the safety rail as the bus swerved.

"What a complete and utter fuck-up," she said out loud. "What a ridiculous, idiotic..." It had become so hopeless, so impossible, that she didn't even see any point in finishing her sentence.

She damped a towel and fixed her make-up. "OK, then, how the hell are you going to get out of this?"

Getting to Stockholm by the deadline was all but impossible. She had no idea if it was worth turning up late, but she knew she should try. However, she could think of one very good reason not to head for Stockholm: the message she'd left on the Nokia. The CSIs would undoubtedly have recovered it from Republik, which meant there would absolutely be some kind of police operation at Stortorget. The probability of getting caught was high. And the *consequences* of getting caught were way, way too high. Either a huge diplomatic incident, or a long stretch in jail; possibly both. Almost certainly both. She thought about the news reports on Dominic's iPad. The city would be on lockdown. It was even possible the authorities would close the Christmas market as a precaution. And Magnus Jonsson, whoever the hell he was, might take one look at the cops and walk away.

She felt her forearms and reassured herself that she still had the components. If she couldn't get to Stockholm on time, she should leave them in a locker somewhere and get a message to Nick Angelis. They could still be used. Something could be rescued from this situation. Then she felt the bracelet: there had to be a way of taking it off, breaking the bonds and slipping away before whoever was monitoring her could respond.

Ingrid let out a sigh: what if they had already responded? What if they could see on a screen that she was nowhere near Stockholm? Her thoughts tumbled over each other, smothering each other, canceling each other out. She was assuming they knew where the drop was being made. And when.

Ingrid turned sharply at a knock on the door.

Her heart jumped. "Just a minute." Had her accent slipped? She ran the water again, buying a minute to compose herself. She unlocked the door. "All yours."

"Oh, hi." Ingrid was caught off guard to find Mare standing in front of her.

"I thought I better check on you. Saw you walk through the bus and, I mean, weren't we supposed to drop you off near the city?"

"*Ja*. I, er, fall asleep."

Mare smiled at her. "You weren't doing much sleeping when I walked past."

Ingrid felt herself blush a little.

"So are you going to stay with us in Malmö?"

"I, er…" She didn't have a clue.

"Because, you know, if you're thinking staying away from your boyfriend… Well, you know, it might make things worse. You know, make him angrier."

Ingrid suddenly felt very protective of her fake relationship: it had absolutely nothing to do with Mare and her interfering tendencies. Mare clearly sensed she had crossed a line. "Listen, sorry, honey. It's not my place, but, well…" She trailed off. "Did Dom tell you to help yourself, you know, to food? There's water, soda."

"Thank you."

"So, you like Dom?"

Ingrid shrugged.

"I mean, it's your life and everything, but, like, well, you know maybe he's not what you need right now." Was she really offering relationship advice? "Obviously he's way better than…"

"Thank you." Did Mare not need to sleep? Could she make small talk forever? "Do you know..." Ingrid yawned, rather more dramatically than was entirely necessary, "do you know what time we get to Malmö?"

"Around eight, something like that. Usually we just sleep on the bus for a few hours, grab an early lunch somewhere, then we'll need to sound check..."

Ingrid had stopped listening. Two hours before they got to Malmö, two hours further away from Stockholm. Getting to Stortorget on time was out of the question. She wasn't going to make the drop. Whoever was monitoring her was going to find her.

"Hey, you look like you could use some sleep—"

"Yes." Ingrid was distracted. "Yes, I should—" She motioned in the direction of her seat.

"You know there's a bunk at the back. It's Dom's. I guess he wouldn't mind."

Ingrid started to move past her, falling against a storage unit as she did so. "Thank you," Ingrid said, "but I..." Her words trailed off as she made her way onto the aisle and back to her seat.

"It really suits you," Mare said.

Ingrid turned.

"Your hair. It suits you."

"Thank you."

Ingrid sat down gently, keen not to wake the keyboard player with whom she'd become a little too friendly. She reached forward and slid his iPad out from the seat pocket. She pressed the home button and swiped. Passcode protected. Damn.

She exhaled slowly: two hours. Heading to Stockholm was risky enough and without the possibility of making the rendezvous there was too much at stake. Leaving the components in a locker in Malmö made more sense. She could head to Riga from there. Within an hour of getting off the bus she could cross the bridge over to Denmark where—she hoped—the cops wouldn't be looking for her yet.

The road outside the window was almost entirely empty and sunrise was still hours away. Her thoughts drifted against the dark shapes beyond the glass. Then, slowly, one particular thought got trapped, circling round and round like a marble on a roulette wheel: two hours was also long enough for the cops at the Freedom Hall to have reviewed the CCTV footage. Ingrid felt a chill rise up from her stomach to grasp her throat: she had to get off the bus.

The moment the CCTV footage linked her to Mare and the band, the cops would intercept the bus. Tentatively, she leaned into the aisle to see who was awake. Mare had disappeared to the back of the bus. A roadie was raiding the cabinets for a snack.

Ingrid bent forward and felt for her ankle pouch. She pulled out several hundred-euro notes and shoved them into her jacket pocket. Before she sat upright, she noticed a coat stored under the seat opposite hers. She checked no one was looking then stretched across the aisle and pulled it toward her.

It was woolen, dark gray. A pair of gloves in one pocket, Samsung Galaxy and a gray woolen beanie in the other. She pressed the home key on the phone: passcode protected. Probably a good thing: she'd only be tempted to take it if it wasn't.

Ingrid carefully put the phone on the floor of the aisle and kicked it, sliding it along the floor like a hockey puck. She stood up, folded the coat over her arm and walked toward the front of the bus, trying not to bash any of the lolling passengers.

"*Hej*," she whispered to the driver.

He said something in Swedish, then immediately repeated himself in English. "You cannot talk to me while the bus is moving."

Ingrid reached into her pocket and pulled out a couple of the euro bills. Two hundred. That should be enough. She held them out for him.

"OK, you can talk."

"Where are we?"

"We will be there in two hours." He was overweight, jowly, his nose embellished with rosacea.

"That is not what I asked." She was speaking so quietly it was hard to disguise her accent. "Where are we?"

He glanced down at his satnav, pushed a button to zoom out. "Here," he pointed, "we are here."

Ingrid looked at the brightly lit display. The names of the towns did not mean anything to her, but she could see that running alongside the freeway they were on was a thin black line. A railway.

"Where is the nearest station?"

He took his eyes off the road and examined her, checking to see if she was crazy. Then he leaned into the satnav, tapped the screen and selected the public transit icon.

"OK," he said. "Hässleholm, nine minutes."

"I will give you this money if you drop me somewhere close. Don't go too far off the freeway. I don't want to wake everyone up. Understand?"

"Yes, OK."

Eight minutes later, the bus left the freeway and started making a series of turns that threatened to stir the passengers.

"It's OK," Ingrid said, "I'll get out here." She studied the satnav, memorized the route to the station, tucked the cash into the driver's breast pocket and dropped into the footwell by the door. It clunked and heaved sideways and Ingrid jumped down into the deserted street, pulling on the woolen beanie as the bus drove away. It would be back on the freeway within minutes. If the police tried to pull it over, by the time they'd checked the bus, encouraged the driver to spill, she'd have a decent head start. With any luck, she'd be in Denmark before the sun came up.

39

Ingrid dipped into the large, tiled doorway of a department store and examined the coat she had taken from the bus. It was a man's trench coat that complemented her new hairstyle perfectly. Not that anyone would see it under the beanie.

Ingrid carefully fished out the components from inside the elasticated cuffs and placed them in the pockets of the woolen coat. Then she unzipped her jacket and saw the hoodie. She needed to ditch that too now that the police would be looking for a woman in River Sticks merchandise.

She pulled the hoodie over her head, and the morning air pierced through her remaining layers like a scalpel. She burrowed into the trench coat and turned up the collar. As she buttoned it, she felt a weight against her left breast. An internal pocket with something inside.

Ingrid reached in, her fingers already too cold to feel the satin lining. The object was heavy and rectangular. A second phone? A wallet? She dipped her hand inside the pocket and smelt it before she felt it. A pack of cigarettes. The Camel Lights were too heavy to just contain tobacco, so she flipped open the lid, her fingers already a little slow with the cold. She tipped the contents onto the palm of her left hand and felt a thud as a heavy metal object touched her skin. A lighter. Antique pewter. She hoped it was a thrift-store find and not a dying gift from a beloved grandfather.

She tipped it back inside the carton, then slipped the smokes inside the inner pocket.

Ingrid buttoned up the coat, balled her jacket and the hoodie and tucked them under her arm. She started walking toward the station, and with each street she turned toward the center of Hässleholm, a few more people were on the sidewalks. It was a small, handsome town with modern retail chains squashed into brick-built stores that would have once housed a grocer, butcher, cloth merchant and apothecary. The paths of flattened snow told her she was getting close to the station and she soon found herself joining the trudge of early morning commuters.

The station was bigger than she'd expected and looked like a cross between a church and a school. While keeping her distance, she scanned the front of the building for CCTV cameras, but the ones she could see were so heavily encrusted with snow they'd be useless.

The large ticket hall was unmanned so the trickle of commuters walked straight through to the platform. Ingrid checked the route map on the wall. She had two choices: either north to Stockholm, or south to Malmö.

South was the better option. She crossed the hall to examine the ticket machine, but as she had neither credit card nor kronor she was going to have to add fare dodging to her rap sheet. She jumped: the pile of rubbish at her feet that she thought was garbage outstretched a hand.

"*Snälla*." Please.

Ingrid looked down at the woman's imploring face, and then to the bags next to her which were covered in slowly melting snow. Dear God, she had slept out overnight. There had been five, perhaps ten, inches of snow. It had been well below zero.

"Please," she repeated. Her skin was dark, her eyes were tired and her expression was one of absolute desperation, though she was not asking for money, only to be noticed. Her dignity was compelling and Ingrid, moved almost to tears, bent down. Behind the woman was a child. The little girl's hair was wet and her eyes were wide with fear and distrust.

This is the European Union, Ingrid thought. This is 2014. How the hell can children be allowed to sleep rough in the snow? How the hell?

"*Hej*," she said to the child, and smiled. She pulled off her hat and both the woman and the child recoiled slightly at the sight of her scalp. Ingrid handed the beanie to the child. "Where are you from?" she asked in Swedish.

"Syria," the woman said.

Ingrid's chest heaved with hurt. A commuter walked briskly across the concourse and pushed open the door to the platform, apparently oblivious to the three people huddled on the floor.

"Do you speak English?" Ingrid asked.

"A little."

"Do you have anywhere to stay?"

She shook her head.

"Do you have family here?"

"No. My husband, he is..." She lowered her eyes and muttered something.

"Where is your husband?"

The woman looked up at Ingrid with brimful eyes. "Prison. But he good man." The woman explained they had fled the war in Syria, crossed the border into Turkey and taken a boat to Greece. Her expression was one of horror as she relived a journey that had seen her family cross an entire continent in search of safety. And yet here she was, desperate, cold, confused and penniless. Ingrid pushed her hands into her pockets as the woman spoke. She held the components tightly in both hands and glanced up at the map above her head. Several people arrived in quick succession: commuters heading for the early train to Stockholm.

"Would you like these?" Ingrid offered her the jacket and hoodie.

She nodded, though they were too small for her and too big for her child. Ingrid feared all she had succeeded in doing was giving her something else to carry.

"I am so sorry."

"You are American?" the woman asked.

Without thinking, Ingrid nodded. *Damn*.

"Obama," the woman said. "Good man." A tear rolled down her cheek as she smiled weakly.

The components in Ingrid's pockets suddenly felt like kryptonite in a strip cartoon, glowing, dangerous, unignorable. She pictured the glowing green stick of uranium in the opening credits of *The Simpsons*. Ingrid looked up at the clock on the wall as more people filed across the concourse. Presumably they all needed to be in Stockholm for jobs that started at nine o'clock? That meant she could get there too, didn't it? She could make the rendezvous. And maybe, just maybe, she could help stop other refugees making the same journey. She had to give it a go. Her best shot.

The ground beneath her started to vibrate. The train was approaching. It was now or never.

"There's some money in one of the pockets," Ingrid said as she stood up, remembering the euros. She waved quickly to the child then sprinted across the concourse and through the double doors. She made it onto the platform just as the Stockholm train pulled in. The LED sign said it would arrive in the capital at eight forty-seven.

That would leave her thirteen minutes to get to the Christmas market. Easy. So long as she wasn't kicked off for fare evasion.

Transcript from Riksdag Committee Hearing 23

December 18 2015

BILUNGS: Obviously I will not be asking you to state your name for the record. But could you please tell us your rank and outline your responsibilities on December 16th last year.
AGENT 54: I am a firearms officer. I work for the Piketen.
BILUNGS: You use the present tense. You still work for the Piketen?
AGENT 54: Yes.
BILUNGS: But you are not on operational duties?
AGENT 54: Not currently.
BILUNGS: And why is that?
AGENT 54: You know why.
BILUNGS: It would be very helpful if you would explain why you are not currently on active duty.
AGENT 54: You know why.
BILUNGS: Very well. [Refers to notes] 'The officer known as Agent 54 has been suspended from duty following the incident...' This is from a release from the Police Authority from January this year '... following the incident in Stortorget on December 16th last year in which officers from Piketen, the Special Operations Unit of the Stockholm Police, shot and killed a member of the public. A full review of the incident has been requested...' And so it goes on. Is that accurate?
AGENT 54: It's accurate that I am not currently on duty, yes.
BILUNGS: And when is the review of your actions due for publication?
AGENT 54: I'd be the last to know.
BILUNGS: Fine. Is there any reason why the pending review should prevent you giving testimony here today?
AGENT 54: No. I'll tell you exactly what I told them.
BILUNGS: And what is that?

AGENT 54: That I was doing my job. The job I was trained to do.
BILUNGS: But you were the officer who fired the fatal shot?
AGENT 54: According to the forensics, yes, the bullet that killed the victim came from my gun.
BILUNGS: And what weapon were you using on December 15th last year?
AGENT 54: The MP5. I was also carrying a SIG Sauer P226.
BILUNGS: What is an MP5?
AGENT 54: A semi-automatic 9mm submachine gun.
BILUNGS: For the record, I am holding up a photograph of a Heckler & Koch MP5. Could you please confirm this is the type of firearm you were using?
AGENT 54: Yes.
BILUNGS: Out of interest, how many rounds of ammunition can a weapon like this discharge in a minute?
AGENT 54: I wouldn't know. A few hundred, probably.
BILUNGS: This particular model is capable of firing 700 rounds of ammunition in a minute.
AGENT 54: Why ask if you already know the answer?
BILUNGS: Is this the kind of weapon regularly used by the Piketen?
AGENT 54. Yes. [Long pause] Though mostly we use the P226s.
BILUNGS: The deployment of submachine guns is commonplace in built-up urban settings?
AGENT 54: We train to use them in all settings.
BILUNGS: When had you last used the MP5 in anything other than a training exercise?
AGENT 54: We routinely use them in anti-terrorism operations.
BILUNGS: So this was a weapon you were very familiar with?
AGENT 54: Yes.
BILUNGS: Tell me, agent, how common would it be for such a high-velocity weapon to be deployed in an urban environment?
AGENT 54: If the Piketen are deployed, we would usually carry MP5s or something similar.

BILUNGS: So there was nothing unusual about using such weaponry in this sort of environment?
AGENT 54: I think we already covered that. [Pause] No.
BILUNGS: What had you been told about the operation in Stortorget that morning?
AGENT 54: We had a multidisciplinary meeting at oh five hundred hours. Positions assigned, signals agreed, tactics discussed. The usual.
BILUNGS: [Sighs] And what was the plan for the operation?
AGENT 54: To shoot and kill as many innocent civilians as poss—
CHAIR: Agent. Enough. It is obvious you are giving testimony under duress but this committee will not tolerate, and nor will the Swedish people tolerate, such flippancy in the light of the death and injury caused that day. [Pause] I am sure that, on reflection, you might want to apologize to your victims for your last remark.
AGENT 54: You know what, I don't want to. I am sick and tired of being the scapegoat for the biggest fuck-up in the Swedish Police Authority's history. I did my job. I followed orders. It's not my fault that the entire operation was planned on the basis of one single, solitary text message found on that phone in Republik. We had no other intelligence. None. We had no idea why we were there or who might turn up. You want to blame someone, blame—
BILUNGS: It is not the purpose of this committee to apportion blame, it is—
CHAIRMAN: I think we should leave it there, don't you?

40

Ingrid successfully avoided ticket inspections with judicious visits to the toilet, and by the time she'd made it through the ticket barrier at Central Station by accidentally-on-purpose tripping and falling into the person in front of her, she had just eleven minutes to get to Stortorget by the nine o'clock deadline. She estimated the square was a little over a mile away, a distance she could normally cover in six minutes.

Running in an oversized woolen trench coat slowed her down more than she'd anticipated. Or she was weak from the lack of sleep and food. Either way, by the time she reached Vasabron, the bridge that led over to the island of Gamla Stan, the clock on one of the huddled buildings on the other side of the water read eight fifty-seven. Ingrid stopped, but not to catch her breath. Uniformed officers were patrolling both ends of the bridge. She couldn't risk bringing attention to herself by running. She was just going to have to be a couple of minutes late.

In the sky, audible but not visible above thick gray clouds, was a helicopter. The city thrummed with pressure. The temperature had risen above freezing and the snow had stopped, but commuters still hurried to their offices without making eye contact. Ingrid did not know if the police presence was a hangover from the events of the day before, but suspected it was because they knew what was going to happen at the Christmas market. Taking a deep breath, and pushing her hands deep into the trench coat's pockets, Ingrid crossed the road and started to make her way over Vasabron.

There were pairs of uniformed officers at each end of the bridge, covering both sidewalks. Eight cops in total. Ingrid's chest felt hollow as she walked past the first pair, trying to look natural, trying not to appear as if she was deliberately avoiding noticing them. She fiddled with the earring that was now decorating her nostril and added a swagger to her walk to accessorize the shaved head.

She made it safely past the first four cops without arousing suspicion. They were paying more attention to vehicles than pedestrians. Midway over the water, Ingrid looked up to judge how much attention she was attracting. It would only take one of them to do their job: after all, she was the right gender, the right height, the right build, the right skin color. And in the right place at the right time. Ingrid slowed: maybe this was a risk too far.

Then she thought about the girl at Hässleholm station, and the desperation in her mother's eyes. She carried on walking, checking over her shoulder just in case there was an escape route she'd missed: if the cops on the other side identified her she'd be trapped on the bridge. *Unless*, she smiled, *I jump over the wall and drop down onto the water just as a speed boat passes underneath.*

But this wasn't a *Bourne* movie and Ingrid's breathing became shallow. Her throat tightened and her stride shortened as she neared the other side of the bridge. One of the cops was looking at her. No, he was staring at her. Ingrid swallowed hard and carried on walking toward him. Another twenty paces and they would be face to face.

Pressing her heels firmly into the ground, Ingrid walked tough. She had a nose piercing; she had a cut above her eye, make-up that was visible from space: she could carry this off.

Ten paces.

Ingrid glanced left and right. Maybe that appeared too casual, too affected? She dared not look at the cop but sensed his posture hadn't altered: he was scoping her out.

Five paces.

Ingrid raised her vision and stared straight at him, almost daring him to challenge her. Such was her ferocity that he took a half-step back. Ingrid picked up her pace and left the bridge, soon hurrying through the narrow cobbled streets toward Stortorget.

The square was pretty much as Ingrid remembered it: dominated on the north side by the hulk of the Nobel Museum, and hemmed in on every other flank by the narrow, brightly painted eighteenth-century townhouses so typical of Scandinavian architecture. In almost every window above the street-level cafés were paper Christmas stars, illuminated through their delicate perforations by a warm honeyed light. No flashing LEDs. No nodding reindeers or waving Santas. Sweden celebrated Christmas with a pleasingly understated aesthetic.

The Stortorget cobbles had been turned into a camping ground of Christmas stalls that were being prepared for another day of selling slippers, jewelry, blankets and sausages to tourists. Several of the stalls were still locked up but a few sellers were opening early, hoping to tempt the tourists lingering over their coffees and pastries in the sidewalk cafés.

Nervously, Ingrid scanned the square, looking for anyone who might be Magnus Jonsson. Was he tall, fat, old, white? With no physical description, she was on the alert for other tells: walking too quickly, shifting from one foot to another, a constant fiddling with clothing or a phone.

The cafés on the west and south edges of the square were bustling, as serving staff delivered breakfasts to tourists who were wearing winter coats and huddling under heaters. Ingrid looked for a man taking coffee alone. There were several, but none gave any hint that he was looking out for a woman in her thirties carrying an illegal arms shipment. Maybe nine o'clock had been a very precise deadline and Magnus Jonsson had already left. She wondered if she should do the same.

Just hanging around made her look suspicious, so Ingrid joined the line at the waffle stand for a coffee. The line was several people deep, in part because there was a new employee being trained. She stood and listened as he took instructions from the frustrated stallholder. The new recruit was incompetent: she doubted he could boil water let alone operate the espresso machine. And then she realized why: he was an undercover cop. Why else would you give a middle-aged man a go at losing you customers? He had to be the only barista in Stockholm who was both over twenty-five and a native Swedish speaker.

Ingrid bit the inside of her cheek: she didn't have any kronor anyway. She left the line, hoping not to draw attention to herself, and started wandering through the stalls that were sporting little white skirts from the overnight snow. Her heart beat so hard she could hear it: the fake barista wouldn't be the only cop. Those single guys sipping coffees in the sidewalk cafés were probably also police.

She felt trapped. Coming to the city had been a mistake. She should have taken the train to Malmö. She could be in Denmark by now. Her jaw started to tremble with the realization that she was in a square in the middle of an island in the center of a capital city: every possible escape route would be monitored and patrolled. There were only two possible ways she was going to get off Gamla Stan. In the back of a police van, or in a body bag.

41

Instinctively, Ingrid's gloved fingers wrapped around the two Perspex tubes inside her pockets. If she wasn't going to get out of Stortorget, she should ditch the illegal weapons components before she was apprehended. Without them, what was she actually guilty of? Stealing a couple of cars? Fare dodging? Maybe she could tough it out and stay silent. Serve a sentence as a Jane Doe. Out in a few years. Months, maybe, if she could pin it all on the fact she'd been kidnapped. Then she remembered firing the gun at the McDonald's employee. She wouldn't get away with less than ten years.

None of the uniformed cops in the square seemed interested in her, and it made her nervous. Why hadn't a police officer stopped her and asked her why she was there? If it were an FBI operation, she hoped her colleagues would have made an approach on the basis of her height, race and age.

She scanned the square and counted the uniformed presence: sixteen officers. And *none* of them had approached her? She began to wonder if it was possible that the police weren't even looking for her. She'd assumed the cops would have worked out who the Nokia had belonged to, but it was less than twenty-four hours since she'd thrown it under the cushions in Republik. The forensics might not be back yet. Ingrid inhaled so sharply she had to stop, finding herself in front of a stall selling brightly colored, oversized lollipops as her head spun with the possibility that they hadn't actually linked the phone to her yet. The cops would know the where and the when from the message, but they didn't have a clue about the who and the what. After the bomb at the museum, the cops were probably only looking out for men of Arab or Somali appearance. Her eyes widened with the realization. She reached out a hand to steady herself on the stall in front of her. She needed to rest. And she definitely needed to eat.

"*God Jül,*" the woman behind the counter said.

"*God Jül,*" Ingrid managed, totally distracted by the thoughts rotating round her head. She smiled at the woman, her face barely visible inside a woolen hat with pompoms dangling from the ear flaps. Ingrid desperately wished she had some of the local currency. Lingering, talking to a stallholder, walking away with a bag of candy: these actions would make her look like a tourist and would buy her a little time to find Magnus Jonsson. Or let him find her.

"For you, or for someone else?" the woman asked.

Ingrid looked into the woman's face and saw that she was apprehensive, making her aware of her appearance. Shaven head, black make-up, a cut above the eye, clearly not been to bed. The woman probably thought she was about to steal something.

"I am just looking," Ingrid said. She smiled broadly, attempting to look as unthreatening as possible.

"Where are you from?" The woman's accent was hard to place. Baltic was as close as Ingrid could get. Another Latvian, or Estonian or Lithuanian.

Ingrid didn't know how to answer and so looked up as the helicopter she had been hearing since she'd entered Stortorget swooped low over the square.

"Crazy," the woman said. "Since yesterday. Absolutely crazy."

You don't know the half of it.

"They don't let people in with their trucks, their vans. Nobody can open their stall today if they can't bring, you know, if they cannot bring in…" The woman searched for the right word in English before giving up.

Ingrid scanned the other people in the square. Only a handful weren't looking at the helicopter as it hovered above them, making the Christmas decorations on the stalls flap noisily in the down draft. They had to be plain-clothes officers. Ingrid puffed out her cheeks and exhaled slowly, her warm breath spiraling out of her mouth like a fire-breathing super-villain from a Marvel comic. It would only take one of them to recognize her. Just one of them to put a hand on her shoulder and ask her to answer a few questions. She needed to get the hell out of Stortorget, get off Gamla Stan and onto a ferry back to Riga. Finding Magnus Jonsson was a problem she could solve in a few hours' time: right now escape was her only priority.

Ingrid remembered to smile at the stallholder before walking away, swallowing hard and shoving her hands deeper into her pockets. *Just keep walking. Get out while you can. Find a locker, leave the components, bust the bracelet, get a message to Angelis and then disappear.*

Something caught Ingrid's eye and made her look up: someone was on the roof of one of the hotels. A sniper. Then she noticed how many of the windows above ground level were open, curtains fluttering in the breeze. Windows weren't generally left open in Stockholm in December. More marksmen. She started to comprehend the size of the police operation. She knew how much planning they normally took and this one would have been prepared in haste. Her jaw tightened. She picked up her pace and headed for the southern side of the square before stopping dead at the sight of a dog walker ten feet in front of her. It wasn't the first one she'd seen that morning. Breathing quickly, Ingrid did a three-sixty. There were three others. In the city center. In the same goddamn square. All walking spaniels.

Sniffer dogs.

Ingrid gulped hard, her throat sore and dry. The cops might not have DNA back from the phone, but the dogs would have the scent. Her scent. If not from the phone, then from the cabin, the

Russell Athletic bag… Even if the cops didn't know who they were looking for, the dogs would. A bead of sweat trickled down between her shoulder blades. Sweat. It was barely above freezing.

Ingrid tried to look over her shoulder slowly, casually, but feared her movements were jerky and nervy. There was another dog behind her. Whichever way she went, she was going to have to walk past one of them.

Stay where you are.

She didn't even have a phone she could get out and pretend to play with. Or a watch she could consult. Hell, she didn't even have any hair she could twiddle round her fingers. She just had to stand there, trying to look as though it was what she wanted to be doing. Then she remembered the cigarettes in her pocket. But she didn't have time to light up: one of the dog handlers was moving toward her. She could see his earpiece now. A curtain in an upper-floor window fluttered in the corner of her vision. The whirr of the rotors burrowed deeper into her ears.

Ingrid undid the top button of her coat and fished around inside for her scarf. He was a big guy. Six foot. Two hundred pounds. She pulled the scarf free of the collar as she turned to look at the other officer. She was short but stocky. Ingrid could outrun both of them, even in the coat. She wrapped the scarf around her neck, pulling the fleecy material up over her chin to hide her trembling jaw. She looked like a punk about to rob a grocery store.

The spaniel over her left shoulder was now only five feet away, sniffing at the base of the adjacent stall. To her right, the dog was seven or eight feet away.

Do you just stand there waiting for the world to end, or do you do something?

Ingrid took a step forward, her right foot almost unbearably heavy. Her left foot was just as difficult to lift, but she managed to move slowly toward the southwest corner of the square. Her heart boomed like a tennis player's on match point.

Just one foot in front of the other. That's all you've got to do.

Ingrid picked up a little speed, but didn't want to draw attention to herself by rushing. Her throat was tight. Her mouth was dry. The female dog handler was three feet to her right. Ingrid nodded to herself: she was going to make it through; the spaniel was diligently inspecting an unopened stall. It wasn't going to notice her.

Just a few more steps then you can break into a run.

Ingrid passed the dog and its handler, exhaling hard as she did so. Then she began pushing through the Christmas shoppers, who were still looking up at the helicopter.

A dog started yapping behind her.

Keep walking. Don't run yet.

The yapping got louder. There was shouting. The crackle of police radios.

Run!

Ingrid powered her way through the stalls and the tourists who were looking to see what the commotion was. Skipping and darting between obstacles, she kept moving as the noise behind her got louder. She could feel the ground shake with footsteps that weren't her own.

Should she grab a hostage? Steal a car? How the hell—how the *fuck*—was she going to get out of this?

A crack of gunfire ricocheted round the square. A single shot. A handgun. Screaming. Everyone was screaming. Ingrid instinctively ducked as she balled her fists and pumped her arms, determined to reach the corner of the square and a road—any road—out of Stortorget.

More shouting. Endless screaming.

Her heartbeat drowned out everything else as she ran, her sneakers slipping on the cobbles, and she swung right, avoiding a gaping-mouthed tourist too stunned to move out of her way. She felt her leg give way under her, felt herself falling, so she pushed down hard on her left foot, turning her tumble to a stumble, and carried on running.

A uniformed officer came round the side of one of the stalls and ran toward her.

Fuck.

Her arms pumping, her legs driving, Ingrid aimed for a gap between tourists, ducking, darting, forgetting to breathe.

Behind her, the shouting and the screaming expanded, mushrooming. The same syllables were being blasted at her over and over again. *Sluta.* Stop.

She kept going, her vision narrowing as she ran toward the street heading south out of the square. She accelerated, sensing she was pulling clear of the cop who was chasing her. She was running headlong at the uniformed officer ahead of her. Her only option was to push him out of the way. Velocity versus weight. She just needed a few more yards to get up to speed.

Another gunshot, snapping the air in two. And another. Automatic fire, ripping across the square. The uniformed officer took cover, crouching behind a stall, opening Ingrid's route out of the square. She willed herself to run faster.

A second burst of automatic fire. A bullet flew off the cobbles at her feet. Then something tugged at her coat. A dog? Ingrid pushed harder, her lungs raw as they heaved in the cold city air. The horror on the face of the woman in front of her confirmed what she feared: behind her someone had been shot. The screaming wasn't fear, it was agony. Her own bullet wound pulsated with the memory as she ran.

She reached the edge of the square and ran down a street that was crammed with trucks and vans. She glanced left and right as she ran, looking for an opportunity to escape. Or hide. There were more trucks parked in the side streets, most with their rear and side doors open for unloading.

She looked over her shoulder: three men in pursuit, two with SIGs in their hands. She swerved toward the sidewalk, putting herself closer to pedestrians, using them as a shield. A TNT truck pulled out at a cross street, blocking the road. Ingrid accelerated toward it, then ducked behind it, putting her momentarily out of sight of the chasing cops.

Something caught her eye. A van parked a few spaces down. The engine was running. Side door open. Man standing next to it. Ingrid couldn't work out why her eyes wouldn't stop looking at it. She checked over her shoulder. The cops still hadn't made it to the TNT truck. Then she turned her vision to the street ahead but her eyes were drawn back to the van. Then she realized why. In red letters on the side of the dirty white van, it said: *Magnus Jonsson, Frukthandlare.*

42

Ingrid leapt through the side door of the van and the man slid it shut behind her. The rear was separated from the driver's compartment by a metal mesh: there wasn't anyone in the front seat and the back of the van was empty apart from a few coils of rope, some flattened fruit and vegetable boxes and a pile of old blankets.

Why isn't he getting in the van?

Outside, the chasing officers were shouting. Ingrid made out something along the lines of 'where did she go?' but their voices were quickly drowned out by the screeching of tires and a fresh invasion of sirens. Her heartbeat pulsed painfully in her ears. She noticed a rip in the fabric near the hem of the woolen coat. That tug hadn't been a dog. It had been a bullet. The skin on her scalp prickled.

They were trying to kill me.

The voices outside got louder. Angrier. Dogs were barking incessantly. The van shook as emergency vehicles raced over the cobbles toward Stortorget. The driver's door opened and the man jumped up into the seat.

"You got them?" He looked at her in the rearview mirror. He was white, late twenties, and gave the impression he had a lot of muscles under his padded jacket. Ex-military.

"Drive," Ingrid said.

"I don't know whether you noticed, but there's a bit of a commotion going on." He had a London accent, and that nasty English habit of trying to make fun of difficulty. "We're not going anywhere, darling."

"Drive," Ingrid repeated through chattering teeth. "They're after me."

He turned his head and looked at her. "Nah, they're just in a pickle cos of yesterday. S'got nothin' to do with you, love."

Ingrid scrambled onto her knees and crouched directly behind him. "Drive." Through the windshield, she could see the street was filling up with ambulances and police cars. "Either you put this van into gear now or we're stuck here for…" Ingrid could hear the dogs yapping outside. "Seriously, just go. Now! Get us out of here."

He turned the key in the ignition and the engine rattled into life. The tick, tick, tick of the indicator was matched by a flashing light in the rear corner of the van. He pulled out and they started moving. Slowly. Too slowly.

"Faster."

"You can see the bloody road. What am I supposed to do, drive right through them?"

"Find a way." Ingrid slunk back down behind the seat, out of view.

He sounded the horn. "This was supposed to be a simple pick-up. No one said nothing about being a bloody getaway driver." A sharp maneuver, and then Ingrid felt the van accelerate. "What the fuck's going on back there? There are dogs and everything."

"Just keep moving. Don't do anything stupid." As soon as she said those words she regretted them.

"What, like bringing the entire Swedish police into what should be a bloody simple handover!" He swung the van to the right, sending Ingrid tumbling against the inside of the door. "You better bloody have them."

"Are they following us?"

"Shit." He slammed on the brakes.

"What?"

"Road's blocked."

"Why?" They couldn't stay still, they just couldn't.

"Just traffic. Gridlock."

Ingrid looked at the back of the man's head as he checked his side-view mirrors several times, then put the van into reverse. "There's got to be another way."

"You can't go back."

"If I reverse I can get down that side street."

"No." She was loud and firm.

"What the fuck is your problem?"

Inhale. "The dogs have my scent. You go backward, they go forward… Game's over, buddy."

He sounded the horn, making Ingrid shiver. "What the hell have you done?"

There was no way to answer that question. "Don't use the horn. Don't give the cops any reason to look in our direction."

He nudged the van forward. "This is fucking chaos."

Ingrid was still breathless from her sprint and her chest heaved with each deep breath. Even inside the van her breath was turned to steam. "What can you see in the side-view mirror?"

The man looked down. "More gridlock. Bunch of cops talking."

"Are they checking vehicles?"

He leaned forward and peered into the mirror. "Doesn't look like it, but I ain't exactly got a Royal Box view." He put the van in neutral and yanked on the handbrake. "We ain't going nowhere."

"You have to try." Without windows in the van's rear doors she couldn't assess the threat herself.

"Nah. Not what I mean. We ain't going anywhere until you hand over what I've come for."

"I do that and you could just open this door."

"You don't do that and it's exactly what I'll do."

Ingrid didn't like being in such a weak bargaining position. "Tell you what. I'll give you two of them. You want the third, you get me out of here."

He turned and looked at her through the mesh. "Show me."

"Deal?"

"Show me the goods."

The voices outside the van got louder and footsteps constantly thudded as the cops searched for her. Ingrid reached into her pockets and fished out the Perspex tubes. She held them so he could see them. "Now drive."

He reached up and unhooked a hatch in the dividing mesh. His expression told her to hand them over. Ingrid pushed them through the foot-wide hole and he snatched them.

The fact that he took them confirmed what she suspected: ex-military, not intelligence or police. An investigator would never have taken the bait. Now he could no longer pretend she had just jumped in his van. He was a mercenary, probably as expendable as she was, hired by a third party through the back doors and corridors of 'plausible deniability' that extended from Pall Mall gentlemen's clubs to beach bars in Jamaica. He threw the tubes into the glove box then put the van into gear and nosed out into the traffic.

"Take your jacket off," Ingrid said. It was a red ski jacket.

"Nice try."

"I'm serious. You give me your jacket, you get off Gamla Stan, you drop me off and I walk away. Trust me, the cops don't know what those tubes are, so the only problem you'll have is if they send a sniffer dog to inspect the van."

"What's in it for me?"

Ingrid took a deep breath. "Think about it. You really don't want me to get arrested. I know what you look like, know you're ex-military, know what vehicle you're driving."

A gap in the traffic opened up and he changed into second gear. Progress.

"Head south."

"Which way is that?"

Ingrid sighed. Surely anyone who'd been in the military would know how to find south? Hadn't he memorized the map before deployment? "Straight ahead."

"Your jacket."

"Jesus, give a guy a chance."

"One sleeve at a time. It's not like we're going fast, then push it through the hatch."

He didn't say anything. Ingrid felt the van slow down. "Now which way?"

Ingrid poked her head above the seats. "Right. Then take a left when you come to a bigger road. It'll be the main road that leads to Södermalm."

"Whatever that is."

Ingrid glanced at the dashboard and saw the satnav. Map-reading was becoming a lost art like basket-weaving and book-selling. The sound of sirens echoed through the city, searing into her skull.

The driver started to remove his jacket, leaning awkwardly as he steered with his elbows.

"Anyone following?" Ingrid asked.

He glanced at his right wing mirror, thinking he was still driving in the UK. Realizing his mistake, he looked left. "Um…" He briefly looked ahead, then back at his left wing mirror. Ingrid tried to angle herself behind him to check for herself but all she could see was the side of the dirty and dented van.

A hard thud. Ingrid was thrown against the mesh.

"Stupid fucker." He'd slammed into the car in front. "Don't worry," he said, horns blaring all around, "I'll get us out of here." He slipped the van into reverse and lurched backwards with such speed that Ingrid was tossed against the door like a cookie in a jar.

"What are you doing?"

"What does it look like?" He accelerated and swerved around the car in front. Ingrid could hear people shouting in the street, and the chorus of car horns turned into a cacophony. The engine roared as he put his foot to the floor.

"You should have stopped."

"You're joking, right?" He weaved through the traffic at what felt like forty or fifty miles per hour.

"Because while you worked your British charm on the other driver, I could have slipped out. Now—"

"Now we've got the cops after us."

Her insides lurched. She could hear the siren. She felt a pressure on her chest. Breathing was hard. She looked around the van. She stared at the tow rope and the cardboard boxes but she couldn't make her brain come up with a way of using them. Hiding under the blankets was the only solution her exhausted head could devise.

You'll find a way. You always do.

She looked again. There was no way of opening the rear doors from the inside, but the side door? She scrambled over to it. There was a lever to slide it open.

When the cops pulled the van over, she could slip out if the meathead created a scene. She looked over at him: he seemed more than capable of attracting attention. He blasted the horn and gesticulated at other drivers as he accelerated south.

"There's a bridge." He sounded panicked, as if the bridge was out. Or blocked.

Ingrid braced herself against the side of the van. She remembered the officers on Vasabron when she'd crossed into Gamla Stan. But instead of slowing, he speeded up.

"Jesus, that was close."

She didn't want to know what he'd just missed. She scrambled onto her knees and peered over the front seats to see uniformed officers on the bridge reach for their radios as they ran toward their parked cars. The van lurched wildly as it left the bridge and swerved onto Södermalm. The island was bisected by a wide commercial avenue lined with stores on both sides.

"Don't worry, I'll get you out of here."

Ingrid couldn't take her eyes off the straight road ahead. One set of traffic lights after another lay ahead of them. Every intersection was a potential roadblock. She looked again at the lever and considered opening it and jumping out into the road. But he was going too fast. There were too many oncoming vehicles. It was suicide.

For a split second she considered it. No jail. No diplomatic incident. A Jane Doe in an unmarked grave.

"Jesus!" Ingrid inhaled sharply as he swerved past pedestrians on a crossing. She scanned the road for an escape. He wasn't going to make it out of the city. No chance he'd even get to the next island. She could hear the siren of the chasing police car and knew it wouldn't be long before another emerged from a side street, trapping them in a pincer movement. Above the sound of the engine was the noise of a helicopter. She held onto the lever, ready to slide the door open and run.

"Should I just keep going?"

They had almost crossed Södermalm and there were no cops manning the bridge over to Hammarby. There was no sign of another police car coming to intercept them.

"Yes," Ingrid said, her head trying to picture what was on the next island. As far as she knew, it was all luxury waterside apartments and recently built roads. He accelerated up onto the ramp and over the bridge, the icy water eighty feet below. If a police vehicle blocked the south side of the bridge, it was all over. Ingrid tried to speak, but her mouth was too dry. She swallowed hard. "Take the next exit."

She could see the off-ramp leaving the bridge and curving down in a wide circle underneath it to the new developments below them.

Ingrid grabbed onto the lever. She'd read about what she was going to do. She'd studied the training manual. Watched instructional videos. But she'd never actually done it. She thought of all the buildings she'd jumped off for fun. All the hours and years of parkour training she'd done. How much harder would it be to drop out of a slow-moving vehicle?

He swung the van to the left and entered the ramp. The curve was tight, forcing him to slow down. Ingrid looked up through the windshield, trying to time it perfectly. She pulled on the lever and yanked open the side door.

"What the fuck are you—"

When the van passed directly underneath the bridge, Ingrid slipped feet first onto the road, tucking her knees and rolling onto her side, spinning out from the ramp and rolling down the hill. Her shoulder slammed into the blacktop. She tucked in her jaw to protect her head and rolled over and over, through the snow, unnoticed by the cops as they chased the van. The ground was steep and she kept falling, while the sounds of the sirens got further and further away.

She lay hidden in the deep snow for several minutes, waiting until the convoy of cop cars had gone past. When there was a lull in the traffic noise, Ingrid pushed herself up, discovering for the first time how sore her shoulder was. She shook the snow from her coat and started walking.

Transcript from Riksdag Committee Hearing 23

December 20 2015

BILUNGS: Please state your name and rank.
NYSTRÖM: I am Inspector Hanna Nyström, Police Sweden.
BILUNGS: Thank you. And thank you for coming today. Can you please explain to this committee how your work relates to the events of December last year.
NYSTRÖM: Certainly. In April this year I was brought in to review Police Sweden's actions on December 15th and 16th last year with a specific mandate to look at how the suspect evaded capture and to conduct a 'Lessons Learned' package so that changes could be made, either to command structures, or the way we handle evidence, or… I had an open remit. Nothing was off limits.
BILUNGS: And by 'suspect' let us be clear, you are talking about the woman who was kidnapped instead of Anna Skyberg?
NYSTRÖM: Yes.
BILUNGS: And, before I go any further, can I assume that you believe the woman who was kidnapped from the Republik café is the same woman who was seen at Stortorget market?
NYSTRÖM: Yes. I was able to create a robust timeline for her. A combination of forensic and CCTV evidence puts that beyond doubt.
BILUNGS: Am I right in thinking you have not published your report yet?
NYSTRÖM: That is correct, but I have concluded the work. And as it is my—and Police Sweden's—understanding that this committee will not be publishing its findings for some time, I am authorized to share certain information with you as my report is due out shortly. In February.
BILUNGS: OK, so let me begin then by asking you who this woman was. Or is.

NYSTRÖM: Ah. That I cannot tell you. We found several DNA samples—the hair in the sink at the Freedom Hall, the Russell Athletic bag—but her sequence did not match any on our database. Ethnic profiling showed her to be of northern European extraction and the specialist we consulted thought there was a probability in excess of sixty per cent that she was Scandinavian. Um, so, yes, after the request was made public for information about her identity, we received in excess of two thousand phone calls from members of the public offering potential names for her. Three names, in particular, kept coming up, but all three women had extremely compelling alibis.
BILUNGS: So you have no idea who she is?
NYSTRÖM: Not quite. We employed a psychological profiler who offered some interesting insights—for instance, he suggested the woman was likely a recidivist with a long criminal record based on her tolerance to withstand stress and the variety of offenses committed. But, obviously, she had not been in custody in Sweden, and there is no record of anyone with her DNA profile having served time in any European penal system.
BILUNGS: So you don't know who she is? She isn't Scandinavian then?
NYSTRÖM: Well, so this is how reviews work. We look at all the evidence and—without the pressure of an unfolding investigation—we weigh that evidence differently. But, yes, you are right, there are many reasons to think that she is not Scandinavian. The first is the items she left behind at the cabin at Järlåsa. The Russell Athletic backpack, for example. We were able to determine that it was a model that had never been on sale in Europe, only in the United States, well, all of North America, and Japan, Korea and a few other Asian countries. The pair of Calvin Klein underwear in the bag, they were widely on sale, but the pair of socks we found in the cabin were a brand called Brasher. They are available from specialist shops in a few places, but they are a British make and they have extensive distribution in the United Kingdom.

BILUNGS: So is she British? American?
NYSTRÖM: Let me say now, I do not know. But... If I may continue. Of course the other item we retrieved from Järlåsa was the missile component. The arms trade tends, I'm sure this will not be a surprise, to be a very male industry and I was hopeful that we would track her down through the arms community. Once the technical analysis showed the circuit board was for the Haze family of weaponry, we started approaching the firms known to trade them, and although her photo was circulated widely within those companies, we did not get a positive identification. However, most of the companies involved were based in Europe, which possibly makes it more likely that she is British.
BILUNGS: It's all very tenuous, isn't it, Inspector?
NYSTRÖM: Yes, I'm afraid it is, Mr Bilungs.
BILUNGS: So we don't know where she came from or where she went to, is that correct?
NYSTRÖM: No, not at all. In the weeks after the bomb and the kidnappings, plenty of evidence—mostly in the form of CCTV—came to light. We know, for example, that she arrived in Stockholm on the morning of December 15th on the 9:30am ferry from Riga, and it seems she left the city by the same mode of transport the following day.
BILUNGS: She was only in Sweden for twenty-four hours?
NYSTRÖM: [Pauses] It would have been more like thirty-one, maybe thirty-two hours.
BILUNGS: I imagine the Swedish people will want to understand how the suspect was able to leave the country. We've heard a lot of testimony here in the past couple of days that has given the impression that every police officer in the country was looking for her. How on earth did she get away?
NYSTRÖM: It is a fair question. The short answer is that around midday on December 16th she changed fifteen hundred euros into kronor at a hotel reception desk in Södermalm. The guy on the desk remembered her because the notes were wet. She then took a taxi to an outlet shopping mall in Sickla where she bought a complete change of clothes. In fact, she bought

two complete outfits. We then understand that she spent several hours in the spa at Sturebadet, where, I assume, she knew there was no CCTV, and at this point no pictures were circulating in the media of her with a shaven head. We then picked her up again, around four o'clock, buying her ferry ticket at a travel agency in the city center; therefore, she did not have to queue for a ticket at the terminal, which the police had under surveillance, along with all major transportation hubs in the country. They weren't just looking for her, of course, but for anyone connected to the events of the preceding day. It was only when a passenger on the overnight ferry to Riga came forward the following week—and he was absolutely certain that he had spoken to her on the crossing—that we even knew she had been missed at the port. She simply strode up, presented her ticket and boarded the ferry.
BILUNGS: So she traveled to Riga? To Latvia?
NYSTRÖM: Actually, we never found CCTV images of her disembarking.
BILUNGS: What are you suggesting? That she jumped overboard?
NYSTRÖM: Well, sir, there is absolutely no evidence for that—
BILUNGS: But there wouldn't be, would there?
NYSTRÖM: [Pause] Given the profiles we modeled on her behavior, I think it's much more likely that she hid inside a packing crate, or climbed into the back of someone's car. Or maybe—remember, she had a change of clothes—she was able to walk out.
BILUNGS: Have you considered a laundry cart?
NYSTRÖM: I'm sorry?
BILUNGS: Isn't that how it usually works in heist movies and slapstick comedies?
NYSTRÖM: I thought, Mr Bilungs, that this inquiry was a fact-finding exercise, not a blame-apportioning one.
BILUNGS: [Pause] Yes, you are correct. Quite correct.

43

November 2016, London.

Ingrid drained her coffee cup and looked at the clock on the wall again. She had already been waiting half an hour and the coffee in the Regency Café wasn't good enough to hang around any longer. Either the woman from the Tate gallery had been held up, or more likely she had changed her mind. It wasn't a surprise: after all, she was asking her to risk her job.

The Westminster café—an old-fashioned 1950s greasy spoon—was popular with politicians and local construction workers, and a line of customers started to form at the counter, the beginning of the lunch rush. She looked up at the blackboard and considered whether there was anything she was actually prepared to eat. If she was in the Regency with a friend, she would happily gorge on bubble and squeak and fried eggs, but she was undercover as the glamorous Natalya Vesnina, one of London's most influential art brokers, and there was no way Natalya would be seen eating fried food. Ingrid's entire outfit probably cost more than the monthly salaries of some of the workers lining up with doorstep sandwiches and cans of Coke. If her contact from the Tate had had second thoughts, she should hail a cab and head back to Mayfair. She stood up, her left foot wobbling slightly on a four-inch heel, and bent to pick up her Stella McCartney handbag from the seat next to hers.

"An Americano, I believe."

It was a voice Ingrid hadn't heard for over a year. No, closer to two years. She took a deep breath, settled her features and turned to face him.

"What the hell are you doing here, Nick?"

"Buying you a coffee?"

Ingrid was shocked by his appearance. The Elvis quiff had been replaced by a buzz cut and his normally tanned skin was sallow, his cheeks hollow. The ever-youthful Nick Angelis looked older. He looked ill. "Go to hell." She pushed past him and moved toward the door.

"Actually, I just came from there." He reached out and grabbed her arm. "Please, let me buy you a coffee."

She turned and looked him in the eye. He was imploring her, his features full of pleading sincerity, but all she could think about was the grief he had caused her when she'd made it home from Stockholm. The interrogations from her superiors, the disciplinary review that nearly cost her career. She looked down at his hand where it grabbed her forearm—he was still wearing his wedding ring—then back up to his newly lined faced.

"Not here."

There was no need to ask Nick how he had tracked her down as it was what he did for a living. The question was: why now? They stepped out onto the sidewalk where the harsh December air made Ingrid pull her pashmina tight around her neck. She took a cloche hat—another designer accessory she had purchased on behalf of the American taxpayer—out of her oversized purse and pulled it on.

"It suits you," Nick said. "The hair. And the hat."

A cab with its light on turned into the street and Ingrid raised her hand. "It used to be as short as yours. Taxi!"

"I know," he said, unusually softly.

Ingrid looked at him as the taxi slowed. She couldn't help but smile at him. For two years she'd wanted to belt him, but now that he seemed frail and penitent that would only make her feel like a bully. The cab driver's window whirred open. "Connaught hotel, please." She had opened the cab door before she realized that Nick hadn't. He really was sick. "I take it you'll ride with me?"

"It would be my pleasure."

Ingrid helped him into the back of the taxi then climbed in, pulling the drifting hem of her pashmina clear of the door before closing it. She sat as far back in the seat as possible, putting the maximum possible distance between the two of them. For the first year after Stockholm she'd rejected all his calls, rebuffed all his offers and resisted the urge to visit his club and punch him in the face. Then, for the past year, she'd wanted answers. The war in Syria hadn't stopped. There had been no peace accord from the Vienna negotiations. And every time she visited her physiotherapist for treatment on the shoulder injury she'd sustained falling out the van, she'd wanted to know if anything she'd accomplished in Sweden had been worthwhile. She wanted to know if the risks he had subjected her to were worth it. But she wasn't about to hit a man whose trousers were now so big for him that they were bunched at the waist under his belt.

"You look, as ever, amazing." He was gripping the door handle tightly. "You can still make me catch my breath." He wheezed just to prove his point.

She was still so damn cross with him that she didn't want to ask him what kind of illness he had, or what his prognosis was. "Obviously none of these clothes are my choice."

"If it helps, I would buy art from you."

Ingrid knew she should ask after his wife, whose name she couldn't remember. She should absolutely mention his hair. She certainly knew she didn't want to be talking to him about goddamned clothes. She wanted to ask him 'why now?' but she was scared of the answer. It had been two years. They weren't close anymore. From the look of him, she feared he was tying up loose ends, making preparations for… God, if he was dying she could be a little more charitable, couldn't she?

"How many millions have you got? I can put you in contact with a Rothko that I think you'd like."

He smiled at her. "You know it would be wasted on me."

It occurred to Ingrid that she had never seen inside Nick's home. She had no idea what his taste was like beyond tailored shirts and alligator shoes. But something in the way he spoke suggested that a clash of artistic tastes wasn't why it would be wasted on him. She couldn't ignore his appearance any longer. She had to say something.

"So…"

"So. Indeed. You may be wondering why—"

The cab turned sharply left, beating the lights just as they changed to red.

"I am," she said. "I am definitely wondering."

"Well." Nick reached inside his jacket pocket and pulled out a thumb drive. "I thought you would want to see this." He placed it on the seat between them and Ingrid eyed it with suspicion. "Please. There's no need to look like that. It's not a Trojan horse. It's not infected with a virus that will bring the embassy's computer system crashing down."

Ingrid stretched out a hand and picked it up. She looked at it closely. "Are you sure I want whatever is on it?"

Nick Angelis pursed his lips. "Yes, I rather think you do. And besides, it's the least that I owe you."

She dropped it into her bag as the cab took a side road, rattling down a cobbled mews. "Are you going to tell me?"

He looked at the taxi driver, then leaned forward. "It's the transcripts from the Borg enquiry in Stockholm." He spoke so quietly she could hardly hear him. "The committee isn't due to publish its findings until the New Year, but I thought you'd want to see them."

Ingrid's heart lurched and she felt the coffee rise in her throat. "They… Do they—"

He raised his hand, weakly, to stop her. "You're in the clear—"

"I am?" She let out a gasp.

"Yes. They have no idea who you are. Your cousin refused to testify."

"Yes, I heard."

He swallowed hard. "Does she know about you? That it was you?"

Ingrid looked out of the window at a parade of boutique shops decorated with holly, fake snow and twinkling lights. For London, the Christmas decorations were discreet and understated. "Probably," she said. Ingrid turned back to Nick and shook her head. "I mean, she must, right? She must have seen the CCTV. Must have joined the dots?"

"So you've not spoken to her about it?"

"No."

"Probably for the best." He leaned forward and tapped on the glass behind the driver's head. "Drop me here, please."

The cab driver indicated and pulled over toward the curb.

"Because there are some things," Nick said, "that are better left unsaid."

And, with that, Nick Angelis opened the door and climbed slowly out of the cab. Ingrid couldn't stop looking at him as the driver pulled away. He kept both hands defiantly in his pockets and tears unexpectedly pricked her eyes: Nick was stopping himself from waving goodbye.

Find out what happens next in...

FINAL OFFER

AN INGRID SKYBERG THRILLER BOOK 6

A shadowy UK-based group has been trying to hack the US elections. When Special Agent Ingrid Skyberg is assigned to find out who's funding the hackers, she finds herself up against an invisible enemy who is extremely powerful and utterly ruthless.

To bring them to justice, Ingrid must go undercover and infiltrate the world of super-rich Russian oligarchs. But money buys all kinds of protection and Ingrid soon realises that by taking on this battle she's putting everything on the line – her career, her future, her life.

In a nail-biting race against time, Ingrid sets out to solve the mystery and unmask the conspirators before they can silence her. Forever.

Available in paperback and ebook.

THE INGRID SKYBERG THRILLERS

Run Girl - Prequel (A novella)

Secretary of State Jayne Whitticker is in the middle of delicate negotiations when her favorite grandchild disappears from Paris.

Special Agent Ingrid Skyberg is hauled out of her FBI training session at Scotland Yard to head the hunt for the eighteen-year-old girl, who the FBI believe is now in London. Will she succeed in her unexpected mission? Or will her failure lead to the collapse of the crucial peace talks?

FREE to download when you join Eva's mailing list.

Fresh Doubt - Book One

A story of lies, secrets and deadly mind games.

Two hours ago, brilliant American psychology student Madison Faber found her roommate lying in a pool of blood. Now she is in police custody and suspected of murder. Madison persuades Special Agent Ingrid Skyberg to find the real killer, but the investigation soon puts Ingrid in danger. Can she unmask the murderer before she becomes a victim herself?

Kill Plan - Book Two

An American trader is poisoned in his office in the City of London. Two days later, a Latvian immigrant is discovered floating face down in the River Thames. These seemingly unrelated crimes are the work of an audacious serial killer working on both sides of the Atlantic.

When Special Agent Ingrid Skyberg starts putting the pieces together, she also puts herself in the firing line.

Deep Hurt - Book Three

In a seedy hotel in central London, the baby daughter of a US Air Force pilot lies lifeless in his wife's arms. Accused of killing the fourteen-month-old in an uncontrolled rage, Kyle Foster flees, taking his eight-year-old son with him.

Will Ingrid find Foster before he hurts anyone else? Or will she succumb to the old demons she's been trying to escape for the last eighteen years?

Shoot First - Book Four

A teenage girl disappears after witnessing a gangland murder in Chicago. Nine months later, and heavily pregnant, she arrives in London only to disappear again.

Special Agent Ingrid Skyberg has just two days to find the girl and get her to testify or else a brutal killer walks free. But Ingrid isn't the only person looking for the girl, and a war that started on the streets of Chicago is about to explode in the peaceful English countryside.

Below Zero - Book Five

Stockholm is under siege. A bomb has gone off, a series of high profile people have been kidnapped, and the city is in lockdown. Unfortunately for Special Agent Ingrid Skyberg, everything is kicking off on the same day she is in town to complete a dangerous assignment that is so secret, and so illegal, that neither the FBI or the US government can ever know about it. Her instructions are simple: no ID, no credit cards, no trace. If she ends up in jail, or floating face down in the harbor, there can be no way of identifying her.

No badge, no gun, no back-up: this time Ingrid is on her own.

Final Offer - Book Six

A shadowy UK-based group has been trying to hack the US elections. When Special Agent Ingrid Skyberg is assigned to find out who's funding the hackers, she finds herself up against an invisible enemy who is extremely powerful and utterly ruthless.

To bring them to justice, Ingrid must go undercover and infiltrate the world of super-rich Russian oligarchs. But money buys all kinds of protection and Ingrid soon realizes that by taking on this battle she's putting everything on the line – her career, her future, her life.

In a nail-biting race against time, Ingrid sets out to solve the mystery and unmask the conspirators before they can silence her. Forever.

Flight Risk - Book Seven

Ingrid is ready to walk away from her life. She wants out of London. She even wants out of the FBI. But when she attempts to board a flight at Heathrow and sneak away without telling anyone, she's arrested on suspicion of causing the death of a man she's never heard of.

Now Ingrid must stay in the country, and the Bureau, to prove her innocence. There's just one problem: she can't remember if she killed him or not

---

EVA'S OTHER BOOKS

The Loyal Servant

Winner of the Lucy Cavendish Prize for Fiction, *The Loyal Servant* is a whistleblower thriller that topped the Amazon political fiction chart. Investigative reporter Angela Tate investigates scandal and corruption in the corridors of Westminster.

The Senior Moment

Sixty-five-year-old Jean Henderson arrives in New York to find her son and his pregnant wife missing from their apartment. When she reaches out to the cops for help, Jean discovers how invisible older people really are and concocts a plan to get noticed: by robbing a series of banks.

The Deadly Silence (formerly The Third Estate)

Thirty-three years ago two little girls disappeared. Today, the man convicted of murder three decades ago is back on the streets as another girl vanishes. Angela Tate covered the first disappearances and is dragged into discovering the terrible truth behind the latest.

GET AN EXCLUSIVE SKYBERG NOVELLA

Want to read more about Ingrid Skyberg? For FREE? Join Eva's mailing list at evahudson.com and receive RUN GIRL, a novella featuring Ingrid Skyberg's first assignment in London for free. You'll also be kept up-to-date when new books in the series are released.

Visit evahudson.com.

ABOUT THE AUTHOR

Eva was born and raised in London. She worked as a local government worker, web editor, dot com entrepreneur, portrait artist and singer. In 2011, Eva won the inaugural Lucy Cavendish Prize for Fiction for her first novel, *The Loyal Servant.* The book was also shortlisted for ITV's People's Novelist Award.

In 2013, Eva published the first Ingrid Skyberg Thriller and never looked back.

To find out more about Eva or Ingrid, please visit evahudson.com. You can get the latest on all things Skyberg by following Eva on Twitter at twitter.com/eva_hudson and Facebook at facebook.com/evahudsoncrimewriter.

ACKNOWLEDGMENTS

I'd like to thank my early readers for their immeasurable input: Stuart Blackburn, Lucy Ruddy, Steve Murray, Hilary Mounfield, Judie Goldstein, Vicki Church and Karen Knox. I'm also very grateful for the cheerleading from my brilliant writers' group: that's you Anna Mazzola, Alice Hiller, Nichole Beauchamp and Jim Stokely. Thanks too to my copy editor Lorraine Jerram (who spotted far too many mistakes!) and to Camilla Bjurlemark for help with all things Swedish.

And to everyone who left a comment on a blog, or sent an email or message on social media, thank you so much for your encouragement. It's a huge privilege to keep Eva's work alive, but it helps to know there are fans out there eager to start reading the next book.

And, Eva… couldn't have done any of this without you. Big love.

Printed in Great Britain
by Amazon

86014158R00174